The Border Reiver

Dear Alice

Nick Christofides

Best wishes
Nick Christofides

The right of Nicholas Christofides to be identified as the author of this work has been asserted by him in accordance with the Copyright, Designs and Patents Act, 1988.

Copyright ©2015 Nicholas Christofides

ISBN 978-0-9930862-6-7

All rights reserved. No part of this publication may be reproduced, stored in retrieval system or transmitted in any form or by any means electronic, mechanical, photocopying, recording or otherwise, without the prior permission of the publisher, except in the case of brief quotations embodied in critical articles and reviews.

This work is a work of fiction. Names and characters are the product of the author's imagination and any resemblance to actual persons, living or dead is entirely coincidental

Published in the United Kingdom in 2015 by Cambria Books, Wales, United Kingdom

Original cover design © M.J.Forster

For Andreas

ONE

The end of the world for one man can be a new beginning for another. For the men who met in that barn, the end was here.

It was January, just above freezing but the Siberian winds swept over the land like Mongol hordes biting flesh with icy fangs. The rain fell like daggers, it rapped off the tin roof of the stone shed.

They were south-west of Wooler, close to the Scottish Border. The Cheviot Hills loomed in the darkness. The howling weather battered the already beaten structure, but there was an orange glow radiating from lights within; offering the warmth of the inn to a traveller.

The heat from the assembled men appeared like smoke, rising from rain drenched coats inside the confines of the shelter. There must have been a hundred ruddy farmers rammed into the barn. They gathered not through choice, it was the fear of change that brought these normally solitary beasts together.

The smell of silage wafted through the space while a muted hubbub filled the airwaves. The rotund, red faced orator who now hushed the crowd was a man named Rowell. He farmed near enough four hundred acres outside Hexham. Fit as a fiddle but well into his seventies the man was flanked by his three sons. As he smashed his fist into his open palm, he bellowed and blustered about the choice these men had to make. Give up their land and livelihood to the local collectives or, with support from

Scotland, fight the land reforms. For most, the decision was already sown in the land.

The howling wind which whipped the shelter foretold the storm that was to come.

In a dark corner sat a hunched figure, head down with white hair hung loose meandering around his weathered brow. His hands were clamped together resting on his lap, swollen and sore from pulling sheep out of snow.

As he opened his eyes, Nat Bell looked upon the throng and although he knew every face, he had nothing to say to one. Some looked towards him for direction, but he bowed his head once more; his mind ready to explode as the evils amplified within his skull.

* * * * *

Three hundred and twenty-two miles to the south, there was another man alone in the midst of a frenzy. Ben Baines was sitting in the ebbing blue hue of the television screen. His elbows rested on his knees, absorbed like a toddler in front of their favourite cartoon. Controller in hand; he was flicking through the channels. His morning routine which had been unchanged for years.

Over past decades, he had watched economies crumble; Islamists threaten the western world; the right wing backlash and now, he was the centre of the storm; Ben Baines and his New Socialist Order.

On screen, the crowds were blowing horns and cheering at the camera in an ecstatic outpouring of joy. The shot panned around to a chubby faced reporter, he had rosy cheeks and thinning wispy hair drifting up off the top of his head; it was not cooperating with gravity.

Baines raised his hand to quiet the other man in his office. As they listened to the reporter speak, his voice was excited, slightly raw and raised to be heard over the throng, he had an ironed out northern accent. The young journalist managed to master the atmosphere and engage the watcher with clarity in his pronunciation and accentuation of the salient details like a seasoned correspondent. Baines would have liked him on the payroll had it not been for the impartial tone of his report, which continued,

"...as you can witness from the crowds around me the mood here on the streets of the capital is jubilant. The Baines era of politics has been legitimised by today's overwhelming results and for tonight at least the NSO can sit back and enjoy their victory.

However unimaginable the New Socialist Order's meteoric rise to power has been it is now that Baines and his ministers will have to back up their promises with action. Their support is unquestionable, but Baines has inherited a country on its knees, bankrupt financially and with a creaking infrastructure.

His land reforms are causing unrest and increasing violence…how long can this charismatic man persuade generations born of Capitalism that his ideology will work…Only time will tell…"

Baines pressed hard on the red button. As the picture closed in on itself, he threw the remote onto the table at his knees. Resting back in his seat, he stared up at the regency coving thirteen feet above his head, his mind racing to construct a more palatable package for the delivery of his land reforms.

Nick Christofides

TWO

The Tyne Valley rolled away to the West. A breathtaking mishmash of organic matter dissected by the churning waters of the river; from this distance just a glinting ribbon winding its way around the undulations of the valley floor.

The wind was tearing its way over the orange and browns of the rugged countryside to the valley sides and the lush greens of farmland on its floor. The trees shaped by this persistent wind bent and arched like claws tearing at the ground and the endless sky a mass of belching clouds fought its way to the farmhouse perched on top of the hill.

Carlins Law was an ancient homestead. It stood as a grand house, enjoying the full force of the prevailing wind but escaping those ferocious northerly winter gales. They hit the farm yard and farm buildings arranged as two sides of a square to the back of the house which itself made the third side. To many, the old house standing atop a rugged hill engulfed by infinite sky would have been a lonely desolate place to live, but not to Nat Bell and his family.

Back when Nat was in his mid-teens, he saw his father killed by the boots of others, over a game of dice, in the Dockers streets of Wallsend in the east end of Newcastle. Nat fled the city after that and he drifted from farm to farm, labouring, until he met his wife's father. Now Carlins Law had been home to him for thirty odd years and his wife's family for six generations before that.

He loved his home it was part of him, he worked the farm and on occasion it damned near killed him but he enjoyed the physicality of the struggle against the elements.

His age was lost somewhere in the passage of time, but the years had taken no toll on his body. He was sinuous and powerful, stood six feet two and straight as an arrow and could work for days at a stretch. He used words sparingly and his wife loved him for it, she yearned to delve deeper into his psyche but even she was only allowed so far. He repaid this distance by an unwavering dedication to his family and home; he was the rock on which their life was built.

His skin was leathered and tanned by the weather and he had a thick shock of white hair and grey whiskers. His eyes were encased in wrinkles from years of squinting into sun and gales. But if you did catch them for a moment the piercing cobalt was a window into the beating soul lying under that gnarled exterior. He had hands like bags of spanners and bones toughened by years of hard labour. It could be said that the longer he lived, the more he became like the countryside he lived in, weather-beaten and hardened but like the water off the hills his eyes shone crystal clear.

It was the middle of the afternoon when he saw the black estate car pull into his driveway. The car was half a mile away, but it was a straight run down the hill from where Nat stood and the drive was unfenced to grazing land either side so a totally open approach. Nat stood in the middle of the gravelled parking area to the front of his home and waited their arrival.

He knew who approached now. He had done more talking in the past few weeks than the past ten years. He knew it was more people from the NSO with smiles and offers, searching eyes and veiled threats. He was doing his best to keep the peace, but he could not give an inch.

* * * * *

The car approached the house at a respectful ten miles per hour, give or take. The speed was partly out of deference and partly the occupants' examination of the possibilities the property had to offer the Hexhamshire Collective. There were five men inside the car. The driver was in his forties, he was a big guy and fit for his age, dressed in a fleece and jeans, his muscular physique was defined; even below the thick clothing he was wearing. He had light brown hair and a few days growth of stubble.

The memory of his face was concentrated on the six inch scar running from the centre of his chin around the right side of his mouth and up to his cheek bone. His name was Gerry and he had been a civilian for twenty painful years now. He gained the scar when shrapnel from a roadside bomb in Afghanistan struck him in the face. He had served as a Sergeant in the First Battalion of 'The Old and The Bold' and had loved his time in.

On leaving the army, he had struggled with civilian life. Having drifted to London in search of work, he had bounced from one bar job to another, struggling to pay rent and secure anything permanent until he had found himself sleeping rough. It was from a bench on Embankment that he first saw the NSO marching on Westminster. He joined the march through instinct more than any belief or knowledge of the ideology and found himself a part of the historic occupation of Parliament Square and College Gardens which lasted for fourteen months. 'The Equity Protest' as it became known by the media was the first example of peaceful dissent by the NSO.

The demonstration showed the growing acceptance and support of the organisation. It was a flashpoint which demonstrated to the country the lack of control and weakness of the government of the time. Westminster was forced to a standstill and parliament had to meet in St Pauls.

It was at this protest that Gerry met Roland who sat next to him in the car. Roland, at that stage, was a politics student racking up crippling debts for a degree which promised little chance of work. He was introduced to Ben Baines beliefs' and the principles of the NSO both academically on his course and informally within the student's union.

By this time, most students believed in collectivism or other strands of anarchism because the idea of professional self-improvement or wealth was now beyond the reach of anyone. The elite had a monopoly on all forms of commerce; there was no hope anymore, no matter how educated or determined a person was. This marginalisation of the young talented generation united them with those from poor backgrounds. The result was a severe backlash which began with rioting but evolving with more sophistication where propaganda of the deed became less violent and far more crushing to government and business.

Roland was an intelligent man of twenty-nine, his slightly rounded face was ruddy in the cheeks and his hair covered his ears in curls. He was athletic and to all intents and purposes a winner. With Gerry at his side, they made a good team as both of them were capable mentally and physically and over the years they had become close friends. Roland had dragged Gerry out of a meaningless existence and Gerry had helped Roland focus and organise with military precision.

The third person in the car was Davey. A twenty-four-year-old from Hexham, who had never worked in his life, not through laziness but because there were currently seventeen people unemployed for every unskilled job in the North East of England.

He had never worked until he became a member of the NSO. After that, he had been assigned a job in a local warehouse which was under the Collectives control. He was the local member of this team. Although he was no great knowledge outside of the town, he had once visited the pub in Great Whittington, but that was as close as he had ever been to this address.

Davey's face was thin and pinched, his hair was cropped and he was as skinny as a pole. He was a boy who could eat as much as he liked because nervous energy would burn away any excess calories. He sat in the middle of the back seat stooped forward and leaning each arm on either side of the two front seats, he was annoying his two companions in the front.

Either side of Davey sat two quiet brooding lumps of meat. Recently assigned to this detail, Steve and Connor were both marines, they had been on active duty in Afghanistan, Syria, Greece and Spain in recent years. They had only met the others a few days previously and were at this stage assigned as security for this small detail.

As they neared the top of the hill, they saw a lone figure, standing, and waiting. The wind whipped at the man's white tresses, his face; a tight mummified grizzle of wrinkles with a grimace showing white clenched teeth. His eyes bullet holes of blue in a sea of crow's feet unblinking trained on the car. He wore the seal skin poncho a friend had given him; it was the best and warmest windbreak and left him totally free to work. Underneath he wore his quilted wax jacket and his long jeaned legs were hoofed in solid work boots. In his right hand, he held a long handled axe. The axe was at ease but it was a foreboding sight and Davey didn't feel at all sure about it.

As they approached he sat back in the seat, instinct, distance between him and the gruesome behemoth waiting for their arrival. The atmosphere in the car had indeed tightened by the time they were a hundred yards out; none of the men in the car had visited this farm before. Gerry piped up

"Oi oi look at this geezer, lock up your daughters."

By the time they hit gravel twenty-five yards from the eerie statuesque figure there was no chat, no jokes, just concentration. Gerry slowed the car to a crawl. He pulled it past the figure, who just stood, only his eyes followed the car. Then a slight turn of the head. As they passed behind him, his head bowed as if now out of his line of vision he had swapped senses to listen to their movements. Now Roland spoke

"Ok guys let's be sensible here, this guy looks crazy. I'll do the talking just keep your distance and remember we are on a fact-finding mission. If he doesn't want to cooperate don't go starting a fight at this stage. Steve, Conor, you guys stay in the car, let's not be too intimidating."

"Oh yeah, we're the intimidating ones," said Conor before adding with a smirk, "Davey, you keep away from that axe."

Davey said nothing. The three men stepped out of the car, crunching feet on gravel. The farmer stood with his back to them, head down, listening. Roland took the lead; the other two fell in a foot or so behind him in an arrowhead formation. They stopped a good six feet behind the man who at this close quarters only proved to be as colossal as he was menacing.

He stood stock still. Gerry and Roland looked at each other briefly then Roland cleared his throat

"We're looking for Nathaniel Bell, is that you sir?"

There was no discernible movement.

"Sir!" Gerry said with a slight elevation in his voice, a little aggression. Roland flashed him a look as if to say 'my show.' The stony hand constricted on the axe handle. The head slowly began to turn to the left until the chin met the shoulder and one dragon's eye captured the three men in its view and in a low, calm gravel pitch he uttered

"You raise your voice at me again boy"

Davey took an involuntary step backwards; the other two men looked at each other and the ghostly figure turned slowly to face down the three of them. His face was more gnarled by weather than by years and his gaze was one absolutely centred on them, the concentration was piercing and unnerving. Roland felt it; Gerry felt it and Davey wanted to run away.

* * * * *

As he stood to face the three men, thoughts raced through his mind, he knew this would be coming. He had read the papers and seen the news. Rowell had warned them of it a few nights previously. After all, it was the only thing people watched on TV now that the country was self-combusting. He had a good idea that he was swimming against a tide that was too strong, he was backed against the wall and he had no answers and no plan.

He studied the three of them and he saw fear but he also saw their conviction, at least in the two older men, the young one cowering behind was no more than a child. He said nothing, concentrated, waited for them to give him direction.

The guy with the scraggly hair and round face said
"Have you heard of the NSO?"
"Yes"
"Were you expecting us?"
"Yes"
"Do you know what we are here to do?"
"No"
"Can I explain? Or are you non-compliant?"
"You explain and I'll tell you whether I comply" growled the farmer
"The NCO is the new government and we want to improve the..."
"Save your bullshit, what do you want from me?"
Nat saw the boys' face change from ambivalence to deadpan in a split second and he knew that he was going to cut through the rhetoric and talk directly,
"We want information from you so we can account for and record what you produce here and the productivity of the farm. Then we will look at how that can be improved. After that, we will calculate how many people could be employed on the farm. How your produce will fit the jigsaw of self-sufficiency for the Hexhamshire Collective, you will either come under the umbrella of the collective or you will be re-housed somewhere else."

Nat's face crumpled in thought, his bottom lip began to protrude and his shoulders rose as if to say 'whatever.'

With that, he turned his back on the men and walked off back to the house. His footing was solid and he didn't look back, he had done with the visitors.

The three men followed him though, they hadn't finished. The older man strolled back around the North West corner of the house and in through the rough old back door, the same route he had passed thousands of times, except now the three younger men followed. He knew they would follow. There was less room in the house. It was a concentrated space; limited movement.

Nat pulled out his chair at the table and he sat himself down facing the three men as they entered his kitchen that smelt of oil from the Aga and the machinery and dirt from the fields.

He was wrought like the gates of a prison. Sitting with one leg over the other at the old oak table where he sat every day, he had his arms lying one on top of the other like a lion basking in the sun. His eyes darted between his visitors attempting to make sense of the situation but trying desperately to hide his emotion. The pose offered a pensive calm, but his eyes would betray the whirlwind of anger within.

The kitchen was warm and inviting with a rich glow from the lights bouncing off the earthen colours of the flagstone floor. The smell of the open fire mixed with the oily tang and the murmur of the wind through the thick walls called for single malt, not the scene that had unfolded.

Nat attempted to tumble the chaos of the situation into some sort of order in his head, but he couldn't quite compute. His pulse was racing and his brow beading, he wasn't sure whether he was visibly quaking with the fear, confusion and overwhelming anger. He felt like a sealed bottle of water thrown into the fire, it was only a matter of time…

"What are your names?" he asked buying time, thinking.

Bemused Roland answered waving a hand at the relevant person in turn

"Roland, Gerry and Davey, now can we get down to business as we have a lot of people still to visit after you."

"What happens if I don't do what you want?"

"You have to do what we want, it is the law. And it is not what I want sir, this is government policy, this is how the country is going to be run from now on."

The old farmer leant in slightly on his elbows concentrating their gaze on his brilliant blue eyes, his face solid as granite

"Do you realise what you are saying, you expect me to hand over my land to a bunch of half cut revolutionaries who have no idea how to work it?"

"Listen, it is time that everyone had the opportunity to earn a decent living. You can't keep all this to yourself anymore; everyone in your privileged position will suffer a little in the redistribution. You will just have to deal with it sir, like the other ninety percent of the population has had to up until this point in time."

"Privilege!" Nat exclaimed in his husky growl with leathered palms and knobbled fingers raised aloft. "You have no idea what you're talking about."

Gerry piped up "These are hard times. You been watching the news? We have orders to bring this and every other farm under government management whether by mutual agreement with the current landowner or by force…"

"What he means is that the NSO are the new legitimate government. If you don't recognise the new system voluntarily this land will be forcibly removed from your possession and whatever rights to it you think you have, will be annulled."

Nat could not believe this situation or how to react for the best. What he could see was that these boys were not bosses, they were a forward party. So he answered with the words he knew were the truth.

"I won't be giving you any information tonight."

"Are you sure about that?" said Gerry menacingly irritated by the old man and staring him down.

Nat's eyes narrowed and focussed on the man, his palm moved slowly to the table as his hand closed into a clench. Gerry shifted on his feet as the adrenalin pumped and he became more at peace with the idea of hurting the grizzled old man. Roland put his hand out to hold Gerry back and was about to speak when the door behind Nat swung open and a young woman entered the space.

She wore thick woollen socks pulled over the bottoms of her jeans, ripped at the knees, which were tight to her athletic thighs. She wore a heavy woollen jumper hanging off her slender but powerful shoulders. Her face was freckled and ivory, her eyes green and her hair an explosion of auburn curls. She had a shotgun shouldered and aimed solidly at Roland.

"He's sure, now fuck off out of this house!" She said without a nerve betraying her.

It was Roland who now raised his palms, and as he did he lent towards Nat and spoke in a hushed voice

"You carry on like this and an enforcement squad will visit and they'll take everything from you" as he said the words he was looking at the girl with the shotgun...Nat moved with the speed of a rattlesnake, with all his bulk and size he grabbed the back of Roland's head with his left hand. Using the table as an anchor with his right, he slammed the man's face into the oak surface crushing his nose and cheekbone. In the same movement, Nat's right hand punched forward with his palm flat into the boys splintered nose. He levelled him in the face and back onto the floor, where he sprawled whimpering with blood streaming from his smashed face.

In one fluid sinuous movement, Nat stood up and moved from Roland to Gerry. Taking one step towards him he snaffled his head as the ex-soldier flailed panicked punches. Nat rolled his head under arm and began to constrict. At first on the skull but then squeezing down around his neck until slowly breathing became impossible and Gerry felt his life on the brink of a precipice. Nat whispered,

"Do you want me to kill you?" Gerry couldn't talk but the blood-curdling rake communicated a 'no.' Nat eased the pressure off slowly ready to constrict again if he felt any fight from the other man,

"Now pick that snivelling little shite up and get off my farm"

Gerry was gasping, he rubbed his throat and stood up, pride dented, angry. Questioning himself as to whether he should have another go at this old farmer. He stood face to face with Nat, eyeball to eyeball, Nat could smell his breath and taste that the man wanted to kill him.

The endless seconds of standoff were disturbed by the spluttering wreckage moaning on the floor and it seemed to focus the minds. Threateningly the man turned slowly with eyes on Nat's until the very last moment, then he picked up his friend with the third boy.

They didn't waste any time getting out the door. Nat snatched the shotgun from his daughter's hand with an angry look at her he followed the men out of the house and stood on the gravelled drive as they got into the estate car.

The two men who had remained in the vehicle turned to look at him and then he saw the men talking, probably arguing whether to come back for another shot at him. But they decided against it as the engine fired up and the car skidded off the gravel firing stones behind it as it went. The soft footsteps of his daughter on the gravel ran up next to his shoulder.

Amber looked at her father "We better work out what we're gonna do when they come back Da"

Nat turned to her, his grimace sent from Hell.

"What did you think you were doing Amber?"

"I..."

"What if they had guns" He turned away deep in thought. His heart was beating trying to think, to plan what to do, he was sure that his home and land were lost to these people. It was true there was nothing stopping this new regime. His immediate conclusion was to get his wife and daughter north of the border into Scotland.

As he stood with his daughter, a mere child with the independence of a woman twice her age, he thought of his old friend in Melrose and his mind was made. If he could get his wife and daughter to Stuart, he could breathe easier and come back to protect his livelihood or at least make sure no one else could steal it from him. As he watched the black car disappear down the narrow winding country road, his eyes raised and he looked out over the Tyne Valley. Dusk was falling, it was ten to four in the afternoon and the light would fail in twenty minutes. He kissed his daughter's head once again and the two of them walked back into the house.

* * * * *

As the car motored towards Hexham, Davey passed Roland a piece of cloth from the boot. Blood was streaming from his broken nose and a gash where his cheekbone had hit the table. A bulbous purple swelling grew on his face and he spluttered with pain. Conor was shouting from the back of the car

"You ok Roland?" Roland raised a bloody hand in acknowledgement and Conor continued "We can't let him get away with that, we should have given him some payback and taken him in"

"We'll come back" Answered Gerry "we need to report it to Truter, let him decide what we do next."

Conor looked across at Steve who gave his friend a knowing look and said

"If you treat the locals with kid gloves they'll learn to fuck you right up. I know it's not your call but if we keep letting these bastards go about their shit the way they want to we will be chasing shadows. And dying doing it; trust me we've learnt that lesson in every shithole we've toured. Next time we get up there we need to sort him out."

"That might be, but I'm not doing anything without Truters say so...that's not worth doing either."

"He's right we wait and return once we have reported to the boss" mumbled Roland through a swollen bloody mouth. Conor stretched forward and rested a hand on Roland's shoulder

"Don't worry mate, he'll get his" he said giving the shoulder a reassuring squeeze and the car fell silent as it sped back to the police station in Hexham.

Nick Christofides

THREE

The office was draped in shadow from roughly head height and above. He didn't like the strip beam lights, or the incessant hum they emitted. At first he was embarrassed by the finery of the antique furniture and fittings in the room. He felt it mocked his beliefs and portrayed him as the type of person he had dedicated his life's work against. The lamps had green glass shades; the desk was walnut and stood like a rhino, the Chesterfields, the regency mahogany sideboard and the wood panelled walls. All these items betrayed him to the trappings of wealth and power.

Nevertheless beggars cannot be choosers, and he had possession of this office building by donation from a party member who was his wealthiest establishment convert. He couldn't argue the fact that it gave his cause a base, a hub and added substance to his movement. He wasn't hiding away in some northern town in an old gym or some such. He occupied a listed Regency building in W1. One thing was for certain; he was not prepared to move into Downing Street at any time soon. His movement would create its tradition not follow those of the enemy.

Behind the desk, hung high on the wall were two portraits painted in oil that illustrated the true nature of Baines beliefs. The solemn bearded faces of Mikhail Bakunin and Johann Most looked down upon the room. Their eyes were unwaveringly piercing the shell of those seated on the other side of the desk. Visitors, whether allies or opponents, to the epicentre of The Revolution.

Two middle-aged men occupied the room, evidently old friends or at least old colleagues. The first sat behind the desk with his chair pushed back, away from it. He was leaning back in the seat; legs splayed and resting only his heels on the floor. His arms hung at ease by the side of his chair. He rested like a rag doll, relaxed. His cohort had just helped himself to coffee at the ornate sideboard, on which he now leaned. He was a hefty man, barrel chest, thick neck, large meaty face. His eyes betrayed his stature though, bulbous yet 'piggy' they made him unattractive. But that was something that had never bothered this man. He took a long deep breath and exhaled loudly, exaggerated and bullish.

"So how are you settling into the new house?" Asked Lucas Start, the man who was standing. The other remained reclining, but his eyes focussed on his company,

"You know, I haven't really thought about it; it's a house, same old problems with moving in and no wife to sort them out while I'm here. Can't see me spending much time there anyway."

"Jesus Ben, you mustn't forget how to live, enjoy your position a bit now, get some women have a party...don't spend your life here creating problems for yourself."

"You amaze me Lucas; we have just led the country in a revolution where the founding belief is common ownership of the nation's wealth. And you want me to start living like a bloody rock star."

"If you have some fun Ben the world will keep turning, look at me I manage the balance..."

"You!" laughed Baines gently shaking his head "you're a bloody power hungry menace" He stopped for a second and then added "who's lucky I'm dedicated to leading the country!"

The two men chuckled. Then the man seated continued

"I haven't left the office in three days; there's too much to organise and the Scots are refusing any diplomatic contact."

"We've been through this Ben, forget the Scots. We've got it under control..."

"Yeah well, until it's controlled I can't relax, we've come so far to be invaded by our very testy and increasingly powerful neighbours." He said with a resignation that war was inevitable.

"Don't worry about it Ben, the Scots won't act directly and The Wall will cut off supplies to any rebels. We will complete it within a month. Our Intel has identified a number of farms that are likely rebel cells. We are continuing to investigate others and will start clearing the occupants in the coming days...it is a non-problem" He exclaimed, palms out, eyebrows raised and a huge smile across his broad face.

"I hope so Lucas...I hope so" He said fingering a file on his desk, his head down, chins doubling slightly with age and lips in a pondering pout.

"Anyway" Lucas added, "all farmers are capitalists, if they don't hand over control of their farms they're enemies of our regime and will be evicted."

"Good, the sooner we get the redistribution completed the sooner we will have a buffer, and we can move on and forget the old system."

As he finished, there was a knock at the door. He sat up straight, tightened his tie, his face changed from relaxed to focus. Ben Baines was quick to his feet; he was around six foot, his dark grey suit was well fitted but not expensive, his white shirt was High Street bought and his tie was dark blue. He was a very handsome charismatic man with a kind face. His dark brown hair was cut short, and his deep brown eyes were accented by thick brows. It was not hard to follow a man like Baines; he had the presence that turned people's heads when he entered the room. And now he had managed, over the course of twenty years to create the most seismic shift in British politics since Oliver Cromwell.

* * * * *

The Regimes men had left over two hours before; Nat was sitting with Amber at the kitchen table, he was sipping a scolding tea and she nursed hers with hands wrapped around the mug. They sat mainly in silence waiting for Esme to return. His daughter would unwillingly do what he said, but he was not so convinced that Esme, his wife, would be so compliant. In fact, he knew he had another fight on his hands, this land was even dearer to her than it was to him. As the latch clunked and his wife entered the room, her curls had been flattened by a brief but heavy shower and her face was muddy, she had been to check on the horses.

"We have to get the fence sorted in the bottom field; Franklyn is giddy enough. I don't want to go chasing him across the Aspinalls' land...but I tell you he is the sturdiest stallion I've ever..." She always chattered. Nat had come to realise over time that it made up for his lack of words. As she placed the bucket she was carrying down she turned and saw her family with heavy faces and immediately she knew something had happened

"What is it Nat?" She spoke as she moved over to him and put her hands around his face "they've been haven't they?" She always touched him; it was a simple luxury that her husband rarely experienced in his physically punishing lifestyle.

"They have," He said looking into her hazel eyes, her lightly freckled face wet and mud-spattered. She was the most beautiful woman he had ever seen. "It is over Esme, we are going to be turfed out if we don't give up the farm so either way we lose everything."

"No...No Nat, it won't happen" She stood up straight and turned away from him, thinking "There will be some compromise, what do they think that every farmer in the country is going to give up their land...no, it won't happen Nat, you'll see, something will give".

"You can't bury your head in the sand Esme; this is happening."

"He's right Mum, but we have to fight, not run" Added Amber

"Don't you start lass, we agreed, you go to Scotland" Nat shot across the room at Amber.

Esme turned to her family "You mark my words, I will not be leaving this farm. Nat you go see Rowell, join them and let's fight. I will happily have Scots soldiers based here if it means it's ours; I will not walk away."

"No one's walking away Esme" Nat replied "But you are not staying here, I won't let either of you stay here. You go and stay with Stuart, just while the trouble starts so we can know where we are. I will be here, and I will join Rowell, I will fight whoever comes onto this farm..."

"I won't go Nat" Esme snapped

"You will! Don't be so stubborn, lass! Losing the farm is bad enough don't make it worse; just let me know you're safe!" Nat raised his voice as his patience wore thin

"And what about you, you stupid man! I want to be here with you...Amber will go; we stay here".

"Amber can you leave me to talk to your mother for a minute?"

"But I want to fight..." She began to argue but Nat was having none of it he turned to her and snapped

"Now girl, get out of here!" She wanted to argue but resisted and left her parents to talk. Nat got up and put his hands on his wife's shoulders

"Esme, look what would happen if this really got bad, what if we both died here on the farm, left Esme with no parents..."

"Don't you talk like that Nat, of course, it won't."

"Maybe it will if we fight, I need you to go with our daughter for that reason only, of course, I'd want you here with me but we have to think of her. I'm sure it won't happen like that, but they were not messing around today."

"Well," Esme turned away, head down, her fingers pinching her lips deep in thought "Ok, ok let's see how this thing pans out over the coming days. If things get worse, I'll go with Amber...Ok?

"Ok, but as soon as things escalate you both leave, agreed?"

His wife looked into his eyes and whilst shaking her head voiced agreement. Neither believed that this could happen; that their home could be taken away from them. But they were fully aware that the NSO knew about their farm and had made many visits now. Something would change at some stage the Regime would have to go through with their promises. Or could it be that they would leave them to live in peace?

Nick Christofides

FOUR

Two weeks had passed since Nat had beaten the NSO operative, and they had no further contact with the Regime. Reports over the internet were proving that the government had underestimated the rural landowners will to resist the land reforms. Farms across the length and breadth of the country were refusing to co-operate and everything had gone very quiet from the NSO's side. Nat was beginning to think that it had been a nightmare or that the regime had simply floated the idea to see if it would work and had now given up the ghost as there was too much opposition. This was a belief that even old man Rowell held.

Nat was out tending their sheep, they were in the thick of lambing and the barn was full. The weather this year was showing mercy. There had been no recent snow, very little frost even. He stood in the top field, above the wood at the northern extremity of his farm, and there were three new lambs with their mothers. The sun was out in an ocean of blue above him, a fresh and optimistic morning he thought as he grabbed a lamb and swung it roughly through the air to kick start its breathing. Life seemed back to normal.

Esme stepped out of the bath; she stopped for a minute as the heat from her soak and standing up had made her light headed. She rested her slender fingertips on the edge of the bath as the dizziness faded; she enjoyed the feeling. Then she padded naked through their bedroom. Passing the full-length mirror she stopped and moved back to look at her reflection. A woman in her forties she was proud of her body and an active life that had maintained her firm round breasts, the curve of her backside and her flat stomach highlighted by visible hip bones. She pretended to smack her bottom and whispered to the mirror

"Still got it, Es!" As she walked over to her dressing table, ringing her thick curls out over one shoulder. She sat and paused for a moment looking at the photo under the glass on her dressing table. The same photo she always looked at when she sat there.

It was a hazy summers evening, and Nat was sitting across from a six-year-old Amber. His face was slightly contorted explaining some important facts to his daughter who sat head cocked to one side listening intently to her father. She adored that photograph it illustrated their relationship. Suddenly she jumped as the heavy bell at the back door clanged. 'Shit.' She thought as the shock waned, Jean and Betsy. She grabbed the first thing that came to hand, one of Nat's heavy woollen jumpers, and she pulled it over her head as she ran downstairs calling out "Coming Jean!"

She had forgotten that friends were coming over to have a look on Ambers tablet at the latest news. She rushed to the back door her hair soaking wet and dripping onto the jumper that hung to her upper thigh, as she clunked the heavy steel latch she spoke apologetically

"Guys, I forgot all about you coming, I've just got to throw some..."

As she opened the door, her words stopped. She immediately tried to slam it again, but a heavy palm hit the other side of it

"Don't worry, don't worry my lovely, it's all right, I'm from the government" came a heavy South African accent. Esme stepped back from the door and pulled the loose neck of the jumper across her chest "What are you doing here? What is this?" her breathing was shallow, and her heart pounded. Behind the man who occupied her doorway, there were at least ten armed men. Most were at this point violating her with dirty eyes caressing her flesh; she was naked other than the short jumper and she wanted the ground to swallow her whole she felt so vulnerable.

The South African spoke again, a smirk appearing across his heavy jaw and eyes darting across her body. He turned to his men "Don't you be scared of these lot, that's security you know, last time we came here one of my boys was pretty roughed up by your old man, is he here?"

Her pupils dilated, and her eyes flickered, "Yes he's in the other room with four farm hands, they're about to go out shooting rabbits."

"Oh, I see," Said the South African with a menacing grin "So your old man is through there armed to the teeth, and we're out here looking all armyish."

Esme nodded, uncomfortably fully aware that the man had seen through her lie.

He carried on, "You better let me come in and speak to him then, we have business to sort."

"He's not here."

"What?"

"I said he's not here, you'll have to come back" The man did not move, so she added, her voice losing confidence, "He's out with the sheep."

"Why'd you lie to me lady?" He said with venom growing in his voice "I'm not the enemy, we all have a job to do, now you step back and let me come in and wait for him." The South African pushed against the door to open it more, Esme held it as best she could and then she saw the look in his eyes. She had seen that look before, she knew it was the look of a man who was about to do something he knew was wrong but couldn't help himself

"C'mon back up little lady" As he pushed harder the door swung open knocking Esme back against the kitchen table. She tugged at the jumper pushing it further down her thighs. He broke the threshold of the door and entered the warmth of the room. His fingers trailed along the sideboard as he skirted to the side of Esme.

"It's lonely for a man up here, you know? Constant quarrels, taking people's homes, kicking them out on the street, hurting them, you know?" As he spoke the colour ran out of Esme's face, she looked forlornly at the men outside the door but their eyes darted away when they met hers. The South African turned and brushed past Esme once more. His hand reached out to the door as he said "Would be nice to feel the touch of a woman, you understand me? Maybe even buy you and the family a bit of time in your home..." Their eyes met as a tear ran down Esme's face, and she frantically pushed the jumper down her naked thighs. He began to shut the door slowly behind him when a man ran up to the door and called after him

"Boss we got company, two cars coming up the drive..."

"Ok" He called. The man's gaze lingered on Esme as he calculated, annoyance flashing across his face as he opened the door again. Then he turned back to Esme, "Tell your old man we're coming tomorrow. We take control of the farm with you in it or without you." He turned to leave the kitchen but at the last moment turned back to Esme and whispered "I'll definitely be seeing you again too my lovely" And he kissed into the air.

Esme sat down in a kitchen chair and burst into tears, shaking uncontrollably with fear. A few minutes later four of her neighbours burst in and wrapped her in their arms.

It was after lunch by the time Nat was powering down the hill towards the farmhouse astride his quad. He saw eight cars on the drive and immediately he turned the throttle as far as he could, and the engine roared. He stopped short of the bottom gate, jumped off the bike and over the gate, running to the house he slammed through the door. Everyone in the kitchen leapt in shock as the door flung open, but Nat had nothing to fear as he saw the faces of old man Rowell, Jean, Betsy and their husbands staring back at him. Rowell's oldest son Barty was there too he approached Nat and said,

"They came this morning Nat, shook her up pretty bad like"

Nat pushed past the young man and knelt down in front of Esme who was sitting at the table

"Did they touch you?" he exclaimed

"No Nat no, I'm ok Hun, I – I" and the tears welled up again she put her arms around him and sobbed into the small of his neck. As she fought for composure, the rest of them told Nat about the visit from the NSO. The fat old man who had spoken in the barn that stormy night in Wooler piped up, he spoke solemnly

"You gotta get both of them off the farm Nat. Jesse took the boys wives up to the cousins in Kielder yesterday. The wife won't budge, but she's got fifty years on you Esme" Turning back to Nat he added "You've been targeted now. You know the Young's over Whitfield?"

Nat nodded "Aye I know him."

"He's dead Nat; they fucking killed him and four labourers including Sammy Clough; he is two weeks off eighty! This is the wild west Nat we are being run off our properties."

"What are you going to do?" Nat asked Rowell

"We're getting organised; we need you; we need men, we're talking to the Scots, and they are getting weapons over the border to our men. We're gonna fight back." The whites of his eyes shone with the grit and determination that fuelled him, he continued "You need to get Amber and Esme North or up to Scotland, it's getting too dangerous..."

Nat gathered his thoughts, "Right you and Amber are leaving tonight, I'll take you up to Stuarts and then I'll be back to meet these bastards in the morning."

"We had the same visit Nat; we are blockading the farm now; we have refused to comply, and they are coming to move us out. They haven't said when but..." Rowell looked at his son "Actually we better get back boy"

The young man nodded at the old, and they both shook Nat's hand on the way out. They left to tend their own troubles. The rest of the visitors followed the Rowell's out shortly after.

Nat sat with Esme quietly waiting for their girl to get back from college. Esme watched her husband as he fell under the spell of deep thought. She saw the farmer in the hard man working out a solution to the problem that had befallen him. Working the land you couldn't let problems stop your progress you had to find a solution. The cocktail of brains and force was a farmer's best asset. And right now her husband was working out how to stop this nightmare. She left him to think and went upstairs to pack a bag.

As soon as Amber bundled clumsily through the kitchen door, throwing her bag on the floor as she did every day and walked over to the Aga. Nat jumped up from the table and intercepted her; he gripped her shoulders, "Go pack a bag, as much as you can for a few weeks but only one bag, OK?"

He saw a faint cloud cross her face as she began to reason but then it passed, and she moved without speaking. She trusted her father; she didn't question him. As the door was closing he shouted after her "Tell your mother to be ready in a few hours."

Nat's mind was spinning; he had to prepare himself for the NSO arriving the next morning as he would be travelling with the women into the night. He had no idea where to begin with a plan, but he was sure that if all else failed he was not going to allow his house and barns to fall into the NSO's hands.

With fatalistic sabotage in mind he spun around and grabbed his coat whipping it over his thick shoulders, the familiar smell of his wax jacket provided some comfort as he charged into the dusk. He moved down the side of the house using what light was thrown out from the windows to help him through the shadows. The weather had been deteriorating throughout the day and was closing in quickly now, the clouds in the sky swirled like a madman's mind and the wind howled through the yard.

Nat reached the trap door to the cellar and with rigid joints and ripping arms he threw the heavy double doors to either side. The adrenalin was pumping. He needed this job done, so he sank deep into single-minded concentration. He didn't even feel the rain hitting his face like a thousand pins being pitched at point blank range. He turned from the cellar and ran across the farmyard to the small bothy where he stored propane gas bottles. There were plenty. He used the quad and trailer to transfer all of them to the cellar.

Next he grabbed his pick axe and crossed to the oil tank which housed the domestic oil for the central heating. Facing the tank he looked over his shoulder to assess the job ahead; it was a good forty feet across the yard to the diesel tank for the farm machinery. He breathed a deep breath, looked at the dirt at his feet and hit it hard with the pick axe. He worked like a metronome, breathing hard, dripping with sweat but showing no sign of pausing or even slowing. His mind was on the job; he could rest later.

The fear, the anger drove him through the pain, in some corner of his mind he enjoyed the pain. He was calling on the same reserves that sent him head first into the snow drift to save his lambs or the slurry pit to rescue his wayward collie. He hacked out a rough trench from oil tank to diesel tank. While he worked he boiled, as soon as he stopped he felt the wind biting at his sweat sodden skin, the temperature was dropping fast, and the wind was picking up.

"What are your plans Nat?" asked Esme as she swept her locks away from her face.

"Get you two to safety and make sure that no-one sits at our table uninvited" He replied as he left the room. Esme could hear his footsteps stomp down the cellar steps.

He laid demolition fuse, he had made it some months before to create space in the quarry for a shelter. Now he laid it in the shallow trench that he had hollowed out. Carefully laying it from the far end to where the oil tank stood. He covered the fuse over with the loose dirt. He punctured a hole in the diesel tank and fed the end of the fuse through securing it with a rag.

He checked his work briefly in the unkind light and heartless weather. It was an elementary set-up; not many variables meant few margins for error.

He turned and ran back to the house and down the cellar steps. The dusty room was large but full of bits and pieces that a family collected over time. With the remainder of the fuse, he took one end and pushed it between the floor boards above. The rest of the length he laid out across the floor reaching the gas bottles which he had shoved through the external trap door.

He threw the rest of the coiled fuse to the floor next to the bottles along with anything else that would burn. When he had set the bonfire, he ran to the barn and wheeled back sacks of AN fertilizer and plastic fuel oil bottles. They joined the heap in the cellar.

When he had finished, he clapped the dust off his hands and stood back from his handy work. He shook his hot head in sadness as well as in uncertainty; he had no idea what he was doing, but he reassured himself it was a failsafe. If everything else were lost, if he lost, his home would not fall into their hands now.

Nat returned to the kitchen where Amber stood with her back to the warmth of the Aga and Esme sat in the armchair next to a roaring fire; both wide-eyed with nerves waiting to leave. His wife looked at him sadly "I've seen what you've done Nat, whatever happens Nat, promise me you will get out?"

"Of course, I promise Es, I'll be up on the hill watching the show" It was half-hearted bravado.

He told them to go and get in the car and wait for him. Then he picked up the phone and dialled a Scottish number. He waited as the ringing tone resonated back down the line. He pictured his old friend sitting in his kitchen listening to the phone ring thinking 'Who's that' and 'If I leave it long enough they'll go away.' But Nat knew he didn't have an answer phone so it would just ring eternally if necessary so he waited it out. Finally, the receiver at the other end was lifted, there was no hello; only silence. Nat spoke

"Stuart its Nat, I need your help."

"Ah, Nat it's you, tell me, no problem" Came back the borders drawl "Are the girls ok? What's happening down there? The news says it's a fucking riot; the countryside is war, farmers killing government troops and vice versa. There's a big debate up here whether we should intervene or leave you English to kill yourselves."

"Yeah, Esme has had a scare, and they'll be back tomorrow, so I want to get Amber and Esme to you if that's ok?"

"No problem, but the border is locked down; the Scottish are massing military there as we speak. Forget the Carter Bar I don't think you'll get through or if you do you'll be stuck for hours. Take the Kielder Road and skirt the eastern side of the reservoir, about three k from the head of the reservoir there is an old stone bridge on a right-hand turn. Park up there and follow the burn north. It's called Bells Burn so that should be lucky! After about one k the burn corners in an easterly direction around the northern edge of woodland. Follow it all the way it leads straight over the border and under a wooded track. When you get to the track, follow it east, and I'll be there."

"How long before you can get there"

"Couple of hours at the outside"
"We're leaving now, thanks eh."
"Leave it Nat and be careful ok."

Nat downed the receiver with a slight feeling of reassurance; he didn't feel quite so alone. Once Amber and Esme were safe, he felt he would be able to concentrate on the task in hand much better. He hurried out to the car. Esme and Amber were waiting, Amber back left and Esme front passenger. The engine was running, and there was already heat emanating from the blower.

"Ok?" he asked as he climbed in, both women nodded. He gunned the accelerator, and they hammered down the long drive. They hardly travelled a hundred yards when Nat's heart sank once more. Racing up the drive to meet them were a set of headlights. His mind racing he thought there can only be five in the car, more likely four. Esme was looking at him, and he nodded down to the foot well where she sat, she leaned in and felt around until her hand appeared with a short-handled axe.

"Pass it over Esme" He said, "And when I get out you take the driver's seat, don't wait to see what happens you drive."

Nat pulled over to the side of the road as the car approached, using the time to explain to Esme the route across the border that Stuart had given them. He lowered his window allowing the driving rain to enter the Jeep as the second car loomed closer at pace. The car only seemed to notice the Jeep late and had to break hard, skidding to a stop. All the occupants of the Jeep sighed with relief as they recognised the small Nissan next to them. The window came down and out came the familiar voice of their neighbour from two miles down the road

"Oh Nat, thank God we found you, they came to our house, six of them. They wrecked the house taking everything and anything, they beat Bob over and again, and they are coming back with a truck for our diesel. Bob's in a bad way Nat, please help us?"

"Calm down Jean, we'll take you to the hospital now…" Said Esme

"No Esme" Shouted Nat "No, we can't spare the time; we have to get you to safety" He looked across at Jean "Can he walk?"

"No Nat, I think they broke his leg or his ankle or something, but his ribs are damaged too and look at his face…he needs a doctor!"

"Ok, turn round Nat" Esme butted in "Take me back to the house with Bob and Jean, I'll patch him up and take him into Hospital in Newcastle. I'll leave them there and make sure I'm back for you in a couple of hours. Go on, we'll be OK. Otherwise, Stuart will be waiting; you can't get hold of him now; he will have left. Go Nat get Amber to safety".

Nat looked at the old couple, and while he cared for them he didn't want to leave his wife. Esme pounced on his hesitation exclaiming

"Come on Nat! We haven't got time for this, I won't leave these people."

Nat bowed to the pressure from his wife his mind chaos.

"Ok Jean, go on up to the house, I'm turning round."

He spun the wheel and turned in one motion, riding onto the grassy verge at the side of the road. The wheels tore up the sodden ground, but the heavy tires found traction and the Jeep began to move with a lolloping action.

At the house they made Bob and Jean comfortable in the kitchen, Amber remained in the Jeep and Nat stood next to the open driver's door as it idled. Esme approached him to see him off, and her beauty gripped his heart like a vice. His head was a mess, and he did not know what to do for the best, but his wife had serenity, a confidence that reassured him.

"Get her to safety Nat, that's the most important thing, we'll be out of the house for most of the time you're away anyway. You'll only be a couple of hours."

Nat saw the flash of fear in those beautiful green eyes, and he gripped her shoulders

"They come back; you take this" He held up a lighter "And you light that fuse poking out of the floorboards in the hallway. Then you get out of there, head up the hill to our place and wait for me there. Do it Esme, with or without Bob and Jean, you stay safe woman".

"Don't be soft Nat, I won't need that."

"Take it anyway"

Nat had one foot in the idling jeep; he turned with one large hand on the door

"You use it Esme, if you need to."

Reluctantly she put the lighter in her pocket and moved in close to Nat; she hugged him tight and kissed him hard on the mouth.

"I love you, Nat."

"Don't worry, you stay safe, I'll be back in a couple of hours."

He climbed into the Jeep fully and closed the door behind him; the window was open from earlier, and Esme approached it and put her hands on the frame. Nat took her hand and squeezed it looking at her face. It was taught with stress glimmering in the dull light; he had nothing more to say, he didn't have any answers or anytime to think this through. He just had to go and get back as soon as he could. He attempted a smile and released her hand. She stepped back and then saw Amber in the back and was overwhelmed by love once again; she pulled open the heavy door and grabbed the young woman's face in both hands

"You listen to your Dad and Stuart, do whatever they say...ok?"

Amber nodded

They both smiled, and Esme kissed her daughters face over and over again. Then reluctantly allowed her hands to slip away from her cheeks, she closed the door and took a few paces backwards with tears welling in her eyes.

Nat's battered old jaw formed as near a smile as it was ever going to manage and with a nod he slammed his foot on the accelerator. The village of Great Whittington was quiet as he passed through. A little too quiet for this time of night.

There was an eerie orange glow in the middle distance to the South East. It was too close to be the lights of Newcastle, and he guessed that it was the paper factory at Prudhoe burning. As he passed the Errington Arms, also boarded up and closed, he entered the dark void heading north, and he thought about the revolution that had swept the country. How unbelievable it would have been to suggest this would be happening twenty years before. Although he conceded to himself that he had witnessed the meltdown over recent years.

His attention was shocked back to the road by the steady stream of cars he came up behind. The silver fans of headlights and red dot eyes of the tail lights wound over the undulations of the straight road for miles and Nat hoped that the border was still open for all these people trying to escape. As he followed the convoy, he could see Amber nodding off in the rear view mirror. It reminded him of her early years when he used to angle the mirror so that he could watch her playing or sleeping in the back of the car while he drove. Esme was heavy on his mind, the traffic was a pain and he ground his teeth in frustration.

The squeak and whoosh of the wipers was the soundtrack to the journey. The mesmerising view of the white lines flashing into sight through the rain and being devoured in the same instant by his jeep made him drift off, but the wrinkles of the road whipped his concentration back.

The straight ribbon of road and lights came to an abrupt end, temporarily as he came upon the brow of the hill that looks down towards Otterburn. They would be turning left at the crossroads towards Bellingham and Kielder instead of right to Otterburn or straight ahead to the Carter Bar. It was this dark wilderness of the border country in which they would lose themselves. Now off the main road the night outside the car was black as death but the rain had broken and he could see some stars penetrating the churning cloud cover. 'Good news' he thought, dryer and lighter for the walk ahead of them.

They were alone on the road now, and Nat could feel the looming emptiness of Kielder reservoir on his right. He opened his window, and he could feel and smell that cold air, heavy with moisture that comes from a large body of water. He sucked up the fresh, invigorating ether; it normalised the situation.

After a few short minutes, he saw the lights of a home on the left and the shadowy outline of the stone bridge on the right. He pulled into the side of the road well short of the house and turned the headlights off. He turned to Amber

"This is it lass, c'mon."

She nodded and opened her door with a crunch and a creek. Nat jumped down from the driver's seat. He moved around the front of the Jeep and went to step up on to the grass verge but his foot slipped on the sodden bank, and he tripped and tumbled into the ditch. Amber jumped from the truck and scrambled down to him. When she found him in the dark, he was chortling to himself and had his hand out

"Well help me up then girl, I'm in this mud like a plug in the bath!"

She shook her head and laughed, clapping her hand tight to his she said

"You auld codger, what'll you do without me around."

"We'll be with you by the time you're awake in the morning."

Nat wiped himself down, took the pack from his daughter, and they set out in the cold night air, at home and in control. Their eyes were now making use of what light there was and the world of shadows unravelled in front of them step by step.

The road continued straight for about two hundred yards then veered sharp right over the old stone bridge. Straight ahead at this point was a rough track which led straight passed the house that they could see, lights on and occupied. Nat whispered to Amber

"Head up the track but stay in the shadows, we don't know whose home and if they're nervous, we could end up shot."

As they walked along the track, Nat nudged Amber and pointed to the fence on the right. The field behind dropped away some ten feet, ample to conceal them from view. They hurried down into the field and once they were moving through the boggy grass they both became more relaxed, the smells and the feel of the land around them and the freedom of the endless sky above.

The wind swirled and beat them but without biting or soaking, they moved quickly through the ankle high grass. They followed the burn that took Nat's family name, a nod to centuries passed when his ancestors would have trod this path on raids north of the border.

The burn was bridged by the rough track that they had left, and the two ghostly figures ducked under the low crossing. The stream led them left along the extremity of a thick immature conifer forest. They kept out of the trees; there was no need for cover, and the going was much easier in the grass.

As they turned north once more the trees ended, and they were running in the open but Nat felt a change in the symphony of the night, there was an alien presence, and it was huge. Similar to the sense of the dark void that was Kielder, this was an elephant in the room. And then it materialised out of the black loomed a shadow against the sky. Nat slowed and walked up to a concrete pillar which rose at least three metres upwards. He felt the cold concrete, as if to convince himself the thing was real. He thought for a minute then looked to his right. He could not see anything in the dark, but he set of striding out about a yard or a metre; the usual way. He counted 'one, two, three' as he stepped and after five strides he hit another pillar. Evidently the NSO were certainly planning on closing the border, once the concrete slabs were set in between each of these pillars; no one would be crossing the border.

Nat thought about all those cars heading towards the Carter Bar, and he didn't fancy their chances of getting through tonight. He noticed history repeating itself; the English building a wall to keep the Scots at bay once more. He realised the threat of a Scottish invasion must be real for the NSO. A chill ran down his spine as he thought of Esme at home; he whistled to Amber, and they set off running north again.

They ran through open ground now, occasionally startling livestock, which kept their hearts pounding. After another mile they hit the dirt track which cut across their path and Nat tugged Ambers sleeve to say 'this way'.

The track was about ten feet wide and ran straight through thick mature coniferous forest to either side. It was relatively clear, but there was no light getting past the giant spiny trees on either side. Nat and Amber moved forward slowly opening their eyes as wide as they could to access as much light as possible. Even though their eyes were used to the dark by now, they could see virtually nothing and so going was rough; stumbling and tripping step after step. Nat was holding his daughters arm. He could feel fatigue setting in. He also began to worry that they were on the wrong path, and he was heading away from Stuart into a thick forest. There was no sky, no view and no way to find his bearings. Getting lost would be a seriously stressful waste of time as he was desperate to get back to his farm.

Suddenly the forest burst into bright white light, and they fell to their knees shielding their eyes. Nat saw the soles of his daughter's feet disappear into the trees. He snatched himself up to his feet and followed. He threw himself over a fallen tree and he crawled along the trunk in an attempt to disguise their position. He stopped and squinted into the alien light, with wet moss between his fingers and wafts of peaty foliage filling his nostrils. They heard a car door open, his hand gripped the handle of his hunting knife.

"Whit the feck are ye dein' Nat, ye auld barst'd" came the exaggerated Scottish wail through the trees. Nat shook his head and got to his feet as Amber chortled and ran over to Stuart and hugged him.

Nat had first met his old friend in the 1990's in the Carts Bog, a pub as old as time. They fought over a woman on their first meeting and spent years at loggerheads. It was when Esme's father died that Stuart turned up on the farm and offered to help with the lambing. After this their friendship evolved into a brotherhood, and they had never let each other down in all the years since.

The big man put Amber gently back down and looked at Nat. In his natural borders lilt he said

"Where's Es?"

"She stayed, some trouble with the neighbours..." Nat replied

"Don't you waste any time now pal. You get back to Esme and Nat, don't be foolish now, get your wife and head on back up here, just for a few weeks while all this settles. Look..."

"Yes man" Nat replied as he stepped forward and clenched hands with Stuart, with his free arm he embraced his friend. Then he turned to Amber and swept her into his arms and held her tight. He stroked her hair and kissed her head.

"You stay with Stu now, we'll be back with you by tomorrow. Listen to Stuart."

She nodded once more but Nat saw the devil flash across her face. She wanted to fight.

He nodded to Stuart, turned back down the track and ran off into the darkness.

He jogged all the way back to the Jeep and jumped into the driver's side breathing hard, sweat beading on his forehead. His was the only vehicle heading south on the A68 winding round and over the hills. There was a steady stream heading north, but only his four wheel drive heading towards the NSO. As he switched the radio on it was like stepping back in time, the stations were the same, the songs were the same and the presenters sounded the same. It was only when the news bulletin came on that there was any evidence of the NSO's influence over the country. Nat listened with horror as he heard the good news stories; the NSO fund new industry, new schools, more doctors...there was no mention of the land redistribution, the chaos in the countryside.

His confusion grew as he began to question whether he had any right to fight the redistribution at all. It seemed like the rest of society was happy with this regime, it seemed as though he was swimming against the tide that was far greater than him. He began to contemplate co-operation if he could stay on his farm. The vice-like pressure on his temples eased as he thought that there may be some positive outcome ahead. At that moment, he decided to broach the meeting with the NSO the next morning constructively.

Once again his car swept passed the Errington Arms, about five miles from his home, all was dark, and all was quiet. The orange glow from the paper factory fire remained strong, but the night looked quite beautiful because of it.

All of a sudden to the northeast, the sky lit up like a super nova. The first fireball rose up into the night and then it was engulfed by an almighty inferno which grew like a black, orange and yellow mushroom belching upwards and outwards.

His throat constricted, his stomach turned over, his chest began to hurt, and his hands grew numb on the steering wheel as his head told his body that the explosion was his house and his wife.

The car swerved as he regained some composure and gunned the big vehicle as fast as he could. With the big tires and soft suspension playing his control at every corner, he struggled to keep the vehicle on the road. He managed to get within a few yards of his gates when a white car came screaming out of his driveway. Nat's headlights flooded the car with light, he saw five ghostly faces. Faces full of menace and adrenalin. Faces from hell. Nat shuddered as he recognised those who were closest; the boy who had squared up to him the night he had fought with them and the scrawny one who had hidden in the shadows. Both had been in his kitchen the day they visited on behalf of the NSO.

His eyes briefly followed the red tail lights disappearing away down the road. Then he slammed his foot on the accelerator and turned into his drive clipping the back of the Jeep on the old stone gate post as the car fishtailed. He watched his house burn as he sped up the straight road. Misjudging his speed, he slammed on the breaks and skidded on the gravel in front of the house crashing into a blue Toyota that was parked in front. He didn't recognise the car. Realising there were still intruders there he grabbed the axe from the foot well of the passenger side of the Jeep.

Nat looked at the inferno shielding his face from the heat. The blustering wind fanned the flames that twisted, licking the night's sky like satanic whips drawing blood in the form of a million sparks splashing out of the darkness.

The house was already a ruin; the roof had either blown off in the explosion or collapsed due to the flames, the rafters were black and broken like giant charcoal sticks. There was no evidence that there had ever been doors or windows in the house and the side wall had completely collapsed. It lay as rubble. Huge stones that once had been part of the structure lay all around.

The heat blistered his face, but he couldn't stop looking, surely Esme ran, surely she was in the barn or better the top wood. He knew she was; he just knew it.

He ran around the front of the house taking the wide swing around the collapsed flank wall. The inferno was raging in the wind; he looked into the molten mass, and it was like the belly of hell.

It was light enough to see but golden flickering with thick shadows and sparks everywhere. He rounded the corner into the farmyard, and the scene hit him like a juggernaut, it was like a war zone there was flames and rubble everywhere.

At his feet lay a man with a close range shotgun wound to the chest. His face was serene with death, but the bloody mess of his chest was visceral and horrific. Nat stopped for a second digesting this new reality.

He looked again and there just outside the back of the house a charred corpse, obviously caught by the explosion. He started over to the body with his stomach in his mouth, working on instinct now with no comprehension. He could see trainers on the feet of the body and his hope was revived. The horror of those hands mummified by the flames, the shrunken sinews pulling fingers into claw-like remnants. He turned away briefly in shock but soon enough his eyes were trained back on the blackened face flesh melted tight into a satanic scream.

He was staggering towards the barns now to look there and then head up to the top wood to find his wife; she would definitely leave for Scotland now that people had died here. They were in serious trouble now, and he cursed his stupidity and rash anger. He had envisaged using this booby trap if they had been forced to leave their land not when there were people in the house.

Then out of the corner of his eye he saw something.

It was almost completely hidden by the wheel of the tractor, but there it was again in the shimmering firelight; a brief flash of auburn blowing in the wind.

Nat's legs buckled, he felt his knees connect with the ground, his hands hit the floor and pushed himself back to his feet and he sprinted the distance to the other corner of the yard.

There behind the Massy Ferguson lay Esme on her side prostrate in the dirt. Her back was facing her husband. Her hair was mostly matted with mud and soot but there was just enough of it blowing in the wind to have given her away. Nat convulsed and threw up, again falling to his knees and crawling the last ten yards to his beloved wife, his tears already soaking his face and chilling it in the night's wind.

Esme was alive, but part of him wished she wasn't. He could see that she had a gunshot wound in her back that must have been as she was running from the house. She had managed to get behind the tractor before the explosion, but most of what she had been through had been inflicted before the chaos, with time and fear and sufferance. He tried not to think, but his mind boomeranged back to her state of undress. The pain ripped at his heart as he couldn't stop thinking about what he had left his wife to endure.

He didn't know whether her injuries were life-threatening, but the blood pooled under her back was horrific, her face was pummelled and she had blood between her legs.

She was shaking uncontrollably. He had no idea what to do for the best, so he ripped his coat off his back. Scooping her frail body up, he wrapped it tightly around her and carried her closer to the flames for warmth. He knelt down with her still in his arms and the heat washed over them.

She opened her eyes and looked into his and at that moment he was inconsolable. He saw Esme's eyes soften as she saw him. Her limp body tightened slightly and her hands gripped his arm.

He scrabbled in the dirt, what to do, nothing or no-one to help, how could he save her?

Then he screamed, animalistic, primeval as he realised he couldn't, she would live or die, but he couldn't influence it. His usual failsafe of brute force was useless now. He had left his wife alone and now she lay dying in his arms.

She moved his jacket to cover her brutalised privates. Every moment a torture that ripped through his soul. It tore all the joy he had ever known from his being and filled the void with a rage and a thirst for vengeance that he could not control.

He howled to the heavens like Frankenstein's monster as Esme choked and spluttered away. The fear had returned to her eyes now as she fought and panicked through lack of oxygen. The shaking was shallower, and the choking whittled away as her eyes became glazed; she was slipping away.

Nat was crying, uncontrollably spluttering words of calm torn between stroking her hair, looking into her eyes and cuddling her tight.

The final moments were punctuated by rakish breaths through blood-filled lungs. Her face calmed as the life drained from her body, and Nat sank his face into the small of her neck heaving with grief and wailing apologies.

They had beaten and raped his wife before shooting her in the back as she ran.

He was finished with life and just beginning with death, whether that be his own or every last one of those responsible for this atrocity.

Nick Christofides

FIVE

His legs were numb with kneeling. Esme's broken body lay in his arms. He had stayed like that for a good hour. She was hardly recognisable. The guilt and loss tore at his flesh; his body shook, and his guts churned. But already the grief was buried, overwhelmed by a burning hunger for revenge. It was part of his makeup to understand that she wasn't coming back, to know the finality of death. His mind boiled with anger. His tears waned, and the cold began to take hold of his body. The rain was coming down again now, so he scrambled to his feet. With her petite body in his arms and he grabbed a shovel and a torch and set off up the hill.

He carried her for over a mile, trudging through the dark. One drenching step after another up the exposed fell and then into the woodland, over the brow of the hill and into the relative calm of the hill's northern slope. The silence was deafening as the wind was blocked by the hillside, it seemed to press against his ears; he appreciated the change, it made life easier. Then he looked at Esme and focussed again. He staggered down the steep bank towards the small burn that had scythed its way through the land and into a deep narrow gorge. It was only a small stream, a relative trickle, but there was a point where the water hit an outcrop of bedrock and pooled behind it exploding over the breach to create a waterfall. It was here that the family would come on summer days. So many memories; there was nowhere else he was going to let his wife rest.

On the southern bank of the river, there was water meadow where when the water was not in flood they would sit amongst the flowers and reeds. At the edge of the field, the thick grass of the rough grazing began its ascent up the slope and about twenty yards up, clear of the flood waterline; there stood a magnificent ancient oak tree. The bulging, heaving trunk grew at an angle from the hillside, and the branches stretched out towards the river and away in search of the sun.

Nat laid Esme's body in the grass, and he took the shovel and began to hack the dirt from a solid cake to a thick muddy mass which he threw to one side in heavy wads. The toil relieved his tortured mind.

He moved over to his wife and knelt by her body, stroking her hair one last time. He kissed her lips and gently swept her off the grass. He closed her eyes and kissed her head once more in silence before laying her in the ground.

He climbed out of the shallow grave, looked with sorrow at his wife one last time and then shovelled fresh sodden dirt directly onto her corpse without uttering a word. His body shook, and his shoulders bounced with an overwhelming melancholy as he buried his wife. He thought briefly that she would be happy to be buried here. No Prayers, he wasn't religious; he sat exhausted on the boulders and thought about his immediate future.

It was past six in the morning; the dark night remained heavy, but the cold air was becoming moist with dew. He realised he was thoroughly exhausted. He knew he had to rest. He hauled his weary carcass to its feet and trudged back up the steep slope, through his beloved woodland and down the fell to the house. When he got there, the flames were still relatively ferocious but had died somewhat from the earlier blaze. Everything from the floors to the walls, from paperwork to the Aga was a mass of charred rubble. He shook his head as he thought about his perfect past life. There were no tears now, no wailing. His teeth ground together in sheer, bitter determination and his head filled with the molten lava of vengeance.

The first thing he went to was his gun cabinet. Esme would never let him have it in the house, so he had bolted it to the wall deep within the barn.

They had found it but had been unable to prize it open. A few feet away on the splintered old workbench he lifted a jar full of screws. He held it up to the light and saw what he was looking for; the keys for the cabinet winked at him through the glass. He opened the cabinet and viewed his limited but amply sufficient arsenal; he grabbed his silenced .308 Winchester and his 28" stack barrelled shotgun. He put the guns on the work bench and piled all the ammunition he had next to them.

Then his head swivelled in search of a bag, he knew it was there somewhere but he hadn't put his hands on it for probably ten years. His eyes scanned the piles and heaps as they had done a thousand times before. He knew he had seen it somewhere, so he dived into piles of material, there were blankets, plastic sheeting, old curtains then he found it under the curtains an old military style canvass holdall.

He placed the guns and ammunition into the flexible bag. Then he rounded up the other supplies he needed; a hammer, a saw, matches, firelighters, two large plastic sheets, three wax jackets. Quickly he moved to the other side of the barn where three thick horse blankets were draped over a trailer, he took two and folding them he stuffed them into the brimming bag. He looked for whatever food he could find. He packed another bag with dog biscuits and some tins of beans; the only food items in the barn. He set off west from the farm, munching dry muddy tasting dog biscuits as he stomped away.

He was heading half a mile west, to an isolated field shelter that he used for his lambs. It was water tight, and it gave him a clear lookout over the approach to his land.

By the time he reached the shelter, the first light of dawn was illuminating the blackness and the eastern skyline glowed deep dark blue. He took out his knife and hacked two armfuls of heather from the earth and then he put them on the floor of the shed as some sort of bed or at least insulation against the bare cold ground. Then he threw one horse blanket over the makeshift mattress and laid his weary bones down, pulling the other blanket over him. As he drifted off to sleep, he could hear the crows waking in the distance and the sheep calling for each other. He fell into a deep sleep.

He woke after about six hours with a jolt. He had a feeling in his stomach that the terrible dream he had just had was reality. The sickness increased as he realised where he was and that the nightmare was true. The life he had been living was over and this was the first day of a new bitter sorrowful reality.

He looked up at the roof of the shelter, pleased with his work, the spiders webs spanning every corner were covered in dust, dry as bones. He slowly moved through the stiffness of his muscles and stood outside the shelter absorbing the beautiful view up the Tyne Valley.

The previous night's storm had now past and although the sun was shining there remained a chill in the air. It was a crisp day. The first thing he had to do today was fill his stomach and dog biscuits weren't going to cut it. Rolling out in front of him was a hillside hopping with breakfast. He took the Winchester and laid down in the opening of the shelter. Although this was akin to cracking an egg with a sledgehammer, he took aim and fired twice. Two rabbits rolled limp across the ground. He stood, leaned the rifle against the shelter wall and walked down into the field. The wind blustered his ears, but he found solace in the exposure of the hillside. The chilled clean air filled his lungs and he felt some control returning to his mind.

The two rabbits lay only a metre apart and he sat down in the thick grass, there was no point in bringing the guts closer to the shelter. Before picking them up, he lay back and watched the infinite sky roll past. The lush tufts of rough grazing gave him even more shelter and he felt encapsulated in the landscape and ultimately alive.

Then he closed his eyes and Esmes battered face came at him from the darkness, he bolted upright and opened his eyes again to the countryside. Still sitting he snatched the first rabbit by the hind legs and unsheathed his knife and laid it in the grass. He held the small body upright and squeezed the lower abdomen to empty its bladder. Then he took up his blade and made a shallow incision just below the rib cage and drew the sharp point down between the rear legs. He then slipped his thumb and forefinger into the abdomen, pushing up and breaking through the diaphragm and there he felt the familiar hard ball of the stomach which he gently extracted. Bursting this would ruin the meal and his day as the rancid stink of a rabbit's belly was enough to make the sturdiest stomach turn.

While he worked, he thought about his wife, he was unsure whether he was in shock or whether he would ever feel distraught again. Yes, he felt hollow but he understood that she was gone; crying over the loss was pointless, meaningless. He knew how he felt, he didn't need to show anyone else love for his wife by crumbling. He felt uneasy that he had come to terms with it so easily and quickly, but he had, that was how he worked.

Using his blade, he removed the rest of the rabbit's innards then slicing through the membrane between meat and fur he skinned the animal. Leaving what he didn't want where it landed in the field he took up the other animal by its hind legs and carried both back to the shelter. He hang-tied the second rabbit's legs and hung it in the shelter then he walked to a glorious beech tree about fifty yards behind the shelter.

He picked fallen branches and with his arms full he returned to the shelter. He laid a firelighter and some scrumpled paper in the grass. Then he arranged kindling around the pile. Then he placed a layer of larger sticks around the kindling in the shape of a tepee. He lit the fire and soon enough the moisture in the sticks was being exorcised in the form of a thick plume of smoke which soon died back when the fire broke into flame. Nat eyed the approach to his land as the smoke could be seen from a long way off, but all remained quiet.

His mind turned back to his breakfast as he fashioned a rough spit out of three sticks and roasted the meat over an open fire. He also opened one of the tins of beans and placed the open tin on the edge of the fire to warm.

He ate as he gazed west up the Tyne Valley towards the chimneys of the chipboard factory in the distance. Which for as long as he could remember was belching out some concoction of gases. Today they were dormant. He wondered what the rest of the country were doing, was there civil war? Were people resisting? It didn't look like it to him, the countryside was quiet, but then he didn't imagine bombs would be going off either way.

It was seven miles into Hexham; he briefly considered walking but then thought better of it; time was against him. He'd take his chances in the Jeep. After gnawing the last of the meat from the rabbit's bones, he put the fire out with loose soil from a nearby mole hill. He walked into the shelter and delved into the canvas bag removing the ball peen hammer he had stowed in there.

He put the tool in the inside pocket of his jacket and put the rifle back in the bag. Then he put the canvas bag into a plastic feed sack to keep it all dry and set off with it towards the house. Halfway up the steady incline he ducked into a small overgrown thicket, in there was an outcrop of rock which had a small cave. He pushed the bag underneath and moved off towards the house with his hammer in his pocket.

His home was now just a smouldering mess of stone, charred wood and melted man made materials. He looked, but his gritty face gave away no emotion. His jaw jutted like a rocky outcrop, his eyes were narrowed against the wind, his whiskers were white as snow and the lines on his face were dark and uniform like a furrowed field.

He stepped up into his Jeep, the keys remained in the ignition but the rear bumper was embedded in the blue NSO car which he had crashed into the night before. He started the engine, slammed his foot down on the accelerator and the powerful engine roared. The vehicle lurched up into the air, but the tyres were true, biting into the gravel throwing it aside and hitting the earth underneath. There was an almighty hollow crack of plastic passing its breaking point and a squeal of metal being torn away as the bumper was left behind. The Jeep tore off down the driveway mostly under the control of its driver.

He entered the centre of Hexham up Preistpopple, the town was quiet. It certainly didn't seem to be engulfed in turmoil, but there was evidence aplenty of the revolution. There were two burnt out shops on the street. There were a few smaller shops open, but the department store had been smashed up and looted all the large windows were shattered and the inside was wrecked from what he could see.

The way he saw it this revolution was a case of complying or be at least ruined, at worst destroyed. There were a few people milling around, he recognised the faces but didn't see anyone he knew to talk to. He parked the Jeep on Beaumont Street, a grand Victorian Avenue with attractive five or six storey buildings built opposite the Sele Park. The road slopes gently north to the magnificent Abbey on which land a church has stood for over a thousand years.

It was at the top of the street, next to the war memorial that he felt was the most exposed, this is where he would wait. He pulled his truck off the road parking across four parking spaces usually full of cars visiting the shops and sites of the market town, but today they were empty. He got out of the vehicle and strode over to a bench positioned at the gates to the park. He pulled his collars high around his neck and buried his hands deep inside his pockets then he sat on the seat and waited, looking out over the unusually quiet junction.

He sat in silence and still for over two hours, watching and waiting, conserving energy and thinking. Only a handful of cars past him by, and no one passed on foot. He didn't recognise anyone which was odd because he knew a lot of people and recognised most in this town. As darkness fell, he noticed the same cars full of younger men passing again and again. This in itself was not unusual but as he didn't know any of the cars or the people he discerned that they were NSO and he knew he was in the right place. He didn't however have a plan, he was simply overwhelmed by a thirst for violent retribution and he would work the rest out in real time.

It was dark now, but the night was relatively still and relatively mild, he had been sitting for hours and he wasn't feeling the chill. He had studied the birds, pigeons and blackbirds, merrily going about their business, he had studied the damage to his Jeeps rear bumper.

Now he was studying the outline of a rotund lone figure shuffling up the street towards him. Then his stomach turned and adrenalin coursed his blood as he caught a flash of white through the corner of his right eye. His eyes darted from the approaching man to a white car which turned into the street and directly passed Nat and his vehicle. He recognised the car; it was the regime thugs that he had seen the night before.

As it cruised past his position his steely gaze pierced into the interior although he couldn't see the occupants he stared as hard, unadulterated and menacingly as he could. The car slowed briefly and then accelerated away. Nat turned back to the person approaching and at a distance he recognised the gait and shortly after the face of his old friend Wes Milburn.

"Nat, I thought that was you, how are you? I heard about your house…"

Before the old man could continue Nat responded "Esme's dead."

Wes eyed his old friend unsure of his state of mind. "I know Nat, the NSO representative told us about the explosion, the booby trap. What were you thinking man? I don't think you can fight them anymore. This is a new system, a new government for now the choice is gone you have to live like the majority of the population want to…I suppose"

"They raped her, she didn't die in the explosion. She died in my arms of a bullet wound. She set off the explosion…"

Wes was absorbing the information, he gulped and stared through the pavement stunned for a second. He breathed out, lost for words he put his hands on Nat's shoulder.

"I-I don't know what to say Nat."

"Just don't give in that easy Wes, what exactly have you given over to them?"

"Well everything, we carry on living in the house but we have a workforce to work on the farm, all produce is collected by officials and distributed to local shops for sale. I get paid a wage according to the hours I work. But so far that's it everything else is exactly as it was. How did your situation get to this Nat…Esme I mean?"

Before he could answer, Nat saw the white car approaching up the hill once more and it had a black car following closely behind it. He knew this was it

"Go now!" he exclaimed to Wes pushing him up off the bench. Wes read the situation quickly from the tone of Nat's order and turned on his heals shuffling off in the direction he had come.

The breeze rustled chill through the naked trees somewhere in the dark behind him and the cold night filled his nostrils with fresh, clean air seasoned by wood smoke from a nearby fire. Nat stood square onto the road, rigid and tall, as always facing his demons head on. The two cars; a white sporty hatchback and a black estate car pulled into two spaces next to his Jeep. They pulled to a stop with a quiet whistle of breaks and the engines cut out one after the other. Nat stood, waiting, his heart pounding but eyes cold and menacing, this is where he wanted to be, this was his showdown and he was in control.

Three of the four doors opened in each car with the familiar dull clunks and out stepped six men. Nat's adrenalin and fear were combining like a horrific speedball, adrenalin taking him up like a racehorse at the gate and the fear paralysing him with that muddy lethargy of overwhelming nerves. So he stood stock still and relied on instinct to take over.

* * * * *

As they pulled up to the curb Roland spoke through the graphic injuries which the farmer had inflicted. They were slowly healing, the left side of his face had been a swollen mass of purple and his nose remained bent to the right. Nat had broken his cheekbone, eye socket and nose on the table and the boy was in no mood for another fight like the last. Political debate was his bag not physical war. He slurred through bulging lips

"It's definitely him again, I'm staying well back this time."

"Yeah, don't worry mate, we'll leave Rudi to deal with this one," said Gerry.

"That's what worries me, he's a bloody psychopath as well."

Davey sank as low into the back seat as he could.

Rudi Truter had arrived in the North East like a whirlwind three months before. He was one of Lucas Starts party enforcers. He had set about organising the party members into teams to action the new system and the redistribution of wealth. He was a ruthless mercenary with no real affiliation to the party beliefs but had met Start at a rally in London years earlier and had been caught up by the violence of the revolutionary struggle. It was his job to bring Northumberland under the control of the NSO and until the previous night things were going well. This headache had occurred when that woman had fought too hard and the retribution had spiralled out of hand. At this point, he only needed to remove this farmer from the equation. Then he could create the history of last night rather than his bosses and the wider public finding out the truth somehow.

* * * * *

Six men stepped out of the cars. As Nat snarled in their direction, now the fuelled blood was coursing his veins and rage was taking over the nerves. The three men who arrived in a black car looked instantly more capable than the three he had met before. They lined up in front of him. The skinny kid with an ugly face and the guy Nat had beaten up weeks before hung back beside the white car. In front of him from left to right; the first man was a thick-set black man wearing a black Gore-Tex jacket, black cargo pants and sturdy boots. Next to him stood a giant man of eastern European origin and who looked as though he had fought with every person he had ever come into contact with. He wore; primarily the same clothes as his accomplice just a variation in manufacturer.

Together though they certainly brought a military image, worse still a Special Forces image to the proceedings. Next to them stood the leader, he had that swagger, the air of authority. He too wore black, his hair was golden and he was tanned but he wasn't soft. Nat could see the coldness in his eyes, he was dangerous and he was the man Nat wanted to break. Next to him stood the man who had squared up to Nat in his kitchen but thought better of taking him on then.

Now the golden man spoke, the Boer guttural tones broke the silence

"Mr Bell, my name is Mr Truter and I'm in charge of NSO security in Northumberland. You are in serious trouble Mr Bell, the explosion you caused at your farm last night killed people Mr Bell."

Nat seethed at how this was being spun, he wanted this guy alone so that he could take time to cause him suffering. Truter carried on

"…it may seem like there is no law currently, but there is and it's me. We still live in a civilised society Mr Bell and although there is new leadership in the country and a little chaos, it doesn't mean we can turn a blind eye to crime. You have to come with us now Mr Bell for the murder of three of our NSO colleagues and the unlawful killing of Bob and Jean Scott and your own wife, Esme Bell."

Nat was reeling, he could see how this story could be believable. But he also knew the truth and the injustice placed more pressure on him, the atmosphere had become so heavy. Like a cornered wild animal and so full of rage, his grip tightened on the ball peen hammer which he had been holding by his side but out of view behind his leg. He stood closest to the smaller paramilitary, about three paces away.

The four men were bathed in the orange glow of the street lights, and their breath was beginning to form condensation as the air temperature dropped. The street was dead quiet and a slight drizzle began to fall. Nat had no plan at all, he had a hammer. They could have guns. He looked at each of the four faces in front of him; Truter was totally relaxed, assured but losing patience with the silence. The other men were watching intently but also unnervingly calm as if this type of situation and far worse were second nature to them. Nat spoke to the smaller paramilitary

"Were you at my house last night?"

"Yes" he replied and as he lifted his chin to give the affirmative Nat saw the deep desperate scratch marks on the man's neck.

"You shouldn't have done that."

"Done what?"

"The woman, my wife…"

Before any of them had time to register the words Nat had taken an enormous step forward. He swung the heavy hammer with every inch of power he could muster meeting the man's temple with a splintering crack underplayed by a dull thud. The hardened steel drove through his cranium with ease and mashed two or three inches deep into his brain. He went to ground with immediate and devastating paralysis.

While his body convulsed as his mind came to terms with the irreparable damage which had just been inflicted, Nat turned the tool again this time at Truter. Although the three men in front of him had been surprised by the speed and unadulterated violence of his attack they were quick to gather their composure and Truter dodged backwards avoiding Nat's lunge. The hammer connected with the shoulder of the Eastern European, who gave an audible wince and fell to one knee. As Nat realigned his body for the third attack, he looked up to find himself staring down the barrels of two guns which were levelled at his head. He understood immediately that this was it, someone was going to pull the trigger.

He heard two shots, but felt no pain and saw no muzzle flash from the guns in front of his face. As Truter and the mercenary turned to see who was attacking them now, Nat turned the other way and ran as fast as he could into the lifesaving darkness of the park. He was no sprinter so he tried to keep changing direction as he went. As he ran he heard three more gunshots; the first whistled past his head. The second slammed into a tree trunk to his right. The third ripped through his left shoulder like a freight train through a car left on the tracks. The force of the impact threw him off his feet and he rolled through the dirt but he was back to his feet in the same motion and he carried on running. It was only after another ten paces that the excruciating burning sensation oozed across his body from the epicentre in his arm. The limited paralysis of the pain lasted for about ten seconds in which he staggered on and then his mind cleared, adrenalin kicked in once again and he was running freely.

He knew this park, he had played in it as a child and he knew that the stream running through it went underground about fifty yards ahead of him. This was his new plan, get into the darkness and pick them off one by one in the confined space if they follow or escape and reorganise if they didn't.

He crouched behind a nearby tree in the darkness to see what his pursuers were up to. They were still under the street lights standing over their comrade's corpse. Two of the men had guns drawn, the eastern European was rubbing his shoulder and Roland and Davey remained cowering by their car. He turned back towards the stream and on the Southern side of the park he saw Wes's old Land Rover tearing off up the street and he realised where those first shots had come from. He owed Wes his life and he wouldn't forget it.

He moved quickly through the shadows holding his shoulder in an attempt to stem the blood but he could feel the warm tacky liquid running freely down his arm, he needed to move quickly.

He climbed the low wall and skidded down the gully to where the stream disappeared into its underground channel. The pain from his arm was ferocious and occupied his mind, but there was nothing he could do about it now and the bullet had passed through flesh so no bones were shattered, so he focused on getting away.

The tunnel was only chest high so he staggered along hunched over, virtually crawling. The river bed was rocky and slippery, there were branches and logs stuck in the tunnel, the ceiling was hard and rough against his back. The darkness made this hell even more challenging and the cold water of the stream filling his boots and washing over his lower arms made the whole adventure more demanding.

He had travelled a short distance into the tunnel when he heard voices at the mouth. He cursed his luck. Then bright torchlight illuminated his surrounds. It washed over him for a split second.

"There" he heard one of his pursuers shout. When the tunnel had been illuminated, he had seen a stout tree trunk left by a previous flood. He flung himself through the small gap between the top of the trunk and roof of the tunnel and in behind it. When the beam finally zeroed back on the spot where he had been it rebounded off the log and he heard a voice say

"Nah…that was just a tree stump," he breathed a sigh of relief which was short lived as the other voice called out

"It wasn't man, I saw something move in there…"

"Well, you get in and have a look then."

"Ah shit…" came a disdainful reply. Nat realised he was back in the firing line.

His breathing was shallow and snatched because he was trying to contain his panting from the sprint. He held his upper half at an awkward angle so as to remain behind the log but also out of the water. It was taxing his stomach, but he knew the small margins were the difference between life and death. He gritted his teeth and took the strain. His grip tightened on the hammer and he waited.

The light from the torch washed over the log and beyond into the tunnel above Nat's head. He could hear his pursuer cursing as he stumbled along the river bed. Whether it was the man he had met before or the other even bigger guy, there was no way they would be comfortable or moving freely in this confined space. Nat felt he had the upper hand.

"There's no room in here Gerry, I can hardly move…I don't think it could've been him down here" The man shouted back to his mate.

"Just check it out to that stump, I know that I saw something…"

The watery steps continued getting closer. Louder more audible over the constant babble of the stream echoing off the roof and around the tunnel. If he were to concentrate on it the noise in the tunnel was maddening but there was no time for that. As Nat peeked through the roots of the tree stump, he could see his pursuers' legs about three feet away and jittery. The torch was flashing all around the tunnel.

Nat looked down at his legs. The beam was illuminating everything. He realised it was time to make his move. He slowly pulled them towards him getting into a crouching position and turning to face the stump. Immediately he felt his calves cramping beneath him. The mercenary shouted to Gerry over the din,

"I've got the log and there's nothing here, I'll take a look the other side then I'm coming back."

To shout to his colleague, the man had naturally turned to face him, shining the light that way too. As his back was turned, Nat had risen out of the shadows like an angel of death, hammer in hand and face like a limestone outcrop in the dark of night. He was hunched ogre-like only a couple of feet from his pursuers face when the man turned awkwardly back towards him.

As the beam of the torch washed over the menacing apparition, both men reacted. Nat swung that ball peen hammer once again and the mercenary staggered backwards in fright. As he fell, he had the presence of mind to lift his gun and release a shot in Nat's general direction, but missing comfortably. Nat, on the other hand, caught the end of the man's chin as he went down. The bone shattered under the weight of the steel and as the mercenary fell into the water, Nat threw himself over the log. Grabbing the big man by the scruff of the neck and looked into the whites of his eyes, illuminated in the shadows by the torch lying close by.

He could see the fear in his eyes, but the rage had taken hold and Nat brought the hammer down once more with a devastating blow to the top of the mercenary's head. He dropped the body into the shallow water and took hold of the torch. He quickly found the handgun nearby on the river bed then he shone the light back down the tunnel, holding it as a rest underneath the weapon he searched for the other man. Nat couldn't see anything clearly but then heard a voice

"Billy, you ok? What's happening?"

Still with no shot Nat pulled the trigger twice down the torches beam. He took one last look then he turned and moved off down the tunnel putting the weapon in his pocket.

Gerry stood at the mouth of the tunnel. He thought about going after him but quickly changed his mind; with no weapon and an increasing fear of the farmer he turned on his heels and made his way back to his boss.

Nat pushed on through the tunnel, hunched over with the torch out in front of him like some hideous jail keeper from a Gothic horror story. The torch made the going much easier than before and he moved along uncomfortably but at a good speed. When he climbed out into the open, it was in itself a small victory as the pressure was released from his back and he could stand straight again.

He dumped the torch as he passed a public bin, preferring to allow his eyes to become accustomed to the night. He moved through the shadows with ease, north through the town towards the river Tyne. He knew that the river was swollen so he headed for the bridge across to the A69 and Acomb. As he came out of the houses past the out of town shops, he found himself in the open areas of Tyne Green and the Eastern edge of the golf course. This was no problem as it was dark enough and he was a shadow moving through shadows. It allowed him a view of the bridge and he could see at least two cars parked on it. He cursed not knowing who they were but not willing to risk another confrontation without any element of surprise and with his arm burning and bleeding.

He crossed the open land and reached the banks of the Tyne and shuddered as he looked into the darkness. He could sense the water in front of him and he knew from where he was standing at the water's edge that the river was higher and more menacing than normal.

He took his jacket off and lay it on the grass, then he emptied his pockets, hammer, handgun, knife, everything and laid them on the open coat. Then he undressed down to his pants and piled his clothes and his boots roughly into the open coat also. The breeze of the cold night air sliced at his skin. He knew there was worse cold to come so he put it out of his mind. He zipped the jacket up around his belongings, clothes and boots, then folded it collar to midriff and tail past collar. Using the sleeves he then tied them together so that he had a tight bundle.

Holding it in his left hand, the injured arm, he tried to lift it above his head. The pain was excruciating but he managed to get it up and rested on top of his head. This left his good hand to help him balance as he crossed the river. He felt happier that the wound was also raised as this may stem the steady flow of blood that he was losing.

He stepped into the icy water which felt heavy around his ankles and got weightier as he moved in. Although he had been inured to the cold, this was a shock to the system. Stoically he trudged onwards without pausing. He fought the shallow panicked breaths that the cold will's upon the body as it tightens the skin, infuses with muscle and makes bone moan in agony.

As he began to come to terms with the situation mentally, he lifted his foot to take a step and his toe collided with a boulder on the river bed. It was so numb there was no pain, but his body was as stiff as a board; the effort to keep his clothes above the water and stay on his feet was exhausting. As his head went under, his good arm flailed in the murky water like a fish on the end of a hook. His brain ached as he regained his footing and he stood for a second to gather composure before setting off once more.

In the deepest part of the river, the current was carrying him downstream with every step. So he turned his back towards the bank to which he was heading. He lifted his bundle with both hands above the water and half swimming half bouncing like an astronaut on the moon he moved across and down the river with the current.

At the back of his mind was the bridge and it was getting ominously close. He was three-quarters of the way across when he was able to regain his footing wholly. He continued with the backwards walk method. This allowed him to crouch down and keep his eyes on the bridge as he was only a short distance from it now and he could see four heads above the walls. They were talking and laughing, he could hear the voices but he couldn't discern what they were saying or who they were. All he was sure about was that he didn't want them to know he was there.

As the water became less than a metre deep, he bounded for the bank. He was shivering uncontrollably now, completely numb and in real trouble of hypothermia. Once out of the water and in the shadows of the trees he untied his parcel and grabbed the t-shirt drying his body and legs as best he could. His skin burned now that it was out of the water as the blood vessels tried to re-heat his extremities. His fingers felt like they would snap off and the carnal ache of chilblains set in.

With the relative heaven of dry clothes, he was quickly stomping his deadened feet through the countryside outside the town limits. His extremities came back to life as he jogged through the cold and the hurt, he crossed the roundabout over the A69 and hit the steep bank that led up to Oakwood and their friend Claire's house. Claire was a nurse and Nat hoped she could stitch him up.

As he trod the quiet road up to Oakwood, his mind raced. He knew deep down that he had to go to Scotland to take care of Amber, escape the violence he was reaping; save what was left of his soul. But he also knew that he wouldn't. He hated his weakness, but he couldn't leave Esme or Northumberland. He mused how different the reality of the situation was from the thought of the same situation before it had happened. He had lost his wife but had no time to mourn. Mourning would get him killed and he had no time to die while those men were still breathing.

By the time he reached the overgrown driveway leading to her diminutive cottage, he was back to normal heat, the exercise had his blood pumping and his clothes were steaming in the night air. His shoulder burned with pain, but he was in control again. He felt strong.

As he approached the front of the house, he was pleased to see a dim light emanating from within. Nat tapped at the wobbly Victorian glass of the front door as he had done on many happier occasions. There was no answer, but he saw the light go out. He knocked on the wood much harder and leant down to the letterbox calling through it,

"Claire, it's me, Nat, come and let me in!"

Almost immediately the light came back on and he saw a shape coming towards the door. Claire opened up

"Nat are you pissed? What the hell are you doing" Then she saw the state of him and his wounded arm "shit, what's this? Are you ok? What happened?"

"Alright, alright, women let me speak man…"

She pulled him with care down the hallway and into the golden hue of her kitchen. A Patchouli joss stick smoked in the corner of the room, the butt of a joint lay in the ashtray and Roy Harper quietly sprinkled his magic across the room. The fire was roaring and the curtains were closed.

Nat slumped onto a kitchen chair "please patch up my arm and I'll explain everything Claire…" As he slipped his coat off, his face grimaced with the pain.

Claire took a sharp intake of breath and her hand covered her mouth as she realised that she was dealing with a gunshot wound. She pulled him up and directed him sitting him back down again in the big armchair next to the fire which was churning out the dry heat that Nat's body craved. He realised then that the clothes he thought were dry were far from it, his trousers were drenched from the tunnel and his top half was heavily damp. It didn't matter now.

She hurried out of the room and Nat closed his eyes letting his head rest on the back of the armchair, drifting with the music and the crackling fire. Claire hustled back into the room after a few short moments, with a bottle of brandy under her arm and a large first aid kit with two glasses on top of it. She placed the items safely onto an occasional table which stood to the side of the armchair. She gently lifted it round so it was next to Nat. Then she grabbed an old three-legged stool from the other side of the fireplace and plonked it with a clump and a screech onto the flagstones.

"Now what the hell happened here then you daft bastard?" She poured two large measures of brandy into the bulbous tumblers. "And here get your lips around that, it'll help the brain, the pain and the shame."

She smiled at him, that familiar smile. Claire was a beautiful country girl, jet black hair, thick and wavy. But it was those voluptuous rosebud lips that sent men wild. Nat wasn't moved by her beauty though, it was her familiarity. She was like a sister to him, and she had been Esme's best friend, a constant, just like his wife. When Claire smiled at him, he was tugged back into reality.

With the warmth of the fire on his face and the brandy in his belly he felt the fatigue, the gravity and the actuality of his new life. But what hit him most in that safe, comfortable environment was the finality of his loss. From this moment forward, every time he ventured into his old life he would be reminded that his soul mate was gone. There were no kind words that could help with that, it was simply a fact and he was left to live with the void. As he looked at his friend he broke down, uncontrollably spluttering out the facts as best he knew them of the rape and murder of his wife and the trouble he had stirred up since.

Claire sobbed openly as she listened, struck dumb by the shock and disbelief. She took gulps of her brandy as Nat's story from the last two days unwound. His tears were soon spent as his initial relaxation and outpouring of emotion past. His eyes were red and hard as he told her about killing the NSO people and that he wouldn't stop until he had got them all, especially the man named Truter.

He realised at that point that he might not end there. His old life would only offer him the feelings that he had just experienced and he couldn't live like that. Crying like a baby. When he finished recounting his experiences, Claire leaned forward and hugged him tight, he reciprocated for a short while then regained his steel,

"C'mon girl, this isn't going to sew itself and I'm going blue here."

"Ok Ok" but as his words registered, her face clouded and she turned to him.

"You should never have fought with these people Nat, you're an idiot, the changes they are making will make life better, I don't know what you were thinking and now…poor Esme, I never even saw her for days…I never said goodbye, never hug her again…fuck Nat you…"

"Alright Claire, I know, don't you think I know."

"What will you do now?"

"Carry on with what I've started, kill those men."

"This is not the Wild West Nat; you can't make your own rules."

"You just watch me. Now please…" He turned his shoulder towards her and she looked at him contemplating whether to carry on. Her eyes washed over her friend, taking him in like a mother looks at her child when she hasn't the energy to argue anymore. She shook her head slightly and began to dress his wound, starting by cleaning it then stitching it. Claire's tears trickled down rosy cheeks as she worked, a dark cloud had settled over her.

"What are you gonna do Nat, carry on killing people until one of them kills you?"

"Or until I feel like stopping, yes" He replied

Claire looked at him puzzled, dumbfounded by his fatalistic tunnel vision. She rolled her eyes and shook her head again

"You're an idiot or you're not thinking straight, what if you get killed? What about Amber?"

"What about Amber? What about you? Look what happened to Esme; these bastards killed my wife. They abused their position and they have started a war."

"What do you sound like man, also where is Amber?"

"She's safe, with Stuart." Claire's eyes flicked up at Nat when he mentioned Stuart. Their romance had started twenty years ago and the roller-coaster had been running ever since, neither settling with anyone else because no one else measured up to each other. But they never managed to commit because they were both pig-headed, Claire loved Northumberland and Stuart had his farm.

Claire gently placed a heavy duty plaster over the fresh stitches and smoothed the edges over his unbroken skin, silent for a moment.

Finally, she looked into Nat's relaxed but melancholy eyes and she put a hand to his cheek

"I'm so sorry Nat, you poor man, I do understand".

She leant forward and they hugged, that much needed human contact; safe, reassuring and good for the soul. He choked up again in the embrace but as they parted his mind moved back to survival. He wanted to get away from Claire as soon as he could so that she would remain safe.

Claire cooked some food for him and Nat showered and dressed in dry clothes that Stewart had left over the years. They were slightly bigger than Nat would have liked but not noticeably. As he wolfed down the food and thought about his next step.

"Can I borrow your car?" He mumbled through a mouthful of food

"No, you can't Nat, that would be great for me wouldn't it. If they caught you driving around in my car and anyway, I need it!" She thought for a second "My brother's scrambler is still in the garage, but I don't even know if it works…"

"That'll do, I've just got to get back to the farm".

He walked out into the cold early morning. It was near four, still dark for a good three hours. He had plenty of time to get back to safety and get some sleep in the field shelter. The weather was reassuringly settled.

Claire's driveway was a rustic cobbled affair and her big wooden garage doors were framed by ivy which twisted and tangled its way up the sides and across the roof of the garage. The lush green of the leaves complimented the weathered and flaking red paint adorning the doors.

He opened one side of the old rotting double doors. The wood was a mushy pulp where it lent on the ground and the hinges were giving very little support so he rubbed another couple of centimetres of door pulp away as it scraped open. He stepped into the dusty garage and turned the light on; it flickered to a dim light. The light was enough to make him raise his hand, to visor his eyes although, more through natural reaction than need.

He shook his head as he looked at the clutter in front of him. He cast his eye methodically over the jumbling until he glimpsed the rubber grip of one side of the handlebars of the bike. He moved in but it took a while as there was no end of potentially useful junk. All to be shifted to free the motorbike from its tomb of household goods. Finally, he liberated the machine and now he wondered at the likelihood it would start.

He checked the fuel tank…half full. Then the spark plugs and the battery there was life in both. He opened the throttle pushed off down the drive and put it into gear, the engine puttered to a start and he was good to go.

He took some bread and fruit from Claire and she had washed his clothes although she had not had time to dry them. He took a small rucksack from the garage and put his old and new supplies in there and set off in the dark. He took the Beaufront Road north out of Oakwood, a steep climb up to the military road running parallel with Hadrian's Wall.

A few hundred yards before he hit the junction with the Military Road as the little bike puttered up the long incline he passed Rowell's farm. There at the end of his drive stood the familiar high beech hedge and grandiose stone gate pillars. He was re-assured to see that the old man had barricaded his gates with the trailer from his articulated lorry on which he had welded side panels fashioned from corrugated iron probably from his sheds roof or sides. It was like something from a war zone. Nat realised he was not entirely alone.

He turned right onto the long straight undulating road running east to West across the country following the Roman Road that ran along the southern side of Hadrian's Wall. There was no sight of headlights in either direction so he revved the engine put his head down and took the bike to its top speed heading east towards home. He had no headlight on the bike, but his eyes were used to the dark and there was some moonlight. Within ten minutes, he was skidding into his driveway.

There was no one on the roads, no early commuters, no night shift workers returning home, no farmers getting a march on the hours in the day. A chilling testament to the change, if previous governments had survived by capitalising on the nation's fears, this new regime was creating fear to dictate to the population.

Nat wasted no time in getting his head down while it remained dark. He slept well, numbed by brandy, full of food and bolstered by the kindness of his friend.

Nick Christofides

SIX

Amber had been exhausted by the time she arrived at Stuart's whitewashed farmhouse. But now she awoke from a deep sound sleep, she had no memory of getting to bed.

Her room was big and beautiful, not through design but the amalgamation of age. She perched on the side of a solid wooden bed, which was painted a nautical colour that some would call blue, others green. Her scruffy rucksack rested on an ivory coloured chest of drawers, the sun burst across the room illuminating an ancient rocking chair with the richest sheen from decades of varnishing. The curtains draped across the large window and the throw resting over the bed were a bohemian tapestry of vibrant patches sewn together. Amber loved the room, as she padded out of bed the silence was broken by the creek of the bare floorboards.

She opened the curtains and breathed in as she absorbed the view. To the front and left of the house stood an old fir tree, robed like a pontiff in needles. This and the rough stone path leading up to the front door gave perspective to the breath-taking backdrop of the meandering valley beyond. The burn frothed and boiled over huge boulders smoothed and rounded by the constant abrasion. The valley sides were steep and in many places the land had slipped giving it the look of a furrowed brow belonging to a green giant. Other than the lush grass and the occasional heather bush, vegetation in the valley was sparse with rocky outcrops piercing the surface. There was a coniferous forest at its head which looked as though it were charging over hillside like a wild army consuming everything that stood in its way.

Amber could see Stuart in the distance laying out hay for his cattle. She stretched, yawned and shook her thick head of hair as if to ready herself for the day ahead. She could not have felt safer, more at home than she did at Stuarts unless she had woken up in her own bed, of course. Gently her thoughts focussed on her mother and father. She felt the rumbling of impatience in her belly. As she padded through it, the old house massaged her senses at every step. There were thick velvety rugs laid over bare floorboards under her feet. The walls and furniture were a cacophony of colour and design. The smell of open fires wafted through the spaces while the silence was only broken by the random creak of floorboards and the harmonic tick of an old clock that she couldn't see.

The metallic thud of the latch reverberated through the wood of the kitchen door. The room was no less enchanting but obviously where Stuart did most of his living as it was chaos. The huge slab of oak that was the kitchen table had a mug and a plate with bread next to it at one end and a motorcycle engine at the other. Every surface was covered with paperwork, tools or foodstuff (animal or human). The rest of the motorbike stood upturned and wheel-less on the flagstone floor.

Amber skipped quickly over the chilly stones and like a cat warmed herself in front of the Aga. She saw tea bags in a jar to her right. She reached the spiralled handle of the Aga's hotplate lid and lifted the heavy covering to a familiar yawn from the hinges and heat washed over her face. She gently put the pot onto the heat and moved along the units to the right in search of a mug. The swoosh and clap of the cupboards opening finally revealed the mugs. She threw a tea bag to the bottom of the cup and followed it with a brimming heaped spoonful of sugar. Habit dictated that she add an extra dab of sugar which she did.

The kettle whistled as she clanged two thick slices of bread under the grill to toast. She would call her parents shortly. She stirred then removed the tea bag and added some milk, not too much but probably more than most people. She turned the toast in short sharp movements before her fingers burnt.

She saw the cordless phone, which must have been forty years old at least, lying next to the motorbike engine. She imagined Stuart taking her father's call the day before. She picked it up and slipped it into the oversized pocket of her thick woollen cardigan. Carrying her tea and toast she crossed the room to the big old armchair nestled in the corner. She kicked two coats and some newspapers onto the floor. She placed her drink on one arm and her toast on the other then sank into the forgiving chair. She absorbed the quiet. The sun had broken the clouds and a bright stream of light cut across the room, illuminating the dust floating through the air.

She pulled her knees up to her chest and took the phone from her pocket. She dialled her home number. It took no time at all before the monotone shrill of a dead line came back down the receiver. She dialled again and again until she was taking a discernible amount of time over each number to make sure it was correct. The same bleak tone came back at her every time. Finally, she pressed the red button once more and tapped the receiver to her chin as she thought. She wasn't overly concerned at that moment, but she could feel her stomach tightening with worry as she tried to find a reason for their phone being down.

She dialled Bob and Jeans number then, just to see, knowing the old couple were most probably still with her parents. Her nerves grew as she heard a dial tone; she listened to it for minutes, her mind elsewhere, being drawn into the void of dark thoughts about what was happening to her parents. The lack of answer from Bob and Jeans confirmed only one thing; the phones were not down.

Her stomach tightened and turned as she registered the situation and realised how out of character it was that she had not received a call from her father this morning or even last night for that matter. She felt sure that he would have been keen to know that they had arrived safely.

She put her mug of tea down gently on the corner of the table and looked around the room as though it was in the kitchen that she might find answers. She saw a pair of welly's at the back door and moved towards them. Pulling the large mud encrusted boots on, she opened the door and ran out into the fresh, invigorating morning air which was still heavy with dew. She crossed the thick grass lolloping in the oversized boots. It was a still brisk morning, birds were singing and the livestock were in animated conversation.

The beauty of the morning was missed by Amber as her worry turned to panic it was her own feet that she concentrated on. She shouted down the hillside to her startled host,

"Stuart, Stuart! I can't get hold of Mum and Dad, their line is dead…"

Stuart turned to see the teenager stumbling down the hill. He waved her back to the house

"Get back in the warm lassie, I'm coming up now."

"But we need to…"

"Don't do it to me now Amber, no one knows what's best…" As he had been working, similar thoughts had been swimming in his head.

"I know that sitting here won't do any good"

Stuart looked at her with resignation in his dark eyes.

"Make me a brew and we'll work out a plan."

Amber stopped, her head dropped and she turned dejected back toward the house and began trudging back up the hill. Stuart grabbed another bale of hay as if it were a pillow, broke it in his hands and spread the grass quickly in front of him. He wiped his massive hands on his jeans and with commanding paces he moved towards the house confident his old mate would get through this latest scrape but also allowing himself to contemplate the worst.

As he entered the kitchen, he kicked his work boots off and stood for a second or too as the warm air washed over his damp clothes. He pushed aside some of the mess on the kitchen table and sat down looking at Amber who was making him tea

"Milk? Sugar?"

"Milk, two sugars please Amber."

She knew how he took his tea. It was an instinctive comment, breaking the silence but skirting the topic that her mind couldn't escape.

She placed his mug of tea down in front of him. Within seconds, it was swept up in one of his shovel like hands while the other coursed through his greasy mop of shoulder length hair. Clearing the strands from his face and exposing the greying areas around his temples and ears. His soggy socks and jeans steamed in the warmth of the kitchen and his sinuous muscles heaved at the material of his plaid shirt. Amber spoke first as she sat back down in the big armchair folding her legs underneath her as she did so

"I want to go back home. I can't just wait!"

"That's exactly what we are going to do Amber, I'm hoping your Mum and Dad will turn up here at any minute. But if they don't, I made a promise to your father Amber."

"That's ridiculous Stuart, the rebels need every one who is capable!"

"Forget the rebels Amber, your parents are our only concern."

Amber rolled her head and looked at the floor, she wasn't going to wait for long.

Stuart looked thoughtfully at the dust particles dancing in the suns beam and allowed the tick of the clock to pace his mind. He was himself unsure how long he could remain without news of his friends. A week? Two? Even those stretches of time were too great, he knew it in his heart, he would not be able to stand back and wait.

His mind moved to the girl, he loved her like she was his own daughter. At eighteen, she was a young woman, could he leave her here if he had to go across the border? He thought to himself; she is too headstrong, too wily. She would be behind him in no time but not with him…no he would take her with him if he went, at least then he could look out for her. He knew it was not a perfect plan, but what else could he do. And he knew that she could look after herself if it became necessary. Nat had taught Amber to hunt and shoot and live off the land at a very young age. She was far stealthier than either of the men; they used to joke that she could stalk a roe deer and catch it with her bare hands.

He looked across at Amber, her eyes burning a hole in the rug as she chewed on a nail nervously. He wouldn't say anything of his newly hatched plan as he thought it better to sleep on it. If there was no news in the morning he would leave for Nat's Farm then.

He stood up "I've got to get back to the beasts, help yourself to whatever you need and I'll be in the bottom field if you feel like working off the worry."

With that, he quietly slugged the last of his brew moved to where his boots lay and tugged them back onto his feet and left the house.

Amber stared at the floor as a tear trickled down her cheek.

Nick Christofides

SEVEN

Condensation hung on the huge sash windows highlighted by the morning sun. Ben Baines rubbed his eyes, he had slept in the office again last night. Now he poured over the papers and nursed a strong coffee. He was not that fond of strong quality coffee; it gave him a headache but after sleeping on a Chesterfield he needed something to kick start his head. He wore a well-cut suit and shirt with no tie, his shirt unbuttoned at the collar.

The media were backing the new regime. There were many positive stories of collective industry setting up across the country; of employment for people who had never worked in their life; class sizes halving and wage increases.

There were also reports of the banks being frozen, personal capital of the rich being confiscated by the government to be funnelled into the system. Companies were being taken over by the government. Put into the hands of collectives with only one change; all the profits were pumped straight back into the government and the business itself as investment or fair wages. Shareholders were abolished, the employees owned the company, they set the wage structures and they had control of the purse strings.

Every employee and board member of every company was free to stay in the role they performed before the advent of the NSO. But those at the top would be paid a fraction of their previous salaries whilst the rest would receive better pay.

The rich had already fled or were in the process of escaping England en masse. Taking with them whatever assets they could move on their person. Everything else had been locked down by the NSO and the threat of retribution by regime enforcers was all too real for those who were not willing to fall into line with the movement.

The revolution was very popular on the whole. Business leaders, landowners and bankers were in such a minority they had no voice against the ordinary people who were desperate for a viable alternative to the previous system.

Although he was well supported, Baines knew there was opposition, even if the papers were not reporting it. There was more and more resistance to his land reforms day by day. It was those who would lose everything if they left their farms and estates who were fighting back. They did not have the capital or a brand to transfer across international borders.

As unrest in the countryside flared, the more Lucas Starts mercenaries clamped down hard on rural communities in an attempt to take control. Baines was continually forced by events to allow Lucas Start more and more power and control over the population.

Starts army had quashed major uprisings in East Anglia, the closest unrest to London. But Cornwall was totally uncontrolled, the NSO could not even venture into the county and Devon was the theatre for a vicious guerrilla war. Wales was becoming less and less contained. The Welsh were being armed by the Irish and the Welsh counter-revolutionaries were getting stronger and more organised by the day. All this trouble was manageable compared to Northern England.

The proximity of Scotland; an aggressive opponent of England and the regime with absolutely no diplomatic relations was the greatest threat to his ideology and his leadership.

Scotland, a wealthy country, heavily militarised after devolution had chosen partnership with its Scandinavian neighbours and the Irish rather than its historical master England. The Scandinavian Arc as it had become known was a group of capitalist countries thriving in an increasingly socialist world. It was history which made Baines most nervous. If ever a dog was having its day it was Scotland and he had read the history books.

Now his poor little country sat at the feet of the Scandinavian Arc geographically and economically and he knew that Scotland could roll into England at any time, he was losing sleep over this fact. He had assurances from the Brazilians, the Argentineans' and the Chinese that this would not happen. In lighter moments, he joked that England had become South America's Falklands and he hoped they would protect their interest like the British had fought for theirs all those years ago.

However, he needed to be upbeat. This meeting did not solely concern the regimes issues, there were a lot of successes within the infrastructure of the country; Baines' domain.

As his government ministers filtered into the room Baines was engrossed in an article buried deep within a more centre standing paper. It was by a young journalist called Rory Jones and it was reporting on the redistribution of land in Northumberland. Apparently, government forces had burned a farm to the ground killing three locals and three of their own in the ensuing explosion. The story carried on to describe retribution by a relative and the murder of two government paramilitaries.

His mood darkened, but he tried to hide his frustration. Lucas Start was far more capable than him in leading the regime through these areas of friction. He had the ability tactically, militarily and he enjoyed the power. Baines did not necessarily thrive on such things and he was all too aware that he had to keep Start under control. He had in no way sanctioned the burning of English farms and murder for non-cooperation.

Baines raised his hand to his gathered colleagues. The jocular hum waned, he began to talk gently and with humility, he congratulated them all on twenty years of work coming together in such a peaceful and popular way. Such a change in society being met by the general population with such positivity was nothing short of incredible. This was his general message. He moved on quickly with aplomb through each governmental department, where the reports suggested they were in terms of his plan and what the next step should be. He was completely up to speed, totally in control. There was however only one conversation he really wanted to have and he moved as quickly to it as was possible, he turned to Lucas Start,

"We are reporting that seventy-seven percent of the population is accounted for at this point, how does this break down Lucas? Who are we missing?"

Lucas had his head down in some papers, his piggy eyes flicked upwards under a sweaty brow

"Well, we are moving around the country systematically. We estimate that of that twenty-three percent unaccounted for around fourteen percent will be in the cities and six in the countryside with the remainder over the border in Scotland or abroad. I think we'll get the rest tagged before two weeks, they can't hide forever."

"Good, but these are our countrymen, not livestock, Lucas, sort your language out and show some respect to the people who brought you to power."

Start raised his eyes to look at his leader who had gained his full attention now, embarrassed by the dressing down. Baines added in anger

"In fact Lucas, I hear you talking like that again and you'll be out of a job."

"Ok Ben, sorry but accounting for more than seventy million people can become rather impersonal. We are on top of the registrations" Start responded with some degree of humility and a great deal of arrogance. Baines looked at him sternly nodding slightly then his eyes moved around the room where he saw his colleagues shift uncomfortably in their chairs. No one wanted a rift at the top, but Baines had an inkling that Start would be followed before him, out of fear mainly. He was all too aware that his leadership was more delicate than ever. Now that his ministers were in power, the temptation of abusing that power for personal gain was in their hands.

His eyes moved to Steve Jones, a career politician who had defected from the Labour Party six years earlier. His remit was industry, coordinating the massive task of reorganising and starting up businesses to support their local areas first and foremost and then the excess being traded further afield.

"Any issues Steve, are you receiving the manpower from Lucas? And do we have the skilled labour locally?"

"Early days but the jigsaw is piecing together well, we have over fifteen thousand businesses to start up over the coming months but we certainly have the manpower. People are hungry for the work and there seems to be no shortage of people prepared to relocate for work. So we are fast-tracking planning for new villages across the country kick starting construction as well as filling empty properties. On the negative side, we will certainly have shortages of skilled labour in the short term; we have no need for salesmen, but we don't have many welders or machinists out there".

"That brings us nicely on to Jocelyn" Baines raised a hand to a large lady with cropped hair at the far end of the table.

"Totally on track at the moment Ben, we have already doubled staffing levels in sixty-eight percent of schools reducing class sizes by half in most. I am liaising with Steve on the construction of twenty-three industrial colleges which will re-introduce blue collar skills into the workforce. Seventeen of those projects are simple refurbishment projects in current schools and colleges so we will see them opening within the year."

"Any issues?"

"A small number of school closures due to local resistance"

"What? Where are these closures?" now Baines addressed the whole room once again. There was a pause and then Lucas Start stepped in with a response.

"Cornwall, just about the whole county, those nut jobs have called for autonomy again, West Wales and Northumberland are the areas where we have issues. It tends to be landowners, farmers and rural communities resisting our land reforms, they are just swimming against the tide but we'll have control in a matter of days."

"What do you mean?"

"Well, we are persuading the population in these small trouble spots to step into line."

"How?" Baines questioned directly as the temperature in the room seemed to rise, Baines stare piercing and shuffling in seats suddenly the loudest noise.

"How what Ben?" Start retorted with some degree of impatience and annoyance. He was a man that people rarely questioned and never in front of an audience. Baines threw the paper onto the table open at the article he had been reading

"How exactly are you persuading the population?"

"We are educating them in our ideology…"

"By burning down their bloody homes and killing them, who do you think you are Lucas, Stalin?"

"Look Ben" Start now the bully with steel in his eye and bluster in his voice. He was aggressive and overpowering "I think you need to leave the boots on the ground to those of us who know how to use a stick as well as a carrot."

"What the hell are you talking about?"

"Ben you are an honourable and even a brilliant man, but if you think that you can take this country without stamping out opposing factions then, you are more naive than I thought you were! Those pockets of opposition will grow and spread like a cancer in our healthy body and one day we'll have barbarians descending from the hills to put us all out of business".

Baines was on his feet now. His knuckles white pressed hard on the table, eyes bulging and red in the face. "I think you need to stop talking right now Lucas, this is not a playground and we are certainly not competing for anything so don't for a second get ahead of yourself…you have finished? Yes?"

"Of course Ben, sorry, I stepped over the line" Start raised his hands nonchalantly in surrender.

"As we all agreed, we leave pockets of resistance alone. We have so much support and so many of our infrastructure changes have been set in place by the general population before we even took power, we do not need to worry about a small amount of opposition. Anyway in this system they will soon see that trade and workers stem from the collectives…they need to be part of it. A cancer can't grow Lucas if it doesn't have a body feeding it. You really worry me Lucas, we are not trying to 'take' this country we are trying to lead it…I am nervous to ask but what exactly is happening on the ground in these areas Lucas, I wasn't aware that we have casualties…less still mortalities?"

Start now became uncomfortable, the Boss had delved too deep, and this was a conversation he didn't want to have. He shifted in his seat and his broad face reappeared to the room with a large smile

"Nothing Ben, it is all in hand, as I said just a few troublesome characters but we are proceeding as we all agreed…"

"Just answer my bloody question Lucas!" Start paused for a moment, then resigned to the question and replied

"We have armed conflict in Devon from Cornish rebels however they are isolated, disorganised and badly equipped so they are not our most pressing problem at this stage. We are at war in Wales, men and weapons are coming across the Irish Sea. Northumberland however is our primary worry, relations with the Scots have never been more strained, arms and men are moving freely across the border but the wall will be finished within the month. The Scottish are courting English landowners in the border counties because if those lands were annexed by the Scots then obviously there would be no land reforms...it's an easy sell. This article is about a rogue farmer who has murdered three civilians and five of our security detail, but this is just one man...we'll find him today."

Baines looked around the room in disbelief "When did this happen and when was someone going to tell me? I don't want to read these things in the bloody paper!"

The room was silent, even Start kept quiet now. Baines pondered the facts. The eyes around the table were lowered, Baines looked on but no one returned his gaze. Start was leaning back in his seat, nonchalantly tapping his pen against sausage like fingers.

"Who is this guy? Is he a murderer, working under the shadow of the system change? Or have we played a part in this situation? We do not need any sort of hero figure fuelling the resistance."

Start saw his opportunity and took it "Definitely the first, he is a crazy old hermit, we visited the farm he blew it up killing his wife, their neighbours and three of our people. That was two days ago. He disappeared into the countryside, we caught up with him last night in a local town but he managed to kill two more of our people...because our people are no good! We need military personnel on the ground."

"Did he escape?"

"Yes he is still at large but he is one man, we'll find him and arrest him."

"Who is in charge on the ground?"

"Rudi Truter"

Baines thought for a long moment, there was nothing to be gained by carrying this on. The lights buzzing overhead irritated him. And the large table creaked as the shell-shocked room shuffled and murmured. This had been planned as a victory meeting full of positivity, but every one of them knew that Baines had dreamt of an entirely peaceful, unopposed revolution and these deaths were hard for him to stomach. Not least because the real enemy, opposing media and politicians out in the wilderness could easily find a way back into the populations minds with a story like this. After a long pause, he spoke again

"Look people, we have done the violence and the fear over the past twenty years, during that time we rioted, disrupted and smashed this country into listening. There were deaths, there were difficult decisions and actions which I am not proud of now but it worked and we changed the system; a feat which seemed unimaginable back then. Now that the country has put its faith behind our ideology we can't let anything de-rail it. You have seen here that every positive action we take no matter how massive no matter how many millions of people it benefits, these changes can be undermined by the smallest or the most isolated problem. A dog can be driven to madness by one flea. Lucas, your people need to find this guy and detain him so that he will face trial, I don't want any more killing, understood?"

"Understood Ben, I'll keep you fully up to date with the situation."

Baines wrapped the meeting up quickly, distracted by this turn of events and eager to get out of that room and back to work. As the members left the room into the vast open plan office beyond where hundreds of bodies busied themselves around workstations. Their aides and secretaries scurried over like loyal dogs.

Lucas Start pulled two of his deputies to one side; both had been in the meeting.

"We carry on with our activities exactly how we were and exactly how we had planned, ok...?"

Both men nodded agreement as Start continued without waiting for an answer

"Our illustrious leader does not share our view that to keep a nation under control there must be fear for the general population. And reward for us. Now get on to Truter. Get that farmer found. Take him out of the equation before he makes a mockery of our security forces!"

Meanwhile in the meeting room, Baines picked up the phone and dialled a number from his head. A cold hard voice picked up after two rings

"Yes"

"Hello, are you ok?" Baines asked hesitantly

"What do you have for me?" came the answer down the line. Baines's head dropped and he thought for a second about persevering then his head nodded gently and he moved straight to business.

"I have a problem in Northumberland, I don't know whether Lucas's people can handle it...sorry really I just have no idea what's going on up there. Can you go up find out what's happening and let me know?"

"Do you want me to sort it?"

"Uh, what...no no just Intel and report back..." Baines seemed knocked by the language from the other end of the phone, it seemed that one way or another it was always your closest allies that one feared the most.

The phone clicked off without another word, Baines looked at his desk, looked at the receiver then placed it back on the main body of the telephone.

Nick Christofides

EIGHT

Nat awoke softly to a stiff cool breeze whistling past the shelter. The morning air full of oxygen was invigorating; he sat on his makeshift bed and looked out to the valley beyond. The first hint of sunrise was pushing the horizon so all he could see was the black block of the land against the deep blue of the earliest of morning skies. So thick and bold were the two colours that it had a distinct beauty in its simplicity. There were no street lights, no headlights and no house lights. No human interference in the poetry of nature and he sucked it up, forgetting for a moment the chaos that had become his existence.

He considered what Claire had said to him. He considered leaving for Scotland, but that felt like betrayal. Betrayal of Esme, of Home. It was a betrayal of all those other farmers who might stay and fight the regime. He wanted to see the life fade from Truter's eyes and he wanted Truter to know he was the reaper. Such was the pain that he felt, the only outlet was carnage.

He sat looking out over the valley, he felt empty. The sun rose, it washed the land with gold which warmed his craggy skin. The breeze whipped those straggles of hair around his eyes forcing him to squint, adding weight to the deep lines around his eyes.

The vast Northumbrian sky opened out in front of him like the vision of Eureka, and the cotton wool clouds hung low so that above his head there were enormous gaps of vivid blue. But as he looked into the distance the covering of cloud seemed to become a solid body punctuating the enormity of the heavens above.

In front of him, the rough grazing land fell away down the valley side. The thick tufts of grass were blown this way and that by the incessant bluster. Two small trees shaped like battered witches hats grew in the field about two hundred feet in front of him, his eyes moved on down to his sheep grazing further down in the more sheltered hillside. His gaze moved on again to his arable fields and he thought how on earth he would manage to turn and seed them in the coming weeks.

He could see across the valley to the far side. The patchwork of greens and browns stretching off into the distance, all that land toiled by local people for centuries under a system which had, on the whole worked. It was not these country people who had swindled and cheated to enormous profits. Change the banking system and huge dominating companies but don't destroy the heartbeat of the country, this was after all his country also.

With those thoughts running through his mind, he decided to pay a visit to Rowell's farm that day, see if he could begin to get consensus on a plan for the rest of his life. The breeze changed direction and snapped him out of his thoughts, he set to making a fire and preparing the second rabbit he had killed the day before.

As he tore the hot flesh from its bones with his teeth and hands and munched it down he was sure, it tasted better than the first he had eaten the day before. The meal seemed to vanish in a flash, but he felt good to have warm meat and beans in his belly. He was sipping on a hot tea and picking at the bones when his eye was caught by crows leaving their roosts in the middle distance, at the edge of his property. This was nothing unusual as crows have to eat too, but this was alongside the road and it was a substantial flock of birds that had taken to the wing. He turned his ear and listened intently and there it was, the hum of an engine, powering along the road leading to his gates.

He looked down at the fire. It was not smoking much, but he grabbed the large circle of turf he had cut away to dig the fire pit and threw it over the embers cutting off the oxygen supply.

He leapt to his feet, snatching up his rifle from just inside the shelter. He sprinted as fast as he could across the open ground, he could see two cars now moving along the lane, not slow but not rallying. It was a race now he had around two hundred yards to make in comparison to the cars three-quarters of a mile. He had to take the upper hand; two cars meant potentially eight or even ten men, he had a full magazine yesterday, had spent two rounds on breakfast so fourteen left in the clip. As he ran he castigated himself for not picking up another box of ammunition. Simple mistakes lead to misery he thought.

He was running across open land as he saw the cars turn into his driveway. If they hadn't seen him now, they were even more useless than the general impression he was building of them. It worked for him if they caught sight of him now because he was about fifty yards from his destination, the copse which curled over the brow of the hill above their home. He felt that if they saw him they would think he was running and they would follow…he hoped.

He had his back to the cars now as he ran as fast as he could up the hill. More of a lollop than a sprint, his ears filled with the wisp of his boots through the thick grass and rasp of his aging lungs trawling vainly for enough air to power his engine up the hill. He couldn't hear the engines now. His large frame broke the tree line and he skidded onto his belly turning to face back down the hill and bringing the rifle sights to his right eye in one fluid movement.

He fought to regain his composure his lungs and muscles burning, the up and down of his panting made ridiculously large tidal swells to his aim through the sights so he put bare eyes on his pursuers. The sweat began to bead on his forehead as he watched the men step out of the two cars, they were the same cars as those he had seen the night before. He put his head down for a few seconds as his breath began to regulate. The damp rich peat filled his nostrils with a sweet smell as the adrenalin began to wane, he looked back at the cars.

* * * * *

Roland was driving the first car with Conor to his left and Davey and Steve in the back seat. Truter and Gerry followed in the black car. Roland was scared, he didn't want to hunt this man down,

"I don't know why we're doing this, we never signed up to become bounty hunters...," he said

"You just gotta do what you're told mate" replied Conor

"I dunno what you lot did to him that night because he was in town last night just to confront us."

"You don't want to know Roland, you're far too delicate" shouted a grinning Steve from the back of the car, Conor turned and gave a conspiratorial giggle to his buddy.

"Fuck you guys this is serious, this fucking shit. This guy is killing people!"

"That's why we've gotta stop him now." Said Conor

"That's why Rudi brought us this time" Grinned Steve

"Yeah well, you should be stopping him not me..."

"I'll have a word with Truter" Smirked Conor

"Ha Ha, I'm sure that wanker will be very understanding" softened Roland as Steve leaned forward and said

"Look Roland, we know what we're doing. Don't worry about this farmer, last night he took everyone by surprise. Now we know what we're up against we can get our game face on and give him as much respect as he deserves."

"I've got no idea what that means but I'll take it as reassuring..."

As the car pulled up the drive Davey exclaimed

"Look up there in the field above the house! That's someone running into the trees!"

The other three craned their necks to look but none saw Nat as he vanished into the copse.

"You better be sure about that Davey, cos if I have to walk all the way up there and we don't find him you won't be coming back with us..." Commented Conor.

"Well, I'm not sure" replied Davey nervously "I just saw something move."

Davey knew what he had seen but opted to put his head back below the parapet. He was scared enough of the two marines and he wasn't going to give them more ammunition to use against him. They were already having a field day on his physical vulnerability and general lack of confidence. He pushed his hands deep into the pockets of his hoody and sank back into the cramped rear seat of the car. Steve next to him sucked his teeth and shook his head at him and Conor in the front simply said "idiot" and chortled to himself. As the car pulled to a stop in front of the burned down house, all four men opened their respective doors and climbed out into the mild morning air.

Rudi Truter pulled his car in alongside theirs and through the open window he barked "Find the bastard now lads, let's put a lid on this". Gerry remained in the car with Truter.

The four of them got to it. Moving around to the back of the car Steve leaned deep into the boot and pulled out two shotguns. One of which he handed to Roland, "here you go mate just squeeze here to shoot and pump here after" he said with a big grin. Conor pulled out an SA80, an old weapon but a good one. He then threw a handgun to Davey, who dropped it much to the marines delight.

"Don't bother taking the safety off that Davey...you'll shoot yourself" Conor called over to him. Roland turned to Davey and whispered "who knows when these were last fired and I really don't want to start shooting people."

"Hey Roland" Truter called over "you come and sit with me, we need to talk and anyway I don't think you're really the killing type." He turned to Gerry who was the other side of the car "you tasted his wife...you go and get him."

Davey and Roland looked at each other and then down at the floor. The latter almost let out an audible whimper, his relief was so great. He felt for Davey too but right now they jogged in separate directions. Gerry ran to catch up with the Marines. He took Roland's weapon as they passed each other. Roland gave him an apologetic look as they crossed, but Gerry smiled at his old friend reassuringly; keen to do his masters bidding. Gerry pushed open the big heavy barn door and pointed the gun into the shadows.

Roland settled into the passenger's seat of Truter's car. He couldn't get it out of his head; what had occurred at the house the other night? It all seemed wrong to him. What had they done to this farmer to cause this reaction? He looked at Truter through the windscreen, looking up into the surrounding countryside as though he were sniffing the air for the scent of his prey. He knew deep down that these people were not what he imagined. This rough edge, this mob like attitude was not why he had joined the NSO.

For him, the NSO was losing its direction and this paramilitary unit was abusing their power. The reality of this struggle was a lot less romantic and far more painful than the riots and protests that were held before the revolution. Also, before he was one among thousands but now the NSO had organised them into small groups; contact with the opposition was far more likely and far less watered down. He found himself on the frontline and he didn't want to be there but he was in a whirlwind and the only thing more ominous than the guy they were looking for was Rudi Truter.

* * * * *

As Nat watched from his vantage point, the four men disappeared into the farmyard while the other climbed into the second car. He looked down his sights and focussed on the one man left in view.

He was the leader from the previous night, he stood in between the open driver's side door and the car itself with one foot remaining in the foot well. He was dressed all in black with a jacket or jumper zipped up tight around his neck. He wore black gloves. His face was tanned, it was a hard face, lean features. He offered no emotion as he scanned the countryside Nat could read his thoughts as he looked around the landscape, they were similar people in many ways. He could see the wolf in him hunting. As Nat put himself in Truters head conversely, he could see this man by the car climbing inside his own mind and narrowing down the possibilities. Nat could see within a few short moments that this killer knew he was in the land and he knew then this fight was going to continue.

* * * * *

Gerry and Davey came out of the darkness of the barn laden with loot that Steve and Conor had packed them up with. Truter exploded...

"What the fuck are you doing you fucking idiots!!" He said as he moved away from his car slamming the door shut in anger.

"Do you think we are here to steal junk, you drop that shit now or I'll shoot you all myself. There are plenty of people out there who would jump at the chance to have your privileges. So you keep your eyes on the task in hand" He stood square to all four men who had the wind knocked out of their sails and stood forlornly. Embarrassed about the armfuls of tat they had just stolen. They dropped the junk at their feet and looked to Truter for direction.

"Now get the fuck into those fields and don't come back here until you have this guy!"

Steve chirped up "Davey, where did you see something move up there?"

Truters eyes were wild now and his face seemed to tighten "What the hell did you just say?" he said with a menacing calmness. All four men stood stock still as the penny dropped. If they were in the bad books before, now they were in serious trouble. Steve realising he was the focus of Truter's murderous gaze pointed at Davey. "He said he saw something move up there when we pulled into the drive, but then he said it was probably nothing."

Truter's gaze moved to Davey; the young man recoiled with fear, judging the situation Truter softened and asked "what did you see Davey?"

"Ugh, I'm sure I saw someone running into the trees at the top of the hill" He looked to where Nat lay.

"Why didn't you tell me about this before?"

Davey hesitated flashing a look at Conor and Steve. Then at Roland, who gave him a reassuring nod from where he remained sitting in the car.

"Because he told me that if we got sent all the way up there for nothing then I wouldn't be coming back down again…"

Truter moved towards Steve, who grinned back at his boss. Truter said nothing but as he approached the marine he drew his handgun. He pistol whipped Steve across the face in a brutal flash. The man went down to one knee with a groan and blood dripped from the gash that had been opened under his eye. He looked up at Truter with a face like thunder. His pal took a step towards Truter, who turned towards him.

"Please try it, I won't kill you. But you'll end up being a lesson for all those foot soldiers who want to question me. I relish the test come on you fucker…" The man stopped in his tracks. "No? Not so confident. Come on you're bigger than me, younger than me, have a go, c'mon!!" Truter strained against the air willing the man to attack. The pause was eternal, but Conor looked to the floor. He backed down.

"Right then now we are back to the status quo you get into your hollow heads that I am giving the orders here. And this is grown up stuff, you don't do what I say, I will kill you. You leave; I hunt you down and kill you. You do as I say and you have a nice trouble free life". His eyes pierced each of the men breaking their will that little bit more.

"Now you arseholes get up that hill and…" turning to the two marines "…you come back down that hill without the farmer and I will kill you".

The four men set off up the hill, Davey and Gerry trudging a few paces behind the others. Davey's weapon was hanging limp by his side. Gerry could hear mumbling from the two soldiers over the wisp of grass under their feet. He couldn't hear the words, but he imagined the bravado coming back now that they were away from Truter.

Gerry shared Roland's feelings of being a prisoner in his own life. He had no control over his destiny, being carried on the wave of this new organisation whose practices were very different to what he had been expecting. He feared for his life and the fear was not being brought about so much from the enemies of the revolution but from its leaders. But he differed from Roland in that he enjoyed the violence and the power. So he followed Truter choosing bravado above brains, but hoping sooner or later an opportunity would present itself for him to escape.

The four men trudged on breathing hard now on the steady incline, they were about two thirds of the way to the tree line, about two hundred yards out. The woodland was becoming detail rather than the wash of a landscape painting. The individual trees were coming into focus, the breeze washed through the branches and the stones of the wall showed their moss covered faces. The men approaching the wood noticed none of that detail.

A tall figure had appeared, rangy with shoulders to hang saddles on, his white tresses blowing west to east and that grimace of clenched teeth; from that distance it looked as though he were smiling. He had a hunting rifle casually resting on his hip, the barrel pointing into the sky. His right hand however held the weapon next to the trigger. He stood motionless as he had done before when Davey and Gerry approached the house the first time. They flashed a nervous look at one another as all four men stopped in their tracks.

"You're a wanted man Mr Bell" Conor shouted up the hill.

"That right?" he responded

"We gotta take you down the hill now, upright or on your back it's up to you."

"You better come and get me then."

"Come on Mr Bell, there's four of us, you can't keep this up."

A lamb was calling for its mother and the crows were barking in the high tops of the trees. The fresh country air filled their nostrils as Nat raised his rifle, smooth, casual without moving his feet. There was no body language to cause alarm. Until he fired the weapon twice, Gerry felt blood and bone and brains splatter his face from ten yards. As Steve dropped to his knees, mouth agape, expression unchanged except for the volcanic eruption which had torn a hole through his head. As his knees thumped into the ground, he toppled forward and flat onto his cratered face. Before the dead man's head had met with the earth, Conor, still facing up the hill, fell backwards as though someone had hit him in the forehead with a baseball bat. Again the breeze carried away atomized blood and gore across the beautiful landscape.

"Now there's only two of you" Nat murmured

It all happened in split seconds but both Gerry and Davey's survival mechanisms had jolted into action and they were both running back towards the farmhouse.

Truter watched the situation unfold from the bottom of the hill, Roland began to go to their aid but the South African knowingly gestured for him to stay where he was. He could see the muzzle flashes from Nat's weapon, and he shook his head as he watched Gerry and Davey turn and run straight back down the hill. He needed qualified men not these headless chickens. He watched and waited for Nat to pick them off. But Nat didn't just pick them off.

Gerry was moving quicker than Davey until a dull thud sounded and he flew through the air as though he had just been hit by a train. He rolled down the hill and came to a stop in a motionless heap. At that point, time began to move very slowly for Davey.

The tears of fear flooded down his cheeks as he came level with Gerry. He looked down at his friend. Still he was running at full speed when something hit the back of his calf and he tumbled through the soft grass coming to rest a few yards further down the hill than where Gerry lay. As he lay in the grass, he was overwhelmed by a feeling of security, all was quiet and he was sheltered from the breeze. But within seconds his leg felt as though someone was holding a blowtorch to the bare flesh. It burned with immobilising ferocity and he wailed like a banshee.

* * * * *

Nat had watched these men approach with weapons brandished and he was consumed once more with rage. An anger that took his soul and buried it deep, all he wanted to do was unleash his pain through merciless violence on the men who had killed his wife.

As they approached he hatched a gruesome plan, the four shots were just the beginning, two heads, one lung and a crippling leg shot. As his hunters lay dying, Nat's eyes remained on the two enforcers who stayed by the car, just watching.

Nat stood just outside the tree line for a short while, resting the butt of his gun on his hip, the barrel pointing straight up in the air, finger remaining on the trigger. He began the slow jaunt down to his prey. As he walked he felt part of the environment, he felt untouchable out here against these enemies. They just didn't understand the land, the nature of open spaces.

His eyes remained on the man who was standing about eight hundred yards away. Nat thought about shooting at him, but his rage wanted to take more time with that man and anyway he wasn't going to waste rounds on a shot he wasn't sure he could make.

Calmly he approached the four men. Strapping his rifle across his back, he bent down without stopping and grabbed the first two carcasses by the scruffs of the neck and pulled them over to where the other two men lay. He dragged the two bodies with ease both men were twelve to fifteen stones each, but Nat's body was accustomed to hauling dead weight. He slumped them downhill of where Gerry was.

Nat then turned to Davey, he was pleading with him for mercy, the tears washed his face wet and he physically juddered with fear. As Nat's massive frame leant over the man who now seemed so frail, so weak. He could see how young the boy was as he looked down into his fearful eyes. He had to remind himself of what the animal had done before he carried on. He punched his fist into the top of his chest taking a handful of clothing he lifted the man like a bale of hay. He moved him like this at waist height and threw him on top of the two corpses. Davey cried out, writhing on the two dead men, repulsed by the idea of lying on lifeless bodies.

Nat turned to the fourth man, checking to see that the men by the car had not moved. He walked a few paces over to where Gerry lay and looked down at the wounded man. Gerry was whimpering and gurgling, his lungs filling with blood just like Esme's had. The sound rattled through Nat's body, opening the fresh wounds and fuelling the rage.

The man full of bravado that Nat had met weeks ago was now broken, whimpering and lost in a hell he would never have been able to imagine before it became his reality. He couldn't manage any words, but the tears rolling down his cheeks and his eyes translated his pleading for mercy.

Nat had no time for compassion now, the war had begun and all he could think about was Esme. He dragged the spluttering boy towards Davey, kicked him onto his front and then scragged a handful of hair and pulled his head up high, stretching out his neck. Blood spluttered out of the man's mouth, Nat raised his head and looked into

Davey's eyes. All the while he kept one eye on the South African, but the man remained still, just watching.

* * * * *

Davey could hardly bear to watch as the grizzled figure slung the miserable wretch that was Gerry to the floor in front of him. Then to his horror the huge man pulled Gerry's head upwards tight.

He watched, incapacitated with fear and disabled by pain. The old farmer, covered in dirt, filthy jeans, dirty brown wax jacket, his huge hands, one holding Gerry's head up fast, the other unsheathing a huge gleaming hunting knife. His wizened face, eyes lost in a heavy squint, teeth gritted and lips snarling, all framed by that shaggy white mane and whiskers. Davey felt the carnal fear that he would if he were face to face with a tiger, this man was the devil himself.

Suddenly Davey realised he still had the handgun in his pocket, he had put it there when he had started running. He slowly shifted his hand as the farmer looked down the hill towards the farmhouse. The next thing he knew was that the massive figure had thrown Gerry to the ground and was looming above him and a huge boot landed in his guts. Davey heaved and bent double, the wind had been literally booted out of his body and he just couldn't catch his breath. On one hand, he panicked to try and breathe on the other it was a relief from the pain of the gunshot wound in his leg.

The farmer rifled through his pockets and relieved him of the handgun. Roughly he sat Davey back upright and slapped him hard a number of times across the face as if to say 'I'm in charge'. He picked the knife up from where he had thrown it into the ground and rested the glinting blade on the nape of Davey's neck.

"Behave boy, and you'll live. Try anything else and I'll gut you like a fish." Their eyes met, Davey looked into Nat's cut glass eyes, cobalt flames like diamonds under a spotlight, demonic and wild "...you understand me."

Davey mustered a stuttering nod, weeping openly. He was lying back against the two dead men, their bodies were still warm but prostrate. Davey put his head in his hands and wept. He looked at his wound through his fingers and he could see the round had exited through his shin. He could see the bright white of bone and couldn't stop himself from vomiting, through his hands and down his front. His brain could not compute all this information at once, it was as if he were having a nightmare and sooner or later he would wake up. But that wasn't going to happen this time.

"Look at me..." growled Nat "LOOK AT ME!" he shouted at the boy who jumped back into the present and looked at him through his tears.

Nat stood up tall, a few paces away now with the wretched figure of Gerry lying on his belly at his feet. The pile of bodies was a few yards back up the hill as he turned towards the Truter, still standing next to his car, looking. Nat stood on the hillside, a wild figure, rifle strapped across his back and large knife glinting in the sunlight. He raised the knife to point it at the man watching from the bottom of the hill and remained statuesque for a long moment. Then he got back to work. Placing his palm on the top of Gerry's head. He hooked his fingers into the top of the injured man's eye sockets and he pulled his head up and back, hard, arching his back to full stretch. Gerry's neck was offered up, tight and ready.

Nat steeled himself against what he was about to do. He swamped his mind with the images of his dying wife, he tried to imagine these men doing what they did to her. Once again the world filled with a red mist, his blood boiled and he craved bloody vengeance. He took his hunting knife and with all his strength he drew the sharp steel across Gerry's neck in one steady, powerful arc. The sound of cold steel slicing through muscle, grizzle and the jugular was never to be forgotten, a noise like no other, high in pitch but smothered, dampened by the flesh and blood involved. He was looking Davey right in the eye when his blade carved through Gerry's jugular.

Davey, confronted by the reality of Gerry's helplessness in the face of Nat's sentient natural force, panicked. He kicked his legs into the dirt pushing his body frantically back against the two dead men on which he leaned. His eyes wild with fear as Gerry's heart, itself pounding with terror, spraying a deep crimson mist of blood towards Davey. Which rained down on him, cloaking him. For what seemed an eternity blood sprayed with unexpected power from the mortal wound.

* * * * *

Truter watched as the scene unfolded, he knew that it took a certain type of mind to be able to slice through another's throat, especially with an audience. And he knew it took a great deal of strength and an intricate knowledge of your weapon to carry out the act in one movement.

As he watched, Nat pushed Gerry's head violently to the floor with disdain and stood up tall on the hill. It looked like a microcosm of a medieval battle, this barbarian slaying all that approached. The realisation washed over Truter that this man was no fly in the ointment but more a viper in his bed.

As the two men stared at each other from a distance. Truter back with a foot up in the car, between the open door and the driver's seat, calm, casually watching the mayhem. Nat with dripping knife in hand, arms hanging by his side, feet apart, Gerry's inert corpse lying at his feet. After a long period of contemplation Truter ducked into the car, he turned to Roland and their eyes met. But both men were speechless, numbed by the visceral barbery they had witnessed. He turned the key, revved the car and drove away without saying a word.

* * * * *

Nat watched them as they left, eyes squinting in the breeze, his heart returning to its regular beat and the carnal blood lust waning, being replaced by a feeling of guilt and disgust. He banished those thoughts to the back of his mind as he took three large strides over to where Davey lay whimpering. The boy was crazed by fear with his hands up shielding his face as though he were about to be struck by a car. Standing over the terrified figure Nat smacked at Davey's arms with his palm, an intimidating gesture knocking them away from his face. As Davey looked up at Nat's eerie silhouetted figure, the big farmer spoke

"What did you expect boy? That I'd run away, that you would hunt me down and kill me?" He leaned down and took Davey by the scruff of the neck, he stood on the ankle of his wounded leg and Davey screamed in pain. Nat then put his arm around his throat and tightened his grip. The boy began to gag and Nat's knife, still in his hand began to sink into the flesh of Davey's cheek slicing a deep gash.

"You stay right here boy or I'll pick you off with my rifle before you get fifty yards, you understand."

With that Nat let the choking man slump back down on top of his mate's bodies and he walked away down the hill towards the ruined farmhouse. The bleak grey clouds boiled above him as he went and a cold wind whipped through the grass.

* * * * *

Davey shivered, his throat raw, his leg in agony and his face bleeding from the fresh wound. His blood only washed over Gerry's which had already covered him. He looked around, he was at least one hundred and fifty yards from the trees. The last thing he wanted was to be hunted down by this psychopath. He lay there staring up at the enormous sky, huge clouds rushing across the vista, the shock rocked uncontrollably across his body. Then he heard an engine, painfully he turned his head to see the farmer coming back up the hill on a quad bike with trailer in tow.

* * * * *

Nat accelerated up the hill like he had done a thousand times before, pulling to a stop next to the dead bodies and the skinny kid. He jumped off the machine and stood for a moment, face in the breeze, checking the perimeters of his area, smelling, watching, listening for anything out of the ordinary. Nothing disturbed him so he turned to the carnage that lay behind him and heaved the bodies like sacks onto the trailer. Finally, he lifted Davey and threw him on top of the bloody mess.

He drove the quad fast back down the hill. Davey's crying was affecting him now, he wanted to help the boy but knew he had to do this, finish his statement. He pulled up next to Gerry's car and pulling him off the trailer, Nat rifled roughly through the dead man's pockets without saying a word to the one who was still breathing. Finding the keys he opened the boot and glanced between the space in the boot and the size of the four men, he shook his head at the conundrum. He grabbed the boot shelf and ripped it from the car. Then he took the bodies up onto his shoulder one by one and laid them like sacks of spuds across the boot, curling their legs up to get them in. Finally, he grabbed the skinny kid who was again pleading with him not to go in the boot. Ignoring him Nat and threw him on top of the others, he was right up against the rear window of the hatchback as Nat slammed it shut in his face.

Nat moved back to the trailer and picked up a piece of sheet metal, a pot of black metal paint, brush and a bundle of pull ties. He put these items in the car and then swung his rifle off his back and placing it in the passenger foot well he drove the quad bike back to the barns. In the trailer, he checked out his latest acquisitions for his arsenal. Two handguns, two shotguns and an SA80. He put one handgun into his waistband and pumped the shotgun and put it over his shoulder and returned to the car.

The back of the car had gone eerily quiet, but Davey was still there, breathing heavily. He drove fast into the centre of Hexham, to the market place where he stopped at the side of the road next to the monument in the middle of the square. There must have been more than twenty people milling around, all of them knew Nat by sight or name and at least ten were now affiliated in some way to the NSO. Not one approached as he began to daub something on the sheet metal. The gathering crowd could see Davey in the back of the steamed up car, his face and hands pressed against the rear-view window. They could see the state of Nat, covered in dirt and blood, wild and unkempt. Some could see the rifle and shotgun in the passenger side foot well through the open driver's side door. Mobile phones were pulled from pockets, some made calls others made videos. Most local people had heard by now that Nat had gone mad or gone rogue, depending on allegiances'. But they had not witnessed any real opposition to the NSO. Until now.

Once he had finished with the paint he left the metal sheet on the roof and moved around to the boot. He opened the boot, Davey immediately started to scream for help, Nat beat him in the face with his fist until he stopped. Then he turned to the crowd and looked for trouble. None stepped forward so he turned again and dragged him by the scruff of the neck out of the car, Davey's legs falling limp to the ground. Nat dropped him next to the monument and he turned back to the car, he saw out of the corner of his eye two men approaching, he knew them. He walked back to the open door of the car and leaned in pulling the shotgun out he turned to the approaching men. They slowed their pace as they saw the weapon in his hands.

"This is not your business, Steven," Nat said to the taller man, they were brothers, policemen from Hexham and now NSO enforcers in the town.

"You know it is Nat, we can't let you carry on like this."

"You can boy or I'll be lying you down next to these four animals. You do what you have to do, but no one is gonna think any the less if you just go back to your office and report this, come back with more of you."

The two men looked at each other, they both knew Nat, more from reputation, let alone the story's people had been telling in the last day or so.

"We'll be back shortly Nat, you've got to be stopped" they turned and ran back to their vehicle and screeched off. Nat presumed it was back to the base to do as he had said. So he stepped up a gear and hauled the other three bodies out of the boot and dumped them roughly on the cold concrete next to the pulp that was the skinny lad.

He attached the bodies, arms to ankles, with the pull ties and then with two more pull ties he hung the sign that he had just written tight around the live one's neck. He stood back and turned three sixty slowly looking at all the faces staring at him in the square, the blood caked on his skin and clothes, shotgun hanging by his side in his right hand. Then, after a moment and within four strides he was back in the car.

He fired up the engine and hammered down Hallstyle Bank out of the town leaving his gruesome message for all to see. The sign, he had written that underlined the bloody misery that was Davey's face, read...

"NO QUARTER FOR NSO NORTH OF THE WALL"

NINE

The cold hard evidence of his activities hit all forums of media very quickly. Recordings from bystanders went viral within hours and he made the front pages within the press.

Nat sat next to Esme's grave as the tide of dusk enveloped his surroundings. He chewed raw beans, the pangs of hunger waning as he listened to rotor blades of a light chopper circling his ruined farmhouse. The murders were like a drug, he wanted more to numb his pain; avenge his wife's murder; teach these people; to slake his bloodlust.

His backside rested hard on the cold ground, his clothes constantly damp, it didn't bother him, he was warm and at home here. The brook babbled under a still sky. Beyond the stream and the distant beat of the rota blades, the wood was quiet. Maybe too quiet.

He suddenly felt that somebody else was present, his eyes looked down at the lifeless pile of stones next to him and he shook his head at the thought, he didn't believe in ghosts. His second reaction was to put his hand on the cold steel of his handgun, he placed it on the boulder next to him and pulled his shotgun up over his lap. Then he reverted back to the absurd and reached down with a big hand, placing it on the stones that lay over his wife's body. The chill of the barren stones transformed the inertia into a frigid wave through his body. There was no paranormal energy there just the temperature of an inanimate object in the cool evening; Esme was not haunting him tonight.

He turned his attention to the increasingly blue/black plethora that engulfed him. His ears pricked and his eyes bulged but there was nothing to see so he dug back into his beans and quashed the hollow pain of hunger in his belly. He shovelled in the sustenance, like a lion at a carcass he wolfed down the meal before any passing hyenas sniffed out the bounty, there was no point savouring cold beans anyway. As he scraped the plastic spoon around the bottom of the tin, he heard it; mute, almost in-audible but a human sound. It was a faint plastic pop. Like the click-pop of an old plastic paracetamol container or even older, he remembered camera film containers. He knew exactly what that sound could have been, he stopped, he stared into the darkness, heart pounding, wild, calling on the height of every one of his senses. Was the hunter becoming prey?

* * * * *

The man in black fatigues had a fully blacked out face nestled in the undergrowth of the wood high up above the ravine. As his eye focussed through his night-sight on the green and black figure sitting next to the makeshift grave. The image cleared in his mind, it registered the legs standing firm in the dirt. The weapon laid across his lap, tin of food in hand resting on lap, grim face with two black dots for eyes. He was stunned at the sight because those black dots were staring straight back down his lens.

In shock, the man at the top of the ravine jerked his eye away from the sights. He stared into the darkness, there was nothing, no outline, no shadow, no sound, just one swathe of dark blue washing over black. Silently holding his breath in check he placed his eye back over the nightsight and the ghostly chill washed over him again. The ghoulish figure sitting in the blackness was staring intently and unwaveringly back at him.

* * * * *

The sun had risen over Greenwich less than an hour before. As Baines leaned towards the huge TV screen in his office. Lucas perched on the arm of his high-backed armchair like some sort of devil on his shoulder. The devil sipped coffee from a mug with the picture of a London bus on it and it read 'I Heart London' in big bold letters with a big red heart in between I and London. Around them; nine colleagues and aides, all focussed on the screen at the front of the room. As Baines flicked through the various news channels, he imagined with horror the millions of families across the country interpreting the disturbing images that they were witnessing.

The reports were on the whole towing the government line on the story, Start had seen to that. The regime had spun the actions of the farmer as a 'violent and dangerous criminal using the revolution as an excuse for murder' and the newsreel was littered with language such as 'heinous crimes'.

However, Baines was no idiot he knew what he was watching and how critical sections of the population would interpret this story; at best this man would become an anti-hero, at worst a cult-hero. He personified the fuel for a fire that was already burning bright, especially in the border counties.

Baines watched the massive figure on amateur video hauling and dragging the bodies from his vehicle as though they were simply sacks of potatoes, his thick white hair and beard framing his tanned face. Baines watched the rugged, statuesque figure going about his gruesome business. He hoped that the feral appeal of the man that he recognised was not universal.

The channel hopped to England Today the only opposition news station claiming to be fighting back against press control. Now the independent news station transmitted through random countries and offered 'the truth' in terms of story to the sectors of the population brave enough to watch it. Baines glanced at Start, both men dreading this report.

The young reporter stood in the market square in Hexham, Baines raised his hand and 'sssh'd' the room, the report continued,

"...the questions must be answered, what led this well known, well liked farmer, family man and popular local figure to start killing people? What happened to his thriving farm? And what has become of his wife? Also, a well-known and well-liked local who has not been seen for a week. This man had never been convicted of a crime, far from it, locals talk about him as mild-mannered, charitable. Certainly no recluse, in fact, a pillar of the farming community.

Questions must be asked of the new government and in particular its enforcement units. Rumours abound in this rural idyll that this farmer's bloody rampage was sparked by the enforcement squads' brutality. Which led to the deaths of Esme, his wife." Esmes beautiful face appeared on the screen and Baines slumped down in his seat. Start threw a hand at the screen as though he were watching a football match and the referee had waved play on to a blatant foul, the report continued "And their elderly neighbours Bob and Jean Maddocks. Although unproven there is an overwhelming opinion throughout this region that NSO enforcers have the blood of locals on their hands. And those locals see the action of Nat Bell as an act of war rather than murder. As this situation unfolds in this volatile region where insurgency is rife, the regime must face up to its shortcomings. Rather than resort to violence, channels of diplomacy must be set up to connect with an ever increasingly marginalised population. This is Rory Jones reporting from Hexham, Northumberland for News Today."

The picture flicked from the reporter's baby face standing in a soggy Mack looking rather bullied by the rain to a still of Nat from that day in the market square. His sapphire blue eyes staring straight down the lens, gritted teeth, white hair streaked with blood from his victims, clenched fists like ball peen hammers and long legs set wide like two tree trunks.

Baines felt as though the colour had drained from his face, a little light headed he tried to gather his composure and face his staff without panic etched in his features. The leader knew about revolution and as he digested the image of this wild man fighting back, he knew it would strike a chord in the psyche of the very people who had brought him to power. He was sure of this because he felt it, he had an affinity with this enemy.

He turned his attention to Start, shock being overwhelmed by anger "what happened to the wife? What happened at his farm?"

Start was prone, pensive, he stared at the floor, elbows on his knees, hands clasped in front of him.

* * * * *

Claire had called Stuart after she had dressed the wound to Nat's shoulder. As she had watched him putter away on the small motorbike, she knew that his friend needed to know the whole situation.

Shortly after speaking to Claire, Stuart told Amber everything, about her home, her father and her mother. Amber had broken down in his arms and sobbed on his shoulder. But in her father's image she pulled herself together and pushed the sadness deep down. That steely look appeared in her eye. She began to demand their return to Northumberland to be with and fight alongside her father. Stuart looked at the young girl, eighteen years old; to him a babe in arms. That was not the way she saw herself.

A few hours passed as the two saw to the animals. It was mid-afternoon when they both sat in front of the news, mouths agape, as they watched her father, his friend dumping the bodies in the marketplace.

Amber looked across at Stuart, her cheeks flushed with colour, her movements twitching with nerves and anger

"I don't care whether you come with me or not...I'm going tomorrow, you won't keep me here Stuart, the man needs our help and so do the rebels. I spoke to Jesse Rowell; we need to join up with them and fight with them" she stated aggressively as teenagers do when they want to make a point.

"hey hey hey Amber" Stuart responded with his hands up "no-ones being kept here, you gotta do whatever you gotta do and I'll be coming with"

Stuart looked back at the television, the blue light washing over his face in the dull room. He knew this young woman would go whether he liked it or not, she would follow him if he went or she would vanish overnight if he tried to stop her leaving. He had known this girl from the moment she was born. She might not say very much, but she was as decisive and determined, or some would say 'pig-headed' as her father and even more capable. She had spent her years independently roaming their land, deep in the environment. Those who knew it marvelled at her ability to disappear in the countryside, she had a gift for nature, she loved it, she was part of it and Carlins Law was her home. Stuart knew that they would be leaving for Northumberland.

"I'm going to pack my bag." She said quietly.

"Amber, I told Nat that I would look after you, I hope you understand that if we turn up there, he's likely to kill me himself!"

"Well, I'm going with or without you…and he'll definitely want to kill you if I show up there alone".

"Jesus woman, you are your fathers' daughter, how do you propose we cross the border?"

"Come on Stuart, I'm eighteen not eight, there is no way that that wall has been completed in the last three days, we just need to find a gap."

"Ok lassie, let's get our stuff together. But we go on one condition, we try and persuade your father to leave with us, he can't win this war he's started. Not one man against the Regime"

"Well, he isn't one man now is he? He's two men and a woman and I think he'll want to fight with the rebels as much as I do. You get me there safe and then you can leave come back up here to safety" she replied with a smile, then she turned and left the room, up the stairs and into her room.

Stuart felt a cocktail of anger, excitement, fear and sadness as he pushed himself up out of his low comfy armchair and went straight to the cold steel of his gun cabinet with a large holdall.

* * * * *

Lucas Start looked at the floor for a long time. Baines didn't understand, he thought the man was about to explode or breakdown so he waited patiently for his closest political friend to decide what he was going to say.

Start had been forced by this menace in the North to act sooner than he had wanted. He raised his head after what felt like an age and looked around the room at his cohorts and his gaze was met by supportive and provocative nods and raised eyebrows. He ringed his hands drew breath and turned to Baines, the man who had carried him to where he was today.

"Ben, you are losing touch with the people, the peaceful revolution will not work. While you have been appeasing the old guard, the population are becoming wild and untamed, twisting our system for their own gain. I am the man who is keeping control. Mine are the shoulders carrying this system and I am the one creating security for our country. This is one man refusing to live the way the society democratically decided to live. There are thousands more like him and we need to crush them. To bring about the change we want we need to force change through martial law. I have been busy Ben, I have amassed our own army. We have been training new recruits for months now and we have been receiving arms and officers from the South Americans. We are now a regime with our own muscle and we are using it to keep control in areas where we are experiencing resistance."

Realisation dawned on Baines, the rug was being pulled from underneath him by the man he had nurtured, supported and pushed through all his difficulties and shortcomings. He had not seen this coming. Until this moment he had been the leader, the talisman and pivotal mastermind of the regime. But in that instant he realised that now that power was the NSO's, he was surplus to requirement. A dictatorship did not need a leader who cared about the people.

He could see that the room of greedy, selfish politicians were following Start. He wanted to explode with anger, his ideology was being manipulated for personal gain, he had to remain calm and figure out a way back.

Start continued "The naivety of your system never took into account the fact that a lot of people out there are simply lazy. They don't want to be empowered as you call it. They don't want to work, they just want hand outs. Men like this Bell character are capturing the imagination of the same people that mobilised our movement. Those who just want to fight. If we don't stamp it out, these pockets of resistance will grow and destroy our regime. I have conscripted many of these people into our army and put those fighters out there to stop further resistance".

Baines sat stone-faced his eyes focussed on Lucas Start.

"Look Ben" Start continued, "I realised a long time ago, although you were our leader and a good man," Baines nearly choked on the condescension "your abilities are floored. When it comes to the tough decisions of security and control, you are allowing the population too much freedom, too much time to think for themselves and take advantage of the chaos.

"But the most important gulf that has opened up between you and us" Start looked around the room, as did Baines to a gang of shifting eyes looking everywhere but into his eyes. "None of us believe in your airy-fairy ideals of equality for all. Why should we organise the country, set up the systems which will govern us in the future and carry that responsibility for the population? Yet we only receive a fraction more in recompense than a builder or factory worker, it's ridiculous."

Baines sat in silence but as it dragged he uttered with disgust

"So this is about money, greed."

"No I like to call it quality of life and power."

"So what now, what do you want me to do?"

Starts face softened, the bully had broken through the wall and he felt subjugation was close, he was high on the thrill of the coup

"You don't need to do anything Ben, we want nothing to change on the face of it. But I will be giving the orders. I want to move out of the shadows with my activities."

"What activities?" Baines asked simply.

"Re-education of the population, military expansion and land reform"

"No wonder you have been so worried about people like this Bell character. It is a sorry day for England that we are now a dictatorship, so far from the progressive government I intended. What are you going to do if I go public, if I say no and oppose this?"

"Just try it and see Ben, I have some powerful allies now. I don't want to see you fall Ben, after all none of us would be here if it weren't for you. But your good work has dealt me cards that I am not prepared to give up. The games have changed as it were. It seems my partners in the south see our little country as quite an important partner in the future. A small but important South American ally neighbouring an ever more powerful Scandinavian Arc. And the overwhelming numbers and size of their armed forces give me the security to thrive in this nest of vipers…a beautiful partnership I think"

"I take the increase in violence is due to your militias."

"Probably, but we are now in control of all land in England and Wales except the border country, Cornwall and the Welsh West. We have conscripted tens of thousands of men into the army in the past weeks and we have amassed a war chest from our ever generous population. This has all been done thanks to my militias."

"I hope you are right Lucas, this is an educated country, people will not settle for oppression."

"That's where you come in Ben. The acceptable face of the regime. The charm to spin my tough love to the masses, after all we know what's best for the country and the population." Start turned to the room and asked their colleagues to leave "I need to speak to Ben alone now."

As the room fell silent and the two men stood facing each other, Baines spoke

"You realise what you're doing here Lucas. Seventy million people will want to see you dead, this country is too established, too educated and too close to the Scandinavian Arc to get away with this. We'll have civil war. Weapons and troops will flood in from Scotland and Ireland. Are you confident in your partnership with the South Americans? My view has always been that their interests lie to their west, India and China is where they concentrate, don't be left to the wolves by an ally who reneges at the crucial hour."

"I'll take my chances" replied Start, a pensive look into the middle distance betrayed the flicker of acceptance that what Baines was saying made sense. Baines took the opportunity to push.

"Your arrogance betrays your intellect as well Lucas, do you really think that we created this revolution, that we cultivated the popular opinion that swept us to power. We only jumped on the back of a population unhappy with the status quo, I developed our policies around what the masses were asking for. That same population will fight you when they realise what you are doing."

"It's done Ben, I have chosen my direction and I will do whatever is necessary to retain power. You can stay with me or not but I can't have you opposing me" his stare came to rest on Ben with an ominous focus as though he were reading Baines mind. Baines thought quickly buying time

"I'll have to think about it." He said rather hesitantly.

"Of course," Start said suddenly with a flash of his hand. He took a few steps across the room looking down at the floor then he turned quickly and his stare landed, "But don't disappear, I don't need anyone else on my wanted list." He uttered with a menacing grin.

Baines returned to his office across a silent open plan space where no one made eye contact and the atmosphere was frigid. He was humiliated and let down, but he was a natural politician and no thug. He knew there were many influential people out there in this country and across the world who would be opposed to Start. He needed to think about his next step, bide his time.

His office was dark, only his table lamp lit a small funnel of light through the air and upon his desk. He picked up the receiver on the telephone between thumb and forefinger and waited as a siren wailed passed his window. He moved papers on his desk into a pile and he looked at the small brass race horse that adorned his office. A present from his father.

As the din receded he dialled the first number in his mind, but this time there was no gruff monotone voice at the other end, it went straight to answer-phone

"Tom, its Ben, call me."

He poked his finger into the receiver and he took a moment to think. Then with a single nod he came to a decision and began to dial a number with purpose. He got halfway through dialling when he suddenly slammed the phone down. He looked out of his office door, his eyes darted around the shadows, and a hundred thoughts rushing through his head; he grabbed his diary and he left the room as quickly as he could.

He could see Lucas Start through the glass wall of the boardroom, he was on the phone, alone, barking orders. He moved as invisibly as he could through the shadows of the open plan office space, out into the main hall and he took the rear stairs down into the empty street behind their party headquarters.

Rain was falling in thick lumps of water, a typical London drenching. It didn't bother Baines, he pulled his collars up high and trained his eyes on the pavement; he didn't want to be recognised. The streets were all but empty in the downpour. He walked for about thirty minutes calculating his next move like a chess master trying to understand the consequences of whatever options were available to him. One thing Baines knew how to do was survive, he had built his party from a marginal anarchist group to legitimate political movement. He had brought anarchism into the mainstream, stamping out the propaganda that the name signified and giving the average man a voice. He would be damned if Start leveraged his dreams away without a fight. But he also knew that only fools rush in. He had time to plan; to build.

By the time he decided on an imminent plan he had found himself at Marble Arch, at the end of Oxford Street, he remembered the throngs of shoppers and tourists trudging the pavements of this famous street. There were a few people shopping but no tourists now and the whole place looked so sad in the dull grey. He walked to the nearest pay phone and wedged his files on the tiny table holding it in place with his stomach. He took out his wallet and found a scrap of paper he had tucked deep down inside it over a year previously. He never thought he would be calling the number but now in the driving rain he tapped it into the public telephone keypad.

"Yes" came the answer after three rings.

"It's Baines."

"Well, bugger me, I hope to God your calling on a secure line or you're a dead man!" The voice was like gravel, it belonged to Trevor Eastman, a ghost, the Kings personal head of security; one of the cogs that make the world go round.

"I'm on a payphone."

"Well, what do you want? I thought Bolsheviks and Royals didn't mix."

"If I thought you were that dumb I wouldn't have called, I want to meet" replied Baines

"Ok, are you in Central London?"

"Yes"

"There's a bench next to the boats on the Serpentine, thirty minutes."

The line clicked off and went dead.

Baines replaced the receiver and turned onto the road, the rain clouds had broken, some rays of sunshine were breaking through. His heart pounded as he once again shrugged his collars up high and trained his eyes on the pavement. Trying to remain invisible to people on the street.

Marble Arch was a ghostly semblance of the frantic activity of previous decades. Like a black and white still from history, only a handful of vehicles passed the white marble triumphal arch. Baines skipped across the road threading between the traffic and crossed the flagstone pavement once busy with tourists, now empty. He made quick time through the open acres of Hyde Park, parakeets lined the branches huddled from the recent rain.

Baines found the bench he had been directed to. As he sat down and looked over the Serpentine, the pedallo's and rowing boats were tied up and all but forgotten, dirty and unloved. There were two characters strapping on skates where in years gone by hundreds gathered to skate, watch and socialise. As he mulled over the idea that this depressing outlook was in some way his making rather than that of the bad weather that day, he was joined on the bench.

The man who sat down dressed in a tailored suit, with overcoat unbuttoned didn't look across at Baines. He was well over six feet tall, well-built and with a handsome, clean-shaven face. His hair was dark and parted at the side. He was immaculately presented; cuffs which stood proud from his jacket no more than an inch; shoes polished, worn but perfectly kept; a Windsor knot in his tie seamless to cut away collars. Baines had never met him, but he knew this was the Kings man. There was a brief moment before the stranger turned and spoke

"This is a little risky isn't? Not everyone loves you Mr Baines, what if you were recognised?"

"Don't you worry about me Trevor, I've avoided being recognised when necessary for years and I have my own security."

Eastman looked around, clocking the huge figure standing amongst the trees about forty yards behind them.

"Aha, I see Pierre is still with you."

"He is, I don't need anyone else…"

"I reckon you haven't got anyone else or you wouldn't have come running to me!" he exclaimed with no half measure of glee.

"I want to know whether we can work together"

Eastman turned to him and with an incredulous look,

"What the fuck do you mean Baines?"

Before Baines had time to answer, Eastman held up his hand

"No, no don't answer that, I'll tell you where you stand: your lot were democratically elected. The King is a figure head he has no way of stepping in on parliament anymore. He might be able to appeal to the population but considering your voters political leanings, I doubt he will hold much sway. Furthermore, you brought down a system which worked very nicely for this country for centuries. Everything you represent is abhorrent. So the answer to your question is nowhere. Our working together is a last resort."

"Look I've got no time for big bruising voices, a danger far greater than my movement is upon the country, I need help but if you have no interest…"

"I didn't say that Baines, we can use you but remember that the best you'll get is the wilderness after this dark patch in our history is resolved."

"Now we're getting somewhere" Ben replied, with an exasperated tone. "We both want to finish Start so a little cooperation would be mutually beneficial" He added

"We want rid of all of you Baines."

"Yes, yes I know" Ben replied with some tedium in his voice "What are the options going forward?"

"The choices are simple, we can take him out of the equation by force or by public opinion...the latter, however will be long and bloody. Force is the line we are currently exploring. You do realise that civil war is looking more and more likely. In itself, this is palatable but the fact that should our country end up at war with itself then the likely outcome is an independent Wales and at least Northumberland and Cumbria annexed by Scotland. That is unimaginable; a result that we must not allow, cannot even contemplate as satisfactory" He took a deep breath and continued "Even contentment in the cities is waning because crime is so rife Baines. And the principal protagonists are your militias; it's as though the country is being governed by a gang."

"And if we choose to speed things up with force?"

"That's where you could be more useful. The security around Start is so tight, he doesn't venture out of his inner circle and he is never seen in public so having you on the inside obviously has its benefits." Eastman looked across the lake "Maybe this will change now that you have been pushed out."

"No he wants me to remain as the figurehead of the regime so I will remain in the limelight."

The two men pondered, neither had a plan at this stage and both were beginning to get restless, they had spent enough time on a park bench in the open. Eastman turned to Ben pulling a mobile phone from his pocket and handing it over.

"There's one number in there Baines and it's secure, use it to contact me. You call me, I will never call you so never answer that phone; if it rings it's compromised. If I need to get a message to you, I will do it another way. Get your thinking cap on Baines, you may have caused this mess but now you have a chance to help put it right before the country is torn apart."

The two men stood and looked at each other, both naturally contemplating shaking hands but rejecting the idea, Eastman spoke again and broke the awkward moment.

"The situation with these land reforms is more far reaching than you think you know. Your vision of self-sufficiency needs a co-operative countryside. They're the ones that put the food on our tables and dispose of our rubbish and produce a lot of our energy. So, now they've stopped playing ball all your workers in the cities are beginning to go hungry, dirty and medieval. You can't take peoples farms and put workers on them who don't know what they are doing. You need the landowners to manage it."

Baines knew all this he couldn't argue he simply responded "It wasn't meant to be like this…"

Eastman continued "I'm sure you were party to the pact he has signed with the South Americans, England is now, to all intents and purposes a Brazilian colony. They are arming, funding and training Starts rapidly growing army. Were you any good at history?"

Baines made no comment humiliated by the freedom he had given Start.

"At School, did you like History?" Eastman said slowly with a supercilious tone.

"Don't fuck around Eastman"

"The Vietnam War and the arms race were the catalysts for the flower power movement, you know everyone dancing around on acid screwing each other the nice way. Well, your era will go down as the antithesis of that. Your lovey-dovey, super righteous ideology has spawned a tyrant. Who, has unleashed a level of bloodshed and degree of control over a peoples the like of which has not been seen since ISIS rolled into Syria…and we all know what happened to them."

"I can see what's happening." Baines eyes were sharp, determined, "Don't underestimate me Eastman, I'll find a way to put this right."

"Ben, most of the people who would react are on the payroll. His first rule is the mixed squads, so your educated followers are now serving in military units next to violent thugs and criminals who are benefiting from the brutality of the regime. Fear keeps the peace better than any other form of control. Start uses those who enjoy the lawlessness to maintain the terror through the rank and file of the NSO, as well as that of the general population. I always told you there are too many variables in society for idealism".

"You just stick to creeping around in the shadows, I'll handle Lucas. You remember one thing; it was me. This revolution. It was me they followed. Not you. Not Start, no one else."

"Maybe, but the last twenty years was nothing in comparison to the mess you've made now."

He turned to walk away and called back over his shoulder

"You make sure you call me; do the right thing."

Ben watched him walk away, as he reached the road a black Jaguar car pulled up fast and he hopped into the rear seat. The car sped off, he could hear the large engine growl as it left the curb. He stood for a moment then looked around quickly as if remembering that he was entirely exposed. He looked at the phone in his hand, slipped it into his coat pocket and began the walk back to his office.

* * * * *

Rain beat upon their faces as Amber and Stuart roared down the country roads on his powerful quad bike. Stuart drove, Amber rested comfortably behind him with their luggage giving her a back rest. The gear consisted merely of a full jerry can, holdall full of weapons, some dry clothes and a small amount of food. Both of them wore ponchos to protect from the driving rain, which flapped behind them like the capes of Victorian horsemen.

When they reached the giant concrete structure of the border wall, the crossing point which Amber and her father had used days earlier was now an enormous grey barrier so they followed along the foot of the wall heading west where the land had been cleared by the construction workers. After about five miles the evidence of building became more apparent and they both knew they were getting close to the end of the wall as it stood so far. Stuart hammered on and the bike chewed up the sludgy dirt until the deep treads bit into traction, he could see the dull grey of the wall disappear up ahead and he twisted the throttle to its full extent.

The super-fast bap-bap-bap of the engine resonated through the trees and their headlight betrayed their position; there was no stealth in this mission. Stuart had the bike drifting in a wide left hand arc around the end of the wall and they disappeared on the southern side of the concrete, on English soil and with thousands of tonnes of masonry between them and the Scottish border.

They were travelling with speed and were twenty yards from the end of the wall when the flood lights fired up and illuminated the whole area. Instantly blinded by the sudden glare Stuart momentarily relaxed his grip on the throttle then pointed the handle bars straight and opened it up once again. They could hear some sort of voice over a loud hailer but couldn't hear the words. They disappeared into the darkness of the woodland along the wall and no one gave chase.

A short while later they slipped out onto the tarmac next to the old stone bridge. The rain was easing off, but the night was pitch black, the cloud cover was thick and dark as a theatre drape. The road was smooth and fast compared to the woodland trails and the heavy peat soil of the open country. Amber hunkered down in the cold of the night exasperated by the speeding bike. Stuart made the perfect windbreak; his solid frame unmoved by the chill or the ups, downs and shifting camber of the undulating road. Like a machine, he looked south.

An hour later Stuart skidded to a stop outside Ambers ruined home. She felt numb in the silence of the night and with the muscle memory of the vibrations from the bike. She pulled her stiff legs down off the bike and stretched out looking into the darkness at the black lump which was her home. Stuart put his arm around her, preparing for tears. But the young woman brushed his arm away, taking a few paces towards the charred ruin, took a few seconds to absorb it in the night's sky. She then turned to Stuart, the breeze blew her auburn curls across her face and she swept them aside with a desicive hand. The moonlight broke the cloud for a moment, her pale complexion glowed in the white light and her young eyes had that sudden steel about them.

"Let's take the bike up the hill, we can hide it in the woods. I know where he will be."

The quad climbed the steep incline with ease and Amber directed Stuart without a word, she wasn't going to compete with the snarl of the engine. As they approached the gate into the wood, Amber jumped off the quad and ran over to the gate which she knew so well. As her hand came to rest on the on the sodden moss covered wood, she could feel the damp foliage filling her nostrils with the smell of the cold night. A voice came calm, almost a whisper on the wind,

"What are you doing back here girl?"

Shocked Amber jumped back from the gate and squinted into the gloom, there only five paces in front of her the huge shadowy figure appeared, it was her father standing in the middle of the path. She ran to the gate and pulled the rope loop over the post freeing the old five bar which she flung back handed, it swung quickly open and she embraced her father.

* * * * *

It was overwhelming love he felt for his daughter. He hugged her tight and long. He found he couldn't speak because he was fighting back tears and he couldn't let go of her because she would see the state he was in. Stuart was standing close and rested his hand on his friends back, Nat finally released his daughter and turned to his old friend. The two men hugged, Nat stood back, his hands still on his friends' arms.

"I thought you were going to keep her in Scotland?"

"She is your daughter pal, you know she would have come on her own…"

"Aye she's stubborn. It's good to see you both" He said with a rare smile and slap on Stuarts' shoulder. It was true, their arrival was easing the loneliness and that eased the pressure he felt. His problems were being halved.

They spoke little as their feet whispered through the dewy ferns and mosses of the woodland floor. Nat was still shaken from the attack hours before. He had taken the three bodies and dumped them again outside Hexham in the darkness of the evening. They were professionals, they carried nothing except their weapons and empty mobile phones.

The early hours brought the cold, cold air. It was on their nostrils like pure oxygen, fresh and invigorating. The night was unmoving and silent, there was about an hour before the sun began its ascent. Nat led them to the little valley where he had buried Esme and made his rough camp.

As they ventured down the steep side of the ravine, the moonlight lit the waters of the stream and the smooth round boulders. While the grass and trees seemed to absorb the silvery light and appeared as thick black shadows. Amber went immediately to her mother's grave and kneeling beside it she placed a laboured hand on the cold stone.

"Tell me what happened?" She said without raising her head or looking at her father, her voice just drifting across the night.

Nat felt his throat constrict and his eyes well up. His heart raced and his stomach churned. He felt his shoulders begin to heave, but he controlled his emotions and fought back the tears, no good would come of showing weakness in their situation. He began picking up kindling to make a fire as he cleared his throat,

"When I got back to the house, I found her dead, she had been shot in the head and she wouldn't have known anything about it Amber."

He knew that his tone was probably not the most convincing and that he hadn't made eye contact with Amber, busying himself with the fire. But then he was pretty sure it didn't matter. Amber didn't reply she quietly pulled her knees up to her chin and pulled her jumper down over her legs. She sat quiet resting her arms on her knees and watched as the morning light began to wash over the valley. Stuart joined Nat at the fire.

"So tell me what it's like, how much fighting?"

"It seems to be escalating daily but to be honest beyond my stupidity I haven't been at too much risk. They seem to be a mixture of thugs and kids with a sprinkling of people who know what they're doing. I think there is a lot of resistance. I hear gunshots in the day but mostly at night and so I can't see that I'm the only one fighting."

He didn't elaborate further, he didn't mention the professionals who almost killed him or the mystery of his protector. He hadn't worked that out for himself yet.

"When did you last sleep in a bed?" asked Stuart

"A couple of days ago at Claire's..."

Stuart's interest sparked up at the mention of Claire, Nat leaned his shoulder across towards Stuart

"...they shot me and she patched me up, she's fine don't worry, keeping her head down."

"We have to get her with us, make sure she stays safe" Stuart said, his eyes embroiled in the dancing flames of the catching fire, the orange glow washing over his untamed features.

"We'll get her, after I finish with the bastards that killed Esme and then we make a break for Scotland until all this sorts itself out."

"It might not be so easy for you now Nat. You are the face of the resistance after what you did, and when everything is said and done what you did will be seen as an atrocity, a war crime."

"Yeah well, I never wanted to be famous, I'll drift back into obscurity long before this misery is over"

"You never know how this will pan out, there is resistance to the regime in Cornwall, Wales and all across the north of England."

"Is that what the news said?"

"Aye that's what it said" Stuart mumbled with a degree of hopeless resignation in persevering. Both men chuckled into the fire as Amber crept over and nestled herself between the two hulking figures. Nat added a pot of water to the flames, as they watched the orange wisps lick the pan, the water began to steam. Nat put his arm around his daughter as the grey-blue light of morning overcame the dark of night.

"It's good to see you my lamb" he whispered.

* * * * *

As they sat in the little valley, sipping hot coffee in the fresh morning, half a mile away a ghostly figure floated silently across the farmyard and into the barns. He felt his way across the dark space, the smell of dust and petrol thick within his nose. He didn't stop to look at what might be in the barn; he was looking for a safe place. He found it in the ladder leading up to the hay loft. He climbed the rickety old wood which creaked wildly under every step and he positioned himself on the edge of the platform with his legs dangling. He perched because he was unsure about the floorboards, he couldn't risk them being rotten and him crashing through and injuring himself so he stuck to the much thicker joist which made the frame of the mezzanine.

He removed the light weight snipers rifle from across his back and placed it on his left, he took the silenced revolver from the holster under his arm and gently put it next to his right hand. He carefully adjusted the weapons so that both barrels were exactly parallel with his thighs; he couldn't help himself, over the years the detail became everything to him.

It was at these moments of calm that he could reflect on his forty-eight years, twenty-five of which had been spent in solitude, in the shadows behind enemy lines mostly. His history was remarkable even in military circles, in fact, if there were no dusty old battered file holding a full account of his service history somewhere in the military records office, his life would be unbelievable. He had a skill for evading death or detection, a lust for solitude and a detachment which meant he carried on where most would break.

He had the same eyes as his brother, but where Baines had puffed and rounded a little due to the comforts of middle age and position, the ghost had wizened. He was no bad man, but he was focussed on his task. His eyes betrayed that determination by offering no emotion, no deviation from the plan; which often in practice resulted in no mercy. Right then he pulled the phone from its case on his chest and dialled the only number he ever dialled. The call was answered immediately.

"Things have changed Tom" Baines spoke urgently, he had not used the agents first name in years.

"Tell me," said the spectre sitting in the darkness in Nat's barn, his voice no more than a whisper.

"I am having some problems here, I have been usurped, but he can't risk kicking me out, I am the revolution, he needs me".

"What about the Establishment, the international community?"

"No and no, I'm adrift."

"You're in the shit Ben, can I stop babysitting this farmer now?"

"No, he is possibly a good distraction for us."

"Who's 'us'?"

"What do you mean?"

"You said 'for us'?"

"Right, I contacted Trevor Eastman."

"Ok well, he will support you while you're useful" There was a pause and then he continued

"What now? No let me have a guess, they want you to carry on as you were, the puppet leader, mole to the very system you sought to change: the irony of power!"

"That will never happen, you know how I love to be written off!"

"What do you want me to do" Whispered the shadow sitting in the hay loft "I'm on this hillbilly, I saved his life today, hope that's OK? But I thought there was no point in you sending me up here if I was just to watch him being target practice for a couple of regime mercenaries. He's been joined by another man and a young woman, from their body language I think it's his daughter. One thing's for sure though Ben, this guy is no Bin Laden, everything he's done so far he has done it alone, with his own bare hands. He is a cold hard bastard, but he's no terrorist mastermind and he's definitely not beaten; he's sitting up there in the woods living his life".

"Just stay on him please, you did good, don't let them kill him, I think he may turn out to be the thorn in the NSO's side or the catalyst to begin a greater escalation in resistance to Starts new regime"

"I'll do my best."

"Ok, Tom and look I'll see you when this sorts out, yes?"

Baines was answered by the dial tone, the shadowy figure perched in a barn in the Northumbrian wilderness had hung up long before Baines finished his sentence. The barn was silent bar a few boards which rattled in the soft breeze. It was a cool breeze that softened the smell of the farmyard to a sweet, pleasant aroma. He ripped open a packet of oat biscuits, peeled back the lid on a small tin of pate and he ate.

* * * * *

Lucas Start reclined in a large leather armchair positioned next to the ornate Victorian fireplace in his office. He had just taken a huge bite of a fat pastrami and gherkin sandwich. The mustard pickle seeped from the corners of his mouth. He could only really enjoy it if he stuffed so much in his mouth that he nearly choked on it. He listened to the animated South African voice through the mobile phone that he held to his ear with his free hand.

"I need heavier weapons and some people who can handle themselves and the weapons! I mean this is ridiculous Lucas, it's like the Wild West up here. I've got insurgents picking us off at every step. They have infiltrated my teams they seem to know what we are up to all the time. Then I've got that psycho up on the hill who is becoming a cult hero. I can't even get close to him because my teams don't have the first idea of military procedures! This is making a mockery of your security machine Mr Start. It's weakening your position and I am losing men to the rebels whilst listening to stories of this marvel living in the hills!"

"Don't worry Rudi" Replied Start swallowing his sandwich and licking his lips "as always I've got this. I'll have weapons aplenty to you within days, including armoured vehicles and light artillery; more than enough to crush your problems."

"What about men? I need people with military experience to keep the idiots I have at the moment in line. Dedication does not mean you know your arse from your elbow, you know?"

"Ok, ok look, we have thousands of men in full military training at the moment, I will see to it you are sent the first trained to crush any rebels in the north. Patience Rudi, the North East, will be your little honey pot, but you have to keep the locals in check long enough for us to get the troops to you."

"No problem, if I know they're coming we'll hold out, I mean Newcastle to Middlesborough we're all sewn up...the beauty of deprivation! All the old industry has fired up again and employing the masses, you'll be reliant on my little patch".

"It won't be your patch unless you contain the resistance...that reminds me as well, I have a small job for you in the interim; find that fucking reporter from last night's report on our farmer and nullify his future comment"

"Fine I'll go to it, I know the one."

Start hung up, looked at his sandwich and stuffed another mouthful to capacity and picked up the paper that lay on the coffee table in front of him. It was a report on the capability of the country for ninety percent self-sufficiency, he read it with excitement. The fact he had just ordered a man's death was history. To Start it was history similar to that which he created when he ate his sandwich.

TEN

Rory Jones had hardly stepped over the threshold as the damp smell of his rather decrepit cottage hit him. He stood in the cramped yet open plan hallway. As one arm slipped out of his damp Mack, he stopped at the mirror in the hallway and looked at himself. A broad grin spread across his face and the pride oozed out of him. He made guns with his fingers and pretended to shoot with a 'piow, piow' then he chuckled to himself shaking his chubby head, cringing slightly at his own actions.

He looked around the pokey cottage with its dusty sides, broken gas fire and ancient radiators. He thought to himself that this was the first time in his career as a journalist that his life was taking a turning point for the better. His report on the Northumbrian rebel was receiving acclaim from his peers and his bosses wanted more. For the first time, he was the lead reporter on a story and this was a big story. It was unusual for a journalist from an editorial backwater got to sink his teeth into such a big story.

He stepped away from the front door and the main part of the house, across the galley kitchen towards the door leading into the garage where he kept a large fridge. He hopped up the three steps to get something to eat, successful or not he still had to eat. As he opened the door, the reassuring jangle of edible goods wobbling rang in his ears and the glow of the fridge light washed over his face. His hand moved towards ham when he heard the click of the lock on the front door. A pleasant surprise he thought to himself as he heard quiet footsteps pad into the sitting room. He had only given his girlfriend keys a couple of days previously and now she was surprising him at lunchtime. He suddenly felt like one of those guys he wished he had been when he was younger, successful, popular, paired off with a pretty girl, dare he say it...'cool.'

Instead of calling out he wanted to savour this experience, she knew he was coming home, he had only spoken to her half an hour or so earlier. Maybe, just maybe she was heading up to the bedroom and he wasn't going to spoil her plans. So he crept to the doorway of the garage and standing at the top of the three cold stone steps he peeked around the door frame. He glimpsed the figure moving slowly, quietly creeping into the sitting room through the door on the other side of the kitchen.

Rory pulled his head back into the garage, his brain locking into an alternative reality. His heart had stopped momentarily, then started again at an alarming rate, he was shaking and he could not control his hands and shoulders juddering. The person in his house was not his pretty girlfriend. The person in his house was a man, dressed in black and he was carrying a gun.

He searched the garage for an escape route. The garage door was blocked by shelving, he had only ever used the space for storage. There was a man-hole cover, no windows and the big fridge; he was not going to hide in there. His thoughts were muddled, too many for his brain to digest. He couldn't move, the front door was already closer to him than the man moving further into the house but his muscles wouldn't react to the synapses his brain was releasing. It was as though his feet were set in concrete. The man looking for him had a gun anyway; he could not outrun a bullet. He began to cry; silently the tears rolled down his cheeks as he stood with his back to the wall, ears pricked to hear every creak and squeak from the old cottage.

He picked up the heaviest thing that he could find within arm's reach. So he stood waiting to club the intruder over the head with a pitchfork as he came up the stairs. He was to the right of the door, feet apart, the gardening tool in both hands pointing at the open doorway, like a soldier in the trenches waiting to run an enemy through with his bayonet.

The seconds felt like minutes, minutes like hours. He could hear hushed creeks and faint bumps as the stranger worked his way through the house systematically. Every so often the house fell silent for what seemed too long and he thought the man had left. But then the ghostly rumours would reverberate through the building once again and his throat would constrict. His eyes felt as though they were about to pop out of their sockets and his ears had taken on a life of their own seemingly twitching independently of each other to pick up every noise. His senses were reacting to the paralysing fear.

Rory followed the man in his mind through the rooms in his house. He pictured the intruder moving up the stairs, impossible to do it silently but he made next to no sound, probably stepping to the very edges of the boards to minimise the give. Then there was an eerie silence as the man must have gone to the far end of the house, Rory's bedroom. This was farthest from the garage and Rory watched the dust drift across the open doorway and he tried to block out the tick of his grandfather's clock. It annoyed him at the best of times, but this was something else.

Then the cupboard door opened in the second bedroom with a barely audible 'click-crimph'. The next sound was the loose board in the third bedroom quickly followed by the cabinet doors, he was no longer being so careful. As the footsteps above his head in the bathroom were no longer soft but regular. Dust fell from the ceiling of the garage after every step, Rory tried to swallow but his throat was dry, his stomach churned and he began to worry that he would be sick.

As the last footstep left the bathroom and the house fell silent. Rory waited for the next sound, sweat beading on his forehead, eyes darting but there was nothing just the click of the clock and the birdsong outside. He waited. Five minutes, ten minutes and still the tortured Rory waited. His arms ached from holding the pitchfork ready, he twisted the handle in his grip so that his arms did not go numb but still no sound.

Rory began to think the man had left. His heart began to settle slightly and his muscles relaxed slightly the pitchfork dipped from horizontal, but then he heard the barely audible scuff of the intruder's boot on the stone steps leading up to the garage.

He had a silenced revolver leading before him in his right hand. No sooner had it split the door frame then Rory's primeval survival mechanisms kicked in; the chubby reporter lunged forward with the pitchfork out in front directed at his assailant's gun. The prongs of the fork happened to thrust either side of the intruder's wrist, but the uncontrollable force with which Rory had lunged had a devastating result favouring the journalist. It pushed the man's gun and arm hard to the left, pinning it against the door frame for a split second before the bones gave way to the pressure and snapped with a horrific crack. The mysterious figure screamed in agony and bent double to take the pain as his weapon skidded across the cold stone floor. Rory lifted the pitchfork high and brought the edge of the prongs down on the back of the man's head. The NSO officer fell to the floor prone. Rory threw the fork to the floor and jumped over his assailant, into the kitchen, out through the front door and into the empty street.

He looked left up towards the dead end, a black cat stopped still with pneumatic perfection, crouched, green eyes staring at the panting mass of human that had suddenly spilled onto the quiet street. Then in an instant it pounced into a darting run and underneath a red car. Rory turned and ran in the other direction down the hill, towards the centre of town. The narrow road made the ordeal more terrifying. There were small terraced cottages to his right and a high stone wall to his left; no escape route so he pushed his legs as fast as they could carry him.

He stumbled out onto the main road through Hexham, The Fox and Hounds pub was in front of him and four hundred yards to the left was the police station. Which had now become the NSO command centre for the area. To the right the centre of town and the market square from where he had made his report the day before. There were few cars around and even fewer people.

He stumbled right running aimlessly towards the town centre when a muddy black pickup truck with a huge bull bar and six lamps mounted on the roll bar above the cab swerved alongside the curb. Rory fell back against the rough stone wall, thinking that the NSO had swooped down to take him. Had he been less panic-stricken he would have registered the pickup as Jesse Rowell's. He leaned across the cab and pushed the passenger side door open, his blonde hair was cropped close on the sides and mopped on top, his face was serious but kind. He was the thinker. His brothers' were the brawn.

"What's the matter with you Rory? You look mental man, running like that..." he stopped as Rory gathered himself and he realised he was looking at someone he knew and could trust. He pushed himself off the wall and jumped into the pickup screaming

"Go go go!"

The big truck growled as it accelerated away from the curb and Rory slumped into the passenger seat, ducking down as the vehicle passed the police station. The truck left Hexham on the Haydon Bridge Road, Jesse spoke to Rory again

"Tell me what's going on Rory"

"They came for me Jesse, they came for me; a journalist. How the fuck is that. He was going to kill me, I saw his gun!" Rory was staring out of the windscreen, tears rolling down his cheeks, gibbering as much to himself as to Jesse.

"Who came for you?" asked Jesse calmly, knowing all too well what the answer was

"They came to my house..." responded Rory losing energy.

"Look, I'll get you safe, you come with the rebels now Rory. You won't be safe in Hexham anymore, they obviously don't want anyone to hear what you have to say. They're killing people in the countryside Rory, you could be our voice..."

"All I want to do is fucking survive Jesse, I am not made for this."

"Tough this is life now, you think any of us saw this coming?"

A short while later the pickup pulled into Claire's driveway. For precisely the same reason that Nat had ended up at Claire's. Due to her friendship with so many of the rebel families and her proximity yet safe distance from Hexham, hers had become the rebel safe house. Arms were being stored in her sheds and she was the field hospital and general hunker down stop off. It was a burden that she was not comfortable with, but she knew these men and women. She was involved.

Jesse dropped Rory in the drive with instructions to wait, he would send someone to pick him up and take him north later in the afternoon.

Rory walked nervously to the front door checking behind with every step. He was scared of the wind in the trees, the gravel under his feet; he was sure that someone was waiting to attack him at any moment. He rapped on the delicate stained glass panel. Claire was worried by the urgency of the knocking at her door, she kept to the shadows, out of sight as she squinted to see who was behind the wobbly antique glass. Suddenly she recognised him as his sweaty red face approached the window to look in.

Claire knew Rory a little, they spoke if they met in the pub, they said hello if they passed in the street, but they were not friends as such. Acquaintances would suffice. Claire was a good ten years his senior.

Right now, she rushed to the door realising that Rory was panicking about something. As she pulled the door open, Rory was holding himself up against the frame, he almost fell into the house already blurting out a string of words that Claire had to translate. She came up with

"Someone's trying to kill me...so scared!"

"Calm down Rory, you need to breathe you're in shock," She said as she glanced outside and shut the front door gently. Rory was pacing back and forth in the sitting room. He was like a zoo animal who had spent too long in a small cage; his pacing was disturbed, erratic and if he wasn't spewing saliva filled sentences he was gnawing at his fingernails. He had always bitten his nails and had little more than patches of nail at the top of each finger. He was a proficient nail biter but hardly had enough nail to bite and so now it looked as though he was simply chewing the ends of his fingers.

"Please stop doing that Rory, it's disturbing and not going to solve anything, now come into the kitchen, I'll get the kettle on"

Rory sat down on the worn old three seater sofa which nestled in the corner of the kitchen next to the fire. The dancing flames of the fire divided his attention. He was recovering some sort of composure.

"Tell me what happened?" Claire said

"Simple really, I went home for my lunch. I thought it was fucking Jenny! I went to have a bloody look and there he was some fucking paramilitary psycho with a gun."

"It could have been a burglar…"

"Could it hell." Rory retorted wide-eyed "he was in the house for a good twenty minutes, didn't touch my belongings and you tell me how many burglars creep around with silencers on their guns?"

"Ok, so you got away…"

"I think I killed him…"

"What? …Rory"

"I hit him so hard with a pitch fork…I was scared."

"Who do you think it could be?"

"NSO I think because of my piece on Nat Bell?"

"What about Nat?"

"You haven't been watching the news have you? He's waging a one-man war on the regime, he's slaughtered about ten of their enforcement squad already, and when I say slaughtered he is exploring the realms of barbarism!" Rory momentarily forgot his problems as he sank into work mode excited about his project. Then his face dropped again "I asked some questions as to why a man like Nat Bell would start killing people…it was aired this morning and then two minutes after I get home this happens. There is no coincidence there".

Claire was about to tell Rory about Nat but kept quiet as she was beginning to grasp the gravity of the situation. She understood all too well that the less Rory knew, the less he could say which might protect him and would definitely protect Nat and herself. Rory continued

"Jesse said he was going to send someone back for me, to take me north, the Rowell brothers are up in Wooler with hundreds of rebels. The NSO has no presence up there, it's safe. I know what's happening here Claire and it is becoming unsafe for all of us. Hexham is becoming a crucial piece of land for the NSO. There is word that the Scots are arming the rebels and the NSO are sending troops north. War is coming Claire and Hexham is going to be the theatre."

"How do you know all this Rory?"

"It's my job Claire, I am paid to know what is going on."

As he said the words, there was a knock at the front door. Her beautiful dark eyes flashed towards Rory. His face drained of blood, the eyes opened wide and his head sank. He knew from Claire's face that she wasn't expecting anyone and it was too soon surely for the rebels to be collecting him.

She gulped and pointed to the stairs without uttering a word. He stole across the room and tiptoed up the stairs taking two at a time. Claire heard the familiar click of the landing cupboard open and shut, then her attention was drawn back to the front door by a more impatient knock. She shook herself down, tried to clear her mind of the fear and called back

"Hang on! I'm coming!"

She opened the front door to four grim looking men, each one carried a gun. The closest, a thick-set, unshaven brute stepped forward into her personal space and with one foot inside the door she was unable to shut it again as her instinct screamed out inside her. He spoke quietly and with a cockney accent

"We know all about you, bitch."

With that he turned the weapon and smashed the butt of the gun into Claire's face knocking her senseless to the floor, she could taste her own blood as she lost consciousness.

* * * * *

Start was hunched over the telephone. He had an elastic band in between thumb and forefinger and he twisted it, watching the elastic curl at the ends like a worm as it wound tight. He spoke calmly but with determination

"Tell me, you have him?"

"Who? ...we have the journalist, not the farmer."

"Well, it's a start, what's wrong with you Truter you sound off, tired or something?"

"I had an accident broke my arm, it's nothing."

"Hmm, you tell me if it's getting too much for you. We need to step up the land reform. Burn out all the landowners if necessary, we need to control food production and we need to secure Northumbria."

"I need more men, there are more rebels daily, we took four rebels today; two had Lancashire accents and the other two were from the Midlands. This isn't a local thing Lucas..."

"What are you doing with the prisoners?"

"We aren't taking prisoners; they're in a ditch off the road to Scotland."

"I'll have more men with you soon; you contain the rebels and get those fucking farms cleared of their occupants. Our grip on power is dependent on what happens in the borderlands".

Start put the telephone down without another word and turned to the men who sat across from him on the other side of his desk.

The first was a man in his mid-forties, dark cropped hair, pale skin and a severe expression. His name was Quentin Harris, Brigadier Quentin Harris and he was the army's instrument of attrition. No one else was able to reduce enemy numbers like soldiers under Brigadier Harris's command. No matter what the odds or the numbers Harris's armies seemed to grind an enemy to dust like a glacier over bedrock. The second man was Harris's boss; General Anthony Beaston. A cold, merciless man, Beaston was small, wiry, not an ounce of fat on his ageing body or his bony face. His mannerisms were super-accelerated and he blinked wildly but he knew the art of war and he understood the nature of stealing another man's hope.

"You two will leave tonight; meet your troops at Aldershot Garrison and get up to the borders. You can station yourselves at Albemarle and the mission is simple; secure Northumberland and Cumbria under NSO control and redistribute every inch of farmland to government collectives."

"We know the mission Mr Start and we have no doubt about the outcome but we need to know two things" Beaston spoke the King's English, mostly through his nose. As his face twitched and rolled as he spoke his eyes remained unnervingly trained on Start, "I'm listening..." said Start

"What are your views with regards the local population and should the instance arise that we are facing Scottish troops do we open fire on them?"

"The answer to both questions is, do whatever you see fit to secure that region."

* * * * *

When she came too, the blood Claire had tasted was like iron; metallic in her mouth, it was now caked around her lips. The swelling felt heavy on the side of her face. Disfigured and in pain she had no strength for the situation she was in. With eyes open wide she could see nothing but pitch black, her mind raced, was she blind or in a room with no light whatsoever. She opened her mouth to speak, but the dull ache exploded into excruciating shards of pain emanating from her jaw travelling through her skull and down her spine. She understood immediately that her jaw was broken. The pain made her whimper which was answered from within the darkness by a shuffling sound and a hollow murmur

"I'm sorry Claire…I – I…" Rory's voice drifted off; there was nothing to say.

She didn't answer. She was prone in the darkness. Her head lolling. Her backside was numb on the cold concrete. Her back against the wall paralysed by fear and one thought travelling through her head; she would rather be dead than face the door to that room opening.

Nick Christofides

ELEVEN

The fire crackled as the sun rose high and its rays began to find their way directly into the little valley. The heat from both sun and fire bathed Nat's face, he had felt the cold the night before and so the warmth was a welcome luxury. A blackbird had joined their party and danced around the camp in search of an easy meal. The constant babble of the stream seemed louder more overpowering this morning. He was not in a good mood.

He gazed over at his daughter. Amber was nestled with her back against the grassy bank, totally at ease in the rough camp; she was intently sharpening her hunting knife. In the early grey light of the day, they had been cleaning all the weapons they had amassed.

They had heard the crack of Stuarts rifle sound off four or five times so they knew they were eating meat that morning. Father and daughter did not speak while they worked, neither were good communicators. He knew from her eyes she had questions, if he was honest with himself he could work out what the questions would be. But she didn't know how to ask and he could not bring himself to talk about the subject.

So as her vivid green eyes connected searchingly with his, piercing the dull air, his tanned hide would crease across his brow. The best he could muster was a thoughtful, reassuring smile before his head, with a slight shake of that white mane, moved back to concentrate on the job in hand. The emotion was all too raw for both, it was all the communication Amber needed and the tears burst the banks of her eyes and rolled silently down her cheeks as she nodded to the old man. She wiped them away with the rough, dirty sleeve of her wax jacket and swept her tight ringlets away from her face. Looking back at her knife, she sharpened it with a renewed ferocity.

He watched the pot bubbling on the fire. The flames danced around it as it brewed, the water churning over and over, tossing the tea bags around as it boiled. As he watched the earth seemingly hiccupped and the pan of water fell on its side in the flames.

Nat looked up into the trees as the roosting crows flew from their perches and pheasant's warbled clucks filled the air as they flew in fright. The forest had been jolted to life by some sort of seismic wave. Then came the rumble of a distant explosion, Nat looked at Amber and without a word they leapt to their feet and started running to the nearest vantage point; the edge of the forest.

They moved quickly through the thick dewy undergrowth, the smell of the fresh morning woodland was rich in peat and leaves. Stuart came bounding out of the trees with four rabbits over his shoulder shouting "what the hell was that!" They ran together, three hunters, like sprinters on a track they moved with ease and fluidity through the barrage of foliage and hazards the forest threw at them.

The three reached the edge of the trees and as they walked out into the wide open expanse of the valley, they looked up to the west. There in the distance, where they were used to seeing the ugly chimneys of the huge chipboard factory they saw a huge thick black mushroom cloud billowing above the factory which was engulfed in flames. The huge piles of wood chip were now burning too, an irrepressible inferno overwhelmed the site.

Nat's eyes surveyed the valley he was so used to admiring. He had never been bored or unmoved by its beauty and ever changing detail. Now it was unrecognisable, the drama was no longer natural. Man had placed his boot on the heart of his valley and the scene he viewed now was like Armageddon. To the east black smoke continued to drift upwards from the ashes of the paper factory, which had been burning for days. In front of them stood the ruin of his home, burnt to the ground with a collection of vehicles littered on the drive and now to the west this latest devastation. He looked across at his friend

"That is no accident."

"It looks like war is here my friend"

"Aye, I thought the paper factory was kids or even the NSO but it must be rebels…I can see it now…take out the employment centres and the NSO will soon lose support if they can't provide people with work."

"Let's go into town and see if we can make contact with the rebels, it maybe we can help one another…" said Stuart

"Agreed" called Amber with enthusiasm.

After brief contemplation Nat nodded and the three started walking down the hill. Each a few yards apart and in a line, half force of habit, half to spread themselves as a target, just in case.

By the house, there was an ever increasing choice of cars. Stuart called out "keys in this one," Nat nodded and held up the carcasses of the rabbits Stuart had passed to him. He turned towards the barn.

No sooner had he stepped into the darkness of the barn than he knew. He smelled the tea and the sweet oats of porridge or flapjack. He didn't flinch with the realisation; he carried on as though it were normal, moving between the farm equipment. It was a route he had trodden a thousand times before to where the rafters of the mezzanine offered him the hooks to hang the kill. He tied the animals from their hind legs to the two thick rusted meat hooks that he presumed had hung meat for centuries.

He knew the feeling of being watched, it wasn't Esme from beyond the grave. The plastic pop in the trees he'd heard the other night. The shots which had killed the two Regime troops who were themselves about to take his own life. The smell of tea and oats in the air. 'Ghosts don't need night sights and they certainly don't need breakfast' he thought to himself as he went back to join the others. The only question lingering in his mind was why the ghost had saved his life.

* * * * *

The spectre had enjoyed the relative lap of luxury the barn had offered. He had even felt comfortable enough to make himself a brew and eat his beloved flapjack there right where he had slept. As his teeth plunged into the rich oats, the barn had shaken under the seismic waves of the explosion then the boom had hit. He jumped up knocking his brew over in the process, he cursed himself as this was a trail and the reason why he should have left the barn before eating.

He looked out of the cracks in the barns timber cladding and he could see the inferno that was the chipboard factory. He knew the farmer would be stirred by the kerfuffle so he eked his view around in a small slit he had found, his cheek pressed hard against the dusty wood and he waited. Like clockwork, his subject appeared at the edge of the wood. As he watched them begin walking down the hill, his mind found its gear and he turned to his predetermined plan.

The tea was now spilt, so he stood his cup on the floor and looked up at the metal frames hung from the roof on which the farmer had stored planks of wood. The ghost then reached up and grabbed the end of the wooden planks and athletically he kicked his legs up and over his head and onto the planks where he lay on his front. He then drew his handgun and quietly screwed the silencer onto it and pressed it to the plank next to his head. He lined up the shot so that should someone discover his cup and walk over to pick it up, his bullet would hit his target. He controlled his breathing and waited. Watching; as he always did.

It was a few minutes before he heard the footsteps at the entrance to the barn. There was no pause as the man weaved his way through the machinery, he hung rabbits almost directly below and then left without inkling there was someone else in the barn. The dark figure left in the barn, silenced weapon at the ready could not understand. He had highly overestimated the man he was watching; the old farmer had been oblivious to his presence.

* * * * *

Nat squeezed into the cramped passenger side of a fifteen-year-old Japanese sports car. His knees pulled up tight to his chest, he looked across at Stuart as if to say 'great choice!' Stuart smiled, turned the key and gunned the accelerator and they raced down the long drive. As they descended the hill Nat surveyed his livestock grazing either side of the driveway. The numbers looked right and they all looked healthy at a glance. As they came to the end of his land, the little car vibrated violently over the cattle grid and they sped out into the country road.

The thick black smoke rose in plumes up into the vast sky and drifted high along the valley creating a menacing darkness to the day. Stuart drove fast, the little car responded well, flying over the undulations of the military road with Hadrian's Wall snaking along the wild country to their right. Every drop and dip in the road sent Ambers stomach through her mouth, she felt sick but knew better than to mention it; any mention of slowing the car to Stuart would have the opposite effect. So she sucked it up and concentrated on the horizon.

It was no time before they all lurched to the right absorbing no insignificant g-force as the little car took a sharp turn without losing speed onto the narrow road leading into Oakwood. Nat's hand grabbed the dashboard, Amber knew the driving was making her father nervous too but he would never give his friend the pleasure of asking him to slow down.

They were about two hundred yards out from Rowell's driveway, where Nat had seen the articulated truck barricading the entrance before. Now there was the familiar blue bus belonging to a local bus company parked at the end of the drive. The bus had rudimentary grills attached to the windows and metal skirts over the wheel arches. They knew this must be NSO. Stuart slowed the car aggressively, Nat's arm took the strain against the dashboard and Amber pressed tight against her taught seat belt. He cruised past the end of the drive at about ten miles an hour giving them all a chance to assess the situation.

Rowell's trailer had been rammed out of the way by a JCB digger, both vehicles now sat dormant on the grass to the side of the drive. In the distance they could see ten to twenty men swarming around the farmhouse which had been set on fire, smoke was billowing out of the first floor. The men around the house were armed and were on the whole merely watching the blaze unfold. As the view of the house was eclipsed by the NSO bus, three heavily armed men stood in front of it. Their stares were long and hard, their three heads following the car in unison as it slowly passed them by. Their weapons hung across their chests, Nat noted that the beaten up black market weapons had gone, they were carrying shiny new semi-automatic assault rifles. The NSO were getting organised. Stuart turned to Nat.

"Do we need to go see the factory?" he asked

"No turnaround down here, Amber you stay put. Make sure the car is side on to them Stuart."

Stuart drifted into the side of the road and then spun the wheel to full lock and the car turned easily heading back towards Rowell's farm they drifted slowly into the entrance. Nat lowered his window as they pulled into the driveway. He leaned his head out of the window as if to ask what was going on. Two of the guards began walking towards them waving them on and shouting 'move away'. Nat pretended he couldn't hear; he gripped the handgun tight as he watched the men approach. He watched the distance decrease with every step making the target larger, the fresh air from the open window doused his face, the adrenaline making the moments feel like slow motion. Like so much of his life recently these moments of reality were so surreal, no time for thought processes or questions, just actions. Simple, decisive, deadly actions.

The little car was still rolling slightly. Nat could hear the purr of the engine and the crunch of gravel under the tyres, there was a slight squeak of the breaks as the car pulled to a stop. The man leading the advance raised his gun pointing it at the car as he approached; he was ten feet from the vehicle at this point. Nat was about to raise his weapon against the man when he noticed a wave of recognition. A lightening in the face of realisation, as the guy on the right, grasped the fact that he was face to face with the 'killer from the hills'.

The man who recognised Nat did not have the killer inside, rather than pointing his gun at the car and squeezing the trigger he lurched toward his friend grabbing his arm to warn him of the danger. In that instant of distraction, the killer inside Nat took his chance. He raised his handgun, up and out of the open window firing two rounds into the nearby body mass of the lead guard. As he fell onto his backside looking at Nat stunned by the brutal reality, the third man came directly into Nat's angle of fire and he squeezed the trigger again twice.

This time, he missed with the first but hit the man in the cheek bone with the second, the small round ripped through his skull. The man was dead before his head bounced on the gravel with a dull crunch. The guard on the right was left now, he was paralysed with fear trying to click the safety off his weapon but his thumb couldn't flick the switch. Nat trained his gun on the nameless man and shot him in the chest. He fell backwards, sitting slumped on the drive staring blankly at the car. As the three stepped out of the car, the life drifted from the third man, his lurid figure remained hunched in a sitting position as the last rakish breath past his blood-soaked lips.

Nat marched over to the body and kicked it to the ground with a fleeting glance over to Amber as though a dead body lying down was more palatable than one in a sitting position. He bent down and picked up an assault rifle and handed it to Amber. Stuart had grabbed one for himself as Nat took the third.

He told Amber to stay by the car and cover their rear, Nat opened fire on the bus peppering the wheels and engine compartment with bullets. Stuart had positioned himself at the gates to the house and was taking single shots at the NSO men at the house. As they began falling to the ground; one, two, three were down when the confusion set in.

At first the NSO began setting positions directed at the house thinking that shots were coming from that direction. As Nat joined Stuart at the other side of the gate, between them, they felled another four before the NSO fighters realised the shots were coming from behind them.

There must have been twenty men to begin with now it was closer to ten and Nat and Stuart had the protection of the ostentatious stone gate posts that Rowell had built. Nat had laughed when he first saw them for the first time, now he rejoiced in their presence as the NSO rounds whizzed and whistled in ricochet off the gaudy stone. Only a few of the enemy dug into positions the rest ran aimlessly for cover or straight at Nat and Stuart in panic. It was a massacre. Nat counted five NSO still breathing and dug in by the time Stuart was able to attract his attention,

"What are we doing? We need to get out of here?"

"I want those dead, what if Rowell is in that house" Nat responded wild-eyed.

"Well, we can't just sit here, there could be others coming, Ambers back there, think Nat, think!" Stuart shouted over the sporadic fizzing rounds, chaos all around even in such a relatively small fire fight.

The clang of shots hitting the bus behind them rang in their ears. Nat knew they had to do something; it was only a matter of time before one of the stray bullets was fired true. Nat took the lead bursting from cover as best he could and leaping behind the trailer which had been barged away from the gates by the NSO.

He lay on his belly between the rear wheels of the trailer and the corrugated iron sheeting which skirted the length of it. He had a good open view over the gardens in front of the house; he could see only the lower back of an NSO soldier lying flat behind a raised flower bed. He lined up the shot and tapped the trigger twice, the red mist of a hit rose from the target.

He raised his eye from the sights and scanned the gardens once again. He saw the muzzle flash of a weapon from within the darkness of a small shed to the far left of the garden. Nat's gun swung the small arc with the accuracy of a machine and he pumped four rounds into the dark space without hesitation. He watched patiently for a few minutes, no response.

Then he saw a flash of movement, two men running towards the burning house, a desperate attempt to escape this hell. Both bodies dropped to the floor as three shots cracked across the countryside from Stuart's weapon. Now the area went silent of gun shots, their ears were filled with the creaking and snapping of the burning building. The breeze pulled the thick black smoke low over the little theatre of war, at least fourteen bodies lay in the dirt.

"Fsst" he heard to his left, Stuart had joined him at the trailer and pointed over to the right where a white rag had been tied around the end of a weapon. It was being waved from behind the stone wall that separated the drive and front gardens from the field to the north. Nat looked at his friend, the two men shook their heads and Nat rested his chin on his rifle for a spell as he pondered the situation. After a few moments, he raised his head and shouted

"What you doing boy?" Then he pulled the weapon in tight and focussed his eye down the sights on the rag, Stuart scanned the rest of the area for a double cross.

"We want to surrender, there's three of us none wants to fight, please."

"You should have thought about that before burning down that farm, was there anyone in there?"

"No, no one, I swear" came the desperate voice from behind the wall

"How old are you boy?"

"We're all seventeen."

"What are you doing out here?" Nat could hear the boy was not local; his accent was from the Midlands.

"Conscripts, we finished two month's training two days ago and we were brought up here, we don't want to fight you!" the voice cracking with fear.

"Ok, all three of you take your weapons and turn them so that the barrel, the shooting end, is pointing at your stomach. One hand on the weapon the other in the air, then walk slowly towards us." Nat tensed as the three figures appeared from behind the wall "We have two of you lined up so no gambling with any sudden movements, two of you would definitely die."

In the background the farmhouse was a raging inferno, Nat was all too aware that they needed to get out of there and he could hear the tuck, tuck, tuck of a choppers rota blades. It was not the heavy, dull thudding of a military helicopter but guessing it was a news crew, he wanted to get away before he was beamed across the world again.

"Get a move on" He shouted

The fearful young men skipped a step as they heard him; trying to walk faster but without making any sudden movements. Nat had no intention of killing these boys; his blood lust was not for innocents. As the three young men drew closer, timidly stepping towards the two giants with weapons shouldered and trained on them. Stuart lowered his gun and walked over to them grabbing each of their guns with fast fluid motions, keeping the kids on edge and under control. Once their rifles were safe he checked them for any other useful items but barring a couple of lighters they had nothing. Nat kept his weapon trained on the three men and said

"Keep walking back to town and on home from there, if we see you again we kill you, no questions asked, no second chance."

The three young men did not need to be told twice; they walked quickly past Nat and Stuart, past the mangled bus and on past Amber, their speed increasing if anything. Nat watched them as they started out down the narrow country road, they moved in single file, their hands had now dropped and were swinging to aid the pace of their march. The pretty road fell away lazily to the left, the tarmac was an elephant's grey, there were grass ditches to either side thick with brambles. The eastern side of the road was flanked by dense coniferous woodland. To the

Western side was a thick hawthorn hedge sitting raised above the ditch on an overgrown grass bank. In the distance, the spire of St John Lee church could be seen rising out of the beautiful ancient trees that gave Oakwood its name. The sun was streaming through the cracks in the clouds and illuminated all before them with a golden glow.

The three NSO conscripts were a hundred yards away when the three loud cracks reverberated across the fell. Nat and Stuart hit the floor, but the shots were not fired in their direction. As they looked, the boys were falling into the ditch to their right scragged by the brambles. Nat looked into the trees where the shots must have come from; Amber sat in the small car between him and the trees. Between him and the sniper. Amber looked at him nervously.

"Get out this side of the car and keep low. Sit on the floor with your back to the vehicle" He shouted to his daughter as his eyes scanned the woodland for any sign of the sniper. Amber shuffled quickly across the front seats of the idling car and fell out of the passenger side door onto the cold dirt where she lay still.

The helicopter was overhead now, the rapid repetitive thud of the rotas pulsed sound waves which washed over them from head to toes. The downdraught whipped up dust and debris all around them and the smoke from the house curled in arcs up into the sky.

The situation was getting worse, they had no idea who or how many people were in the trees beyond their car. To all intents and purposes they were pinned down which was inextricably linking them to the carnage that lay behind them. Something, the news crew above them, could easily paint as a massacre.

Amber covered her eyes from the whirlwind, Stuart looked at Nat, who pointed to the car and got to his feet staying low he ran a curving run to the car. As Nat's back slapped against the cold metal of the vehicle, he sat next to his daughter. Stuart pushed himself to his feet and followed suit.

All three were now sitting; backs against the small car looking up at the circling helicopter which suddenly banked to the right and set off back towards Hexham. As the din died down and the dust began to settle, their attention once again turned to the trees on the other side of the car. Both men turned slowly and looked through the car into the thick wall of foliage

"I can't see anything in there" whispered Stuart

"No we've got to listen."

As the rotas of the helicopter became a distant throbbing, the rustle of the trees became the loudest sound. The breeze ebbed and the two men listened intently for a man-made sound. The stand-off had lasted too long before they heard the snapping of sticks and the rustle of foliage. Nat looked at Stuart in wonderment as the racket coming from the trees he half expected a mountain gorilla to appear.

"Don't shoot me Nat" bellowed a thick Northumbrian accent from the trees. The rummaging in the bushes became louder and louder, cracking and swishing. Stuart looked at Nat in wonder, Nat shrugged and they watched not sure what to expect. Then as the final leaves parted two muddy figures appeared. Old man Rowell and his wife were visibly shaken, weary but smiling at their old acquaintance.

The eighty year old farmer had a hunting rifle strapped across his back; his wife carried a walking stick.

They walked across the road, their brains giving the synapses that, in a person thirty years younger, would lead to a jog. Nat, Stuart and Amber got to their feet and stood watching the old couple approach, they didn't move around the car. The Rowell's shuffled over to them, Rowell was a man standing five six with boots on. His wife was a clear half a foot taller than him. She was slender and elegant in comparison to her husband. His face was round and ruddy, his grey hair floating in the breeze, his corpulent stomach sat on broad hips but it was the two fingers missing from his right hand that drew the eye.

"Looks like we've been dealt similar cards Nat" she said softly as she put her hand on his shoulder and kissed his cheek.

"Everything's changed now Susan, you ok?"

She smiled at him with vivacious narrowing eyes in response then looked down at the dirt and turned away back to her husband.

"We won't lie down" grunted Old man Rowell "Do you know why they came here…did this?"

"They want to get rid of the landowners…control the land."

"Aah, maybe that too…it was my boys who organised the attack on the chipboard factory. They've got an army growing by the day, we're gonna fight Nat and you should join us."

"Where are they…are they safe?" Amber butted in; Jesse being a friend of hers.

"Aye lass, they're up Wooler way, based there the Scots have been training them and giving them weapons."

"How many are they?" Nat asked

"I don't know man, hundreds, maybe thousands, I don't keep track they say there are more and more joining every day, coming up over the Pennines through Haltwhistle and Carlisle. Labourers, country folk from Cumbria, Durham, Yorkshire, even further I think, all joining up with our boys"

"Ok, you come with us now, we have a car you can take. Get yourself up to your boys and stay safe up north don't come back, you're too old for this hell Rowell."

The old man's stunned gaze drifted past the three of them and on towards his burning home. The fire was raging now, the cracking and snapping of wood reaching breaking point. The whoosh and roar of gas canisters and petrol cans sporadically excited the fire. The bodies of the NSO fighters littered the land in front of the inferno. Susan Rowell, sturdy and dignified took the hand of her forlorn husband and showed him to the car. Stuart and Amber busied themselves with collecting the weapons from the dead soldiers and filling the boot of the small car.

As they wound down the lanes back to Carlins Law, Rowell's wife, sitting squashed on the driver's side of the back seat, talked of the increasingly violent purges by the NSO. The camps in Slaley forest holding those who refused NSO orders or had shown some degree of resistance. She went on to mention the latest NSO arrest, the local woman and the journalist dragged from her home in Oakwood by NSO thugs. Nat flashed a concerned look across at Stuart as the big Scot turned in his seat and the mood in the car chilled

"Who was the woman?" He asked pointedly

Unaware of any connection the old lady replied "it was the nurse Claire."

* * * * *

Baines perched, arms folded, brow furrowed; pensive. Start was ensconced in paperwork at the head of the boardroom table. Searching eyes darting from report to advisor and back again; with questions providing accompaniment to the visual waltz. Baines studied the new look leaders of England. There were just two of his left-leaning comrades left in the room, one of them Start.

The rest were radicals and extremists who he had known on the edges of the political spectrum for years, but he would never have imagined them gaining any sort of influence over governance of the country. But right now he watched as Lee Mannion reported to 'the boss' on security in the capital city.

Baines watched the small muscular man talk about his 'population controls' and security squads as though they were legitimate means of governance. All the while he watched he could not get the image of this man giving a Nazi salute at a rally out of his head. The image had painted the front pages ten years earlier when he was the leader of the British National Alliance the right wing fanatics who had gained some marginal success in the troubled years of the financial crisis. Now Baines watched this dangerous little man speaking at his table, in his cabinet and it made him sick. He was the puppet leader watching on as gremlins controlled his machine and he was powerless to intervene.

The room turned to watch the news, the sound was low as they saw an aerial view of beautiful rugged landscape. The dark oranges and reds of the heather, highlighted the lush greens and the basalt outcrops accented the scene with ancient greys. It was, however, not the countryside that drew the eye to the picture. But the flaming carcass of the burning house in the centre of the picture, the thick grey-black smoke drifting off to the bottom right of the screen.

The film closed in on two gunmen hunkered down behind the wreckage of an articulated trailer. As the helicopter circled it whipped up the smoke into a wispy valley, momentarily leaving a clear view of the scattered corpses littering the land in front of the house. The news flash on the bottom of the screen read ARMED CONFLICT CONTINUES TO RAGE IN RURAL NORTHUMBERLAND.

"Turn that fucking thing up" raged Start

'...the scene one and a half miles north of Hexham, the town in Northumberland that is becoming the frontline in the fight for power in England. As history repeats itself this idyllic part of the country has once again become the fault line of war. The battle continues less than one hundred yards from Hadrian's Wall. The great barrier created by the Roman Emperor to keep the Celts at bay and in a location well-trod by the warring clans of Scots and English families known as the Border Reivers. That is the historical backdrop for the fighting that rages today between rebel forces and NSO militia. Sources suggest that the rebel army is being organised by three local brothers named Rowell and the ruthless insurgent Nat Bell the known murderer of four government militias and suspected killer of many more..."

A hushed silence descended over the boardroom as the NSO officials were absorbed by the newsreel. Parliamentary 'Office' was new to all of them. With the country in a state of chaos under the sweeping changes of dictatorship and the lawlessness of Starts militias, none of those present felt any measure of control over the situation, except Lucas Start.

The corners of his mouth turned upwards as beads of sweat gathered on his forehead, his eyes sparkled with excitement as he watched the report. The husky reporters' voice oozing sex and solemnity in equal measure continued "…the burning building is, in fact, the Rowell family farm and reportedly the headquarters of the rebel cell. It is unknown whether any rebels were killed or even present within the property, but none have at this stage been detained. It is evident from our pictures that there were a number of NSO fatalities…"

The sound went down once more as Starts narrowed eyes searched the faces in the room. He was waiting for panic, waiting for wavering of confidence or conscience. He caught the glimmer of insecurity in a couple of the faces before him and he took the opportunity to speak.

"I can see worried faces people but don't worry about civil war, quite the opposite; embrace it. Yes, none of us want deaths either to our own people or the general population but sacrifice is necessary to bring about change. As a country we are bankrupt, we need the industrialisation of war; the manufacture of armaments and vehicles, the employment of the army and the investment of aid from our foreign allies. Furthermore, we need to get back what is ours in the North. Scotland belongs to England and once we win the war on English soil, we can reunite Scotland and England under the NSO. We know the Scots are arming these terrorists so they have begun the war that we will end".

He turned the television off, threw the controller onto the papers which lay before him and stood to face his colleagues in silence, waiting for a reaction. His head hung between his thick set shoulders. He looked up slightly, eyebrows raised, forehead wrinkled, he looked towards his two military advisor's. Baines stood arms folded his head shaking slightly, "You'll take how many of our innocents to the grave in an unnecessary war?"

Start ignored the question and spoke to his military men "Give me some good news you two. I need an army on the ground in that god forsaken armpit of the country. I need these rebels crushed, annihilated so that the population realise that we will react to uprising in the harshest way..."

"The army has been deployed Under General Beaston's command. We currently have three squadrons in convoy on the M1, they are well armed with small arms, rocket-propelled grenades, mortars and four 105mm field guns."

"I want another thousand men on the ground up there." He stated "So that means get your backside in gear; I want them on the road today. Once these idiots have been crushed I want garrisons set up south of the Scottish border."

TWELVE

Their tightly packed car raced around the country bends, Stuart bubbled and churned like molten rock ready to blow. As Nat drove the muscles in his jaw tensed and released, tensed and released. He was desperately trying to work out where Claire would be, he understood she was bait and so his mind kept returning to the police station; it was the obvious answer. Stuart spoke
"What will we do then?"
"To be honest with you Stuart, I have no idea, they'll be waiting for us, if she's in a cell, I don't know" Replied Nat. Silence fell over the car once more, but only for a second or two before the guttural drawl of Old Man Rowell rumbled into the front of the car
"I'll tell you what you're going to do, you're going to turn around and come and join my boys at Waters Meet."
"What the hell are they doing now?" Nat asked
"They're preparing to attack Hexham," said the old man with pride and belief "they're going to beat those bastards and re-take our town."
"What? Armed with their shotguns?"
"No you daft bastard, the Scots have armed them and there are hundreds of them, maybe thousands from all over, so turn the bloody car round."
"Mind your mouth Sam!" Rowell's wife blasted across the car at him turning to Amber, who sat quietly next to the window. She mouthed the words "sorry lass" at the young woman with a swift shake of the head. Amber

returned a smile and turned to look over the countryside as it past the window.

Nat nodded thought and chewed his gums. Then he spoke,

"We'll take the weapons from my farm, then join your boys Rowell."

They drove the rest of the way in silence, living in that moment so different from life before. No one person in the car knew what they would be doing that night apart from trying to survive and trying to find Claire. As he drove Nat thought about his livestock the hours he had put in, caring for beasts, the planning he had carried out, the blood and the sweat he had given in building his farm. He understood now what his father meant when he said 'look after your health and your family because everything else is no more than an illusion.' Everything he had known of society was now altered, changed and different. And his stomach turned; he hadn't looked after his family. His foot pressed harder on the accelerator as the anger blossomed in his gut and the car drifted into his driveway.

"We'll see you at Waters Meet, tell your boys." Nat said to Rowell and threw him the keys

Stuart grabbed a tarpaulin and was unloading the captured NSO weapons onto it. Rowell and his wife walked either side of the car and climbed in, the old man labouring to get his round being into the driver's seat. As Stuart closed the boot, the engine sprang to life and the little car zipped away.

As they watched the small car streak down the rough gravel, Amber gazed up at the woods, her woods; the woods she knew better than the route from bedroom to bathroom. Nat turned to see her looking and he spoke softly but urgently,

"I know lass, don't let him know; look away now. Go, with Stuart, store the weapons and flank around the wood from the east, we'll flush him out."

As he spoke he gestured up to the top field with his shotgun and once finished he trudged off up the hill, he broke the gun and rested it over his forearm. He made eyes across the open grass but as he approached the wood he became one with his surroundings.

His mind absorbed and calculated, the squirrel gnawing on an acorn and song birds busying themselves to his left betrayed the lack of potential predators lurking in the thick undergrowth there. The silence and lack of movement to his right were like a neon sign to Nat advertising the presence of an alien. Nat knew the visibility in the wood was down to about twenty metres so whoever had eyes on him; they were close. He respected the visitor as he was good enough to be invisible by eye. Nat moved on through the wood on one of a small network of well-trod paths they used to walk and hunt.

* * * * *

The Ghost had been hiding in the rafters when the farmer had interrupted his breakfast that morning. When the two men and the girl had driven off, he lowered himself down and out of the shadows and picked up the cup of tea he had left behind. He moved out into the open and enjoyed it sitting on the stone steps of the burned-out farmhouse he sipped his brew and watched the black satanic smoke billowing up from the raging inferno caused by the explosion. He also listened to the tat-tat-tat and the pup pup of distant gunfire. He was pretty sure that the three who had just left would be involved in the fighting...the timing all stacked up.

When he heard the car returning, he quickly cleaned his space and broke for the woodland where he now watched the giant grey haired brute come towards him, conserving energy by trudging methodically with that wide gait. He was deep in thought; Baines' man was surprised again that someone with his ability to survive was totally oblivious to the fact that he was being watched. The other two vanished around the hillside to the east carrying a load of weapons from the boot of the car in a tarp, but the agent was more concerned with his subject right now. The farmer was a few hundred yards away when the watcher slipped his mobile phone from his pocket, he pulled up the only number logged in it and hit dial. Baines picked up immediately.

"Tom, what's new? It's getting out of hand up there now, the rebellion is gaining strength...Start is sending an army..."

"Not now Ben, quickly, has anything changed with the farmer, I have the opportunity to take him out he is alone, do I have the green light?" he whispered

"NO!" Baines shouted then collected himself. "No, this rebellion is good for us, chances are it may build and destroy Start. Just watch him. Protect him but stay invisible, if the regime does invade the area I don't want you being taken out as a rebel."

The phone clicked off without another word and Baines stood alone and silent in his creaky office once more.

Tom shook his head as he slipped the phone back in its pocket. Baines had no idea really; this was a holiday compared to Hawija in 2015, he was not worried about the NSO or the rebels for that matter.

The farmer laboured through the thick wet undergrowth, he was oblivious to his surroundings, head down his mind in another place and time. Tom thought to himself that the old man would have to get over whatever it was that occupied his mind. Sooner or later some NSO marksman would be putting a bullet in his head if he didn't sharpen up.

The farmer passed about twenty-five yards to his west. Foliage whooshing, sticks cracking and brambles scraping across his clothes as their barbs tried to cling on like a thousand fingernails. Tom followed in relative silence. The two men were nearing the Northern edge of the trees, the farmer slightly ahead and to the west of Tom but in clear view. He was about to break the tree line when he slumped his big frame down on a tree stump and sat still staring out across the open country to the North. Tom lowered himself to his honkers and looked, rain water from a previous shower dripped and splashed when the breeze caught the leaves high in the trees. A wood pigeon called out to the south of their positions. The wet, muddy smell of peat and decaying foliage filled his nostrils as the farmer sat like a gorilla in the jungle.

The log on which the farmer sat was the bow of an old oak; broken and quickly becoming part of the land, ferns grew up, around and on it. The rich green of the moss carpeted the rotting wood. The sun broke through the clouds and stabbed shards of hazy gold down onto the rolling acres beyond. The farmers hunched figure in that most beautiful of setting would have given Constable a worthwhile subject. As his mind drifted it dawned on him. Tom realised that the man must have been injured, he had to have taken a round and he was bleeding out. That explained his lack of care, his clumsiness.

Tom watched him closer, his big head and white mane hanging forward making him look headless from Tom's position. He watched those broad shoulders closely. Moving up and down with every laboured breath. As he concentrated he was sure that the respirations were becoming shallower, more laboured...that was the moment he felt the chill of cold steel on his Adams Apple.

"Don't you fucking move" came the soft voice of a young woman. Tom's blood turned to cement rendering his body rigid, not with fear but calculation, this is where he came into his own; his thoughts were lucid; his body awaited instruction from the grey matter.

It is not easy to cut someone's throat; he knew it was both physically and mentally hard, involving a great deal of hacking and pints of blood. He had never met a young woman capable of stomaching such horrors; so he raised his arms in surrender.

As the first synapses began to order his hand to grab his attacker's arm; the undergrowth about ten yards in front of him exploded in a thunderous roar. Standing before Tom and Amber was the huge frame of Stuart with a semi-automatic weapon pointed at the forehead of the ghost.

"Please try that, she won't have to do the killing then..."

Tom's arms dropped again, he knew when he was a hostage and he knew how to get through it. He looked at the big Scot, his long straggling dark hair was wet and stuck to a face filled with threat and promise, the man was not playing tough. His eyes were dark, thick-set and heavy, his was a face you could love in friendship or fear in animosity for all the same features. Tom knew what to do; submit and say nothing.

* * * * *

Nat leapt from his perch. As he ripped through the wet foliage, he pulled his handgun from his pocket. His eyes were crazed and Amber drew her knife away from Tom's neck and stepped back from the prisoner fearing a side of her father she had never witnessed before. Nat's visceral intent was clear as he approached, his old friend backed off slightly in surprise,

"Control yourself Nat, he's alone we need to know who he is!" said Stuart urgently

Tom did not flinch as Nat approached and pistol whipped him across the face, lacerating his skin on his cheekbone and sending him tumbling into the dirt. Nat stood over the ghost, breathing heavily, thinking his next move after the fix of violence. Tom returned the look calmly. With no threat, no aggravation he slowly reached into the pocket where he kept his phone, as he did so Nat's knee came down hard on his forearm pinning it across his chest.

"It's my phone, I'm getting my phone!" exclaimed Tom "you call the number on there..."

Nat leaned over Tom, close now, they could smell each other's sweat and he stuck the barrel of his handgun into his prisoner's eye socket. He then lifted his weight and his knee off the man's chest, leaning his weight through the barrel of the gun into Tom's eye. The man winced with pain. Nat crouched and his big hand delved into the small pocket where he found a mobile phone. As it powered up he looked down at his prisoner and pressed the barrel harder into his eye; pinning his head in the dirt.

Tom spoke as calmly as he could muster

"There is one number in the phone, call it and tell the man who answers who you are."

Nat pressed the green button and put the phone to his ear. It was answered immediately

"Tom, I haven't heard from you twice in one day since we were children..."

Confused Nat looked at the man at his feet, he recognised that this was a professional, something to do with the security services but he seemed far too slick for NSO. He felt the voice on the phone was familiar but he could not place it.

"This isn't Tom," Nat growled, he heard the gulp down the line. He felt the pause, then the shuffle of panic probably whoever was on the other end sitting down or standing up the brain giving orders that the body misreads in an attempt to buy seconds and think.

"This is Ben Baines, where is the man that you got the phone from"

Now it was Nat's turn to panic, his jaw clenched and Tom winced as the barrel of the gun was pressed so hard into his eye socket he felt the cold steel against his eyeball. Tears of pain, anger and hatred welled in Nat's eyes and it was Tom who first whispered 'no' at that point. Nat looked down at the man beneath him; the cogs in his brain beginning to move

"I've got a gun pointed in his face" Nat replied distracted and sounding distant; dangerous.

"You think that I am the enemy but I'm not, I am no longer the leader of the NSO quite the..." Baines continued down the line

"Shut up you fucking animal, you are the reason for all of this. You are the reason..." Nat looked across at Amber and flicked his head gesturing for her to disappear. He then looked at his old friend who looked at him quizzically. After a moment realisation ignited his face

"Hang on Nat wait that's not you..." exclaimed Stuart

The psychotic mists enveloped Nat's mind he could see revenge for his own torture right at the heart of the regime and he spat down the phone

"You became my enemy..."

"Don't do it, please don't do anything...He's my brother!" begged Baines from his London offices

"When your people..."

"Don't you fucking do that Nat!" shouted Stuart

Tom squirmed under the farmer's weight, but his knee was firmly positioned in the centre of Tom's chest, he was unable to free himself as Nat mumbled...crazed.

"My wife."

As he uttered the word Nat pulled the trigger, the dampened metallic snap ended the chorus of 'No' ringing out from Stuart, Tom, Baines and Amber.

The wood fell silent, the phone line fell silent and Nat's heart fell silent. He felt an immediate release of his pain. But he also felt an instant self-loathing for taking a man's life in such cold blood. He had no time to digest his actions before Stuart was onto him, a giant fist breaking the skin above his eye and knocking him off his feet. Stuart grabbed the phone and hung up. He screamed at Nat

"We could have used him to get Claire back you selfish, stupid bastard! Esme is fucking dead you idiot, are you a fucking murderer now? You're no better than those fuckers...You've got a daughter you got to start thinking! What have you done, Jesus" he threw his hands through his hair and turned a tight circle as though he were looking for an answer.

"You probably just killed us all"

Nat knew his friend was right, he sat stunned. He was so tired, he just sat staring at the forlorn body of the man he had just murdered. Stuart stepped over to Nat, grabbed his collars and lifted him roughly to his feet. He looked him in the eye drawing the farmer's attention away from the body

"Who was on the phone Nat?"

"It was Ben Baines," He said in a whisper. As Stuart let go of his jacket and turned away, looking at the floor, the weight of the name he had just heard etched all over his face. Nat added, "He said that that is his brother" Nat pointed at Tom's body. Stuarts' hands ran through his thick hair again and he paced, mind racing and blood boiling he exclaimed

"You have got to be fucking joking me, you just killed the brother of the leader of the NSO. We have got to be screwed; this place is going to be crawling with an army looking for you".

"Now he knows how it feels to have someone taken away."

Stuart slowed down regaining some composure, he looked down at the dirt and kicked at it.

"This changes things for me Nat. We go into Hexham tonight, get Claire and then I leave with her and Amber. I'll take them back across the border and you can come with or stay...up to you, but I'm not staying here."

"I'm not going back to Scotland" Came the acerbic voice of Amber from a short distance. Stuart looked at the father and his daughter, both staring at him with solemn but unwavering faces, muddied, wet and ashen, they were not going to be persuaded. Stuart looked to the heavens and turned on his heels and walked away from both of them, uttering over his shoulder

"You'll make a bloody murderer of your daughter now will you?"

Nat called after him

"We have to make them see that we will not flinch, that we can hurt them too."

But he was all too aware that his justification was unconvincing. As he spoke, Amber walked over to the agent's mobile phone, she switched it off and put it in her pocket.

* * * * *

Baines stared at his phone, no real tangible emotions except anger and hatred; his brain still working overtime to arrange the facts. He heard the farmers voice, he had seen how brutal the man could be; he knew his brother was dead.

He looked around his room, the meaningless grandeur. So far from the rioting street politician he had been, so far from the people he had set out to benefit. He resigned to the cul de sac power had sent him down. He was doing deals with the old regime, being controlled by his own extreme elements and had no control whatsoever over benefiting the general population he had always wanted to serve.

Something had just switched on in his belly, a furnace of energy; a new cause...as Lucas Start bowled into his office the two men looked at each other and Start smiled.

"I haven't seen that look since our days in Parliament Square Ben..."

"That farmer just killed my brother."

Lucas paused for a second; unsure whether to trust his old colleague but he could see the sincerity and focus in his eye and he knew they had a shared goal once more.

"I want to see the rebels in the north hunted down Lucas and I want that farmer hanging from a tree!"

Start looked at Baines perplexed, there was not a hint of acting in Baines, he was solemn, genuine and determined.

"I can see it now Lucas, there is no place for my ideals. The dog will always bite the hand that feeds it sooner or later unless, of course, we can control the dog. I will commit to your vision Lucas."

Simple as that, the pendulum had swung, Baines had steered a new course. The two men stood for a moment, eye to eye. Baines evoking sincerity while Start calculated the play. Until the latter broke the silence

"Oh, I don't doubt that now Ben" The two men shook hands and Start turned to leave the room then turned back "What's changed Ben? Apart from your loss, why join me now?"

"I've changed Lucas, I have changed" He replied with assurance and determination. Start looked thoughtfully into the middle distance as he turned again, raised his hand and gave a wave as he left the room in acceptance of the explanation.

THIRTEEN

As the shadows of evening became longer the weather was drawing in. A deep blanket of cloud bubbled in the sky and a wet wind blustered signifying rain in the air. The three rebels were seated around a small fire; they ate a gamy pheasant. The woodland was quiet around them, it seemed to feed off their dark moods. They didn't speak until Nat threw the last of his bones into the fire and said
"Better get set in the field shelter, looks like rain coming."
"Aye" Replied Stuart; he didn't look at his friend as he got to his feet.
The two men sat side by side in the field shelter as the rain began to come down. As the light began to fade they looked out over the valley that they knew so well. The chipboard factory continued to burn, there was no electricity running as not a single light shone across the whole landscape. No cars were on the road. The Tyne Valley had become a war zone and as night fell people hunkered down.
They said nothing to each other. All the time that Amber was away from them they sat in silence and that didn't change when she struggled up the hill with the heavy holdall. She placed the bag in front of the two men on the dry earth in the shelter and then she reached inside the bag and took one of the new NSO guns. She also took six full magazines. She moved over to the far corner of the shelter and began taping the magazines; two together head to toe.

They cleaned the weapons in silence keeping a close eye for approaching traffic.

Nat was consumed by an emotional deep freeze, Amber wanted desperately to hug him, to have him back but she was also damaged by witnessing his cold-blooded killing first hand. She didn't have the words to mend such situations, they communicated by actions, by working together on the farm, there was never great dialogue in their family.

There was no need for words between Stuart and Nat, they were bound to each other through history. Nat knew he had disappointed his friend but never questioned his loyalty and he was sure Stuart felt the same. The three of them understood one thing very clearly; they shared the same all-consuming reality. Events were moving so fast they had no time to stop and contemplate the fact that a few years previously this situation in this country would have been unimaginable. Everything had changed and they just had to keep moving and remain one step ahead.

Amber watched her father; he was drinking tea and staring out across the valley. The rain was coming down in thick grey waves like a plague of locusts wafting across the countryside. The tanned and creased hide of his face was like a lump of varnished oak. Those blues eyes pierced his crow's feet like two sapphires set in a carving, his white teeth shone through that perpetual grimace even in the fading light. Then he spoke,

"She's got to be in the police station."

After a momentary pause to digest Nat's sudden statement, Stuart answered

"How the hell will we get her out of there? Or more to the point how will we get in there?"

"That is the question." Nat pondered.

"There is no way the three of us can get into the police station and survive. It is bound to be full of NSO, we need to go to Waters Meet, join others like us" Stated Amber.

As his words trailed off, all their ears pricked to the sound of engines, Nat flashed a look at Stuart; maybe the fight was coming to them. Dusk was in its full, deepening throws, but there were no headlights accompanying the rough growl of engines. They hunkered down in the shelter, heart rates increasing with every nearing grunt of the accelerator.

Both Stuart and Nat filled magazines with rounds as their eyes fixated on the bottom of the driveway, both hoping that the engines would die away into the distance. Both disappointed when they began counting the trucks into the driveway; one, two three, four, five, six! They came fast each tailgating the truck in front, losing little speed around the sharp turn into the drive. All the vehicles were large four by fours. Nat turned to Amber handing her the 33 rifle and directing,

"Go get yourself in the tree line, if they start coming up the hill start shooting and don't stop until they're gone or you run out...ok? Go quick"

She turned and swung the weapon onto her back and ran North East towards the trees. Nat and Stuart set off to the south-east to meet the visitors at the ruin of the farmhouse. As the vehicles motored up the long drive the two men ran down through the wet grass, its undulations testing their every step as the incline of the hill pulled them faster than their limbs could manage. Just as the vehicles were pulling up outside the tumbled stones, Nat and Stuart fell in behind the stone wall which ran west away from the Northern end of the barn.

Sitting with his back flat against the wall Nat looked across at Stuart, who was kneeling at the base of the wall looking back for the next call. They could hear the engines die, they heard the crunch of footsteps on the gravel. Nat nodded to Stuart and both men rose, leading with their weapons. They had them trained before the top of the cold, wet stones were tucked into their armpits.

The men who had stepped from their trucks scattered as the arms came into view. Running back behind the big metallic chunks, skidding on the gravel all arms and legs. All the fuss unnecessary. Nat recognised the Toyota up front. Rowell's youngest son called out

"Mr Bell, Its Jesse Rowell you helped my dad today"

"I know who you are" Nat responded bluntly

"Can we talk?"

No response

"It concerns Claire" he came back again

"We're listening" called Stuart immediately

"You two can't take on Hexham on your own, it is crawling with NSO and you will be massacred. We are attacking tonight and what if one of ours shoots you in the confusion?" He stepped out from behind his truck, he was a blond ruddy twenty-something. A closely shaven head to the sides with a limp Mohican covering the centre of his scalp. And now he stepped a few paces closer, still a good distance from the wall but the subconscious communicated the fact that they were about to be party to coveted information.

"We have over a thousand men down at Waters Meet, we are going to attack the town tonight, drive the NSO out of Tynedale and start the civil war proper from the north. Word is that the Cornish and the Welsh are fighting. We have the backing financially and with weapons from the

Scots. All through the north of England, people will join us if we can show some momentum."

"None of that means anything to me..." Dismissed Nat

The boy paused as if conjuring up the courage then he responded

"What happened to your wife Nat was terrible and we all want revenge for that, but I know Amber too, I care about her...don't you? Lots of these people joined the rebels because of what happened to you, don't let them down, don't let your daughter down and don't let them win by committing suicide."

"Listen son, you wind your neck in...All we're interested in is getting the girl back."

"Ok Ok, you stay up there living in a tree for the rest of your days... But you know one night someone will come and cut your throat or they'll just burn you out sooner or later..."

"Come on Nat you stubborn bastard, we'll be much more likely to get Claire safely with them."

Stuart climbed the wall and jumped down the other side, he walked over to Jesse Rowell and held out his spade like hand

"I'm Stuart, his brains," he said with a smile on his face and a nod back up the hill to the stone wall that Nat remained behind.

As he sat with his back to the wall, he looked back up the hill to his beloved woods. The grey film of dusk over the land, the damp smell of wet grass and rain in his nostrils, his clothes sodden and the semi-automatic weapon in his hands. As his daughter broke through the tree line and walked down the hill towards them, he had a moment of clarity in the storm that his life had become.

There was more to his life than killing those men that had had a hand in Esme's murder.

He pushed himself off the cold moss covered stone, out from the cover and back into the cold breeze, the great wide open. He pushed his stiff limbs up over the stone wall and a few stones tumbled as he slid down the other side.

His old bones rocked as he stomped towards the car, he rested his weapon on his shoulder as he walked. The young men ventured from the cover of their trucks and began to clap their hands for him. His grimace thickened and he awkwardly waved a large hand for them to stop. The reality of his new life was becoming evident, he had become a cog in a larger machine now, larger than his farm, larger than his life. He didn't want it, he wanted Esme to be the start and finish of his breath but his experience now was that life had moved on.

He looked into the young Rowell's eyes and he saw the boy feared him. Neither said a word as they shook hands. As Amber joined them and greeted friends among the men, Nat stood aside, feet wide, hands in the pockets of his muddied padded wax jacket, his shining white mane wet, greasy and slightly matted. His head was spinning, as he watched his daughter moving through the young people and finally to Jesse in front of him who she hugged tight and exchanged some soft words. Nat looked to his left; Stuart stood next to him. Shoulder to shoulder they would stand against the NSO.

* * * * *

Rudi Truter was in pain, he sat in a dark room in a quiet corner of the police station. Both bones in his arm had been broken by the journalist. They had brought a doctor to the station to put a cast on it. He had done as good a job as he could, but the pain was excruciating. On top of that Truter's other elbow was sore too; he had visited the journalist in his cell and made short work of the man's baby face with his good elbow. He was waiting for his latest round of pain killers to kick in before he went back to kill both the prisoners, they were of no use to him and keeping them there simply created a security issue. The pain was beginning to dull when he heard a voice in the corridor calling his name, he called back and the voice returned telling him that Ben Baines' office was on the telephone. Everything else could wait. The man handed him the phone and Truter pressed the receiver to his ear. He didn't recognise the officious, nasal tone of the aide's voice on the other end, there were no pleasantries.

"Mr Truter?"

"Yes"

"I'm calling on behalf of Mr Baines; he has been disappointed by your lack of ability in containing the rural community in your region."

"I've got one man on a killing spree and an untrained group of terrorists making home-made explosives, once I get more men I will crush both the problems..."

"The way we see it, is that you have allowed the creation of a local hero in opposition to our cause and the destruction of the largest employment facilities in the area. You do understand don't you that our ideology is primarily concerned with getting people working."

"I'm fighting a war here with kids and thugs for my army, I can't do everything myself. Once I have the trained reinforcements in position, I will get the area secure and under our control."

"Did you know about the rebel force congregating at Acomb? I think that is about two miles North of where you are..."

Truter balked, "What twenty farmhands with shotguns?"

"No Truter, hundreds at least, maybe more armed by the Scots. This job has become too big for you Mr Truter. A gentleman called Beaston, General Anthony Beaston will arrive this evening with more troops and he will relieve you of your command and find a role for you to fill."

Truter paused for a second and then opened his mouth to argue his corner but as he did so, he heard a calm click as the aide hung up. He was now out in the cold, wounded physically and mentally. Worse than being bottom of the pile he had failed.

He put the phone down on the table in front of him. He looked across the room, the felt carpet, toughened plastic chairs, the ancient metal filing cabinet which stood under a clipboard littered with police bulletins, guidelines and assorted rubbish akin to any office noticeboard. This noticeboard however was a historical item, a window into the past, as there was no police force now.

* * * * *

They took the black estate car that had been driven by the man whose throat Nat had cut. They followed the speeding convoy of four by four's, Nat was driving and he was doing his best to keep up with the young drivers who were taking full advantage of the empty streets. They wound down the steep bank from Oakwood like the cars of a roller coaster and onto the roundabout giving access straight into Hexham, left to Newcastle and right to

Carlisle. The A69 was the highway linking Newcastle to Carlisle on opposite sides of the country and all that lay in between.

The convoy looped the roundabout and hit the long ramp onto the motorway at pace. They were doing well over seventy as Nat mulled over the wisdom in using the main roads. The speed of the journey couldn't be argued, but the noise of the seven engines and their respective headlights was like sending a rocket across the dark, still countryside and hoping it wouldn't be noticed.

The convoy left the motorway pulling right, across the oncoming but empty carriageway losing some traction and adding a squeal from some of the fat tyres in front. It whooshed seven times into the straight road leading into the small quiet village of Acomb.

They passed the bus depot which was now ablaze, Nat knew the reason; their buses were being used by the NSO...but not anymore, five of them burned where they stood. The journey continued down a left hand turn, the narrow road which lead to the river. The convoy stopped in the middle of the road a good mile out from the river, Nat bumped the car up onto the verge behind another. There were cars and people everywhere, hundreds of them. Everyone was armed, some with shotguns and hunting rifles but others, most, were carrying new shiny military hardware such as automatic rifles, heavy machine guns and some had hand held rocket launchers. Stuart was nudging Nat, pointing at the new weapons and repeating "It's gotta be Scottish Army gear, aye Nat look it's gotta be from the Scots".

As they got out of the car, the atmosphere hit them. The sound of boots on the tarmac and the metallic clicking and grinding of weapons were the only sounds, but due to the sheer numbers involved those sounds made a swarm like din. The vocal silence was eerie, but the atmosphere was so tense, electric and heated to boiling point. They could see in the faces around them that they were fired up and itching for a fight.

Nat barged and thugged his way through the maelstrom, the heaving mass of men and women, young and old, marginalised by the regime, hungry for revolt and baying for blood. Stuart trod on at Nat's shoulder, Amber floated in their wake. He followed the young Rowell, he didn't know where to, he just followed through the chaos down the muddy path towards Waters Meet. The beautiful meeting point of the turbulent South Tyne and the languid North Tyne rivers. A spot Nat had been in the past to swim across the frigid waters from Kielder Reservoir that filled the North Tyne to the milder natural flow of the South Tyne.

Unrecognisable this day, the ground was being churned up in the thickening crowds. As they burrowed their way further into the army, the noise of energy barked and hollered from every direction. Through the trees came lights glowing and an ever-present sound; the steel grinding and springs clicking the metal of weapons being readied. They were the sounds heard over a dull, hushed drone of lowered voices.

Nat could see in the faces around him a steady determined concentration driven by fear and desperation. There were accents from all over the country but predominantly the Northumbrian lilt and borders Scots came through. Many of those marshalling small groups into units were Scottish and the weapon being carried by most of the people present was the SAR90 the standard assault rifle of the Scottish Army.

Nat caught the nod from Stuart, he had been right, both men realised that the Rowell's were being organised and armed by the Scots military. They suddenly felt a reassuring acceptance that this was an orchestrated revolt against the regime in which the Scots wanted all the players, especially those who had recently courted some fame or infamy depending on your viewpoint. The leathery farmer didn't care, he wanted to save his friend and kill whoever was left of the raiding party; he was a willing pawn.

They approached the tunnel under the disused railway line, there was a fire burning and so the crowds within it glowed with a flickering orange and gold. He saw Old Man Rowell sitting to one side while his eldest belted out instructions to those around him. Nat and Stuart nodded to the ruddy round-faced old man and passed the circle around the fire absorbing the image of those young men coming to terms with the gravity of the unfolding situation. Rowell's eldest, Phalin, raised his gun in the air acknowledging the newcomers and returned to his rant.

Like the eye of the storm the three came to rest with their backs against the side of the tunnel, still, calm, watching the human commotion before them. Amber checked her weapons she had a new automatic weapon taken from the NSO, a handgun and of course the hunting knife her father had painstakingly taught her how to use.

"What do you think?" Nat asked Stuart

"We go in, get Claire and fuck off" replied Stuart

"You think they'll win?"

"Maybe…who knows? But I don't want to be in town when the air force arrives."

"Aye"

Nat looked down at his daughter; she looked so young for a moment. He put a big hand down on the auburn curls covering the back of her neck

"You stay close to me and him OK. If you're not next to one of us, you're low to the ground and in shadow OK."

She looked up from where she rested on her honkers and smiled nodding briefly.

Nat looked around the milieu, these moments of reality never as paralysing as the thought of them. For those few seconds, he picked out faces that he recognised, farm hands, labourers, gamekeepers, his postman, a few weeks previous this scene would have been inconceivable. Now these men and women prepared to fight as an army for a region which was theirs through the blood and sweat of generations before them. These were the people who believed in the regimes original message, before it had been rapidly warped and abused by those in charge. It dawned on him then that these people would never stop fighting. That the NSO would never contain this part of the country because these people had no choice, this land was their blood and they had fought over it for centuries. They were exactly like him, one and all.

Calls came across the line and the army quietened down, slowly beginning to form some sort of procession, bottle necking its way up the steep bank and onto the disused railway above their heads. Calls of 'stay off the bridge' came from above as the sheer weight of numbers could cause the old structure to collapse. Nat, Stuart and Amber joined the procession, now eerily quiet, the heat and smell of all the bodies and the electricity of expectation filled the air with a feral energy. As he climbed the slope up to the railway line, Nat heard the roar of powerful engines through the trees. The headlights danced between the branches and he realised the Rowell brothers, or whoever was organising this army, had made preparations for some kind of vehicular support for the men on the ground. A short man whose head Nat was looking over caught his eye,

"That's John, Rowell's middle boy; he's a great fighter but wild; he's off to raid the food banks out at Whittonstall".

"What do you mean food banks?" Nat asked

"There's no trade anymore as far as food is concerned, it all goes straight to Whittontsall, where it is stored and distributed through the Northeast…all fresh produce. It's well you stopped farming Nat; they take it all now."

"This John don't we need him tonight?"

"Don't worry if we need him he'll be there, he blew the factory…he won't let us down. He's like you Mr Bell."

Nat looked down at the man in front of him, caught out by his comment and with no idea what to say in return his eyes moved on down the column without a word. They began the two-mile journey south to Hexham as the convoy of vehicles rumbled off to the east. The march was slow going as the column compacted and stretched like a concertina. There was little talk.

The rain clouds had parted. The deepening night sky was as clear as a dark sapphire cut to a million points as the stars blazed down on them. After twenty minutes or so Nat noticed up ahead the column becoming more congested and people dropping out briefly to the left before re-joining the army. He couldn't make out what was going on in the failing light but slowly they drew closer and up alongside an old hawthorn tree. There, someone had left a battered guitar with a note scratched onto the rosewood which read 'hands off…I'll be back for this'. Surrounding the guitar others had left their most treasured possessions from wedding rings, necklaces to photographs and clothes. As they passed, Nat saw Amber break from the crowd. As she hung her mother's necklace upon the tree, she turned to look at her father, his eyes piercing but he bit his tongue, he didn't feel or care for any superstition.

After an hour, they reached the river and crossed in single file over the ruin of the old railway bridge. All that was left of the iron structure were four massive stone pillars and two huge girders spanning the river. The river was not deep or raging, but it was a good twenty feet below so each person gave the person in front plenty of room. As they stepped off the other side Nat, Amber and Stuart were still together. They looked around them, there must have been four or five hundred people on the bank of the river with the same amount still behind them crossing and waiting to cross the bridge. Nat tapped his two companions and began leading them off into the shadows when teams ran along the banks telling the force to fan out all along the river in readiness to sweep into town over the golf course.

Nat wanted to head due south passed the clubhouse down the main drive to the golf course meeting the Haydon Bridge road about three-quarters of a mile west of the police station where Claire was being held. It seemed that this plan closely resembled the main forces and so he stayed with them adjudging the three of them could slip away at any point.

* * * * *

"Why aren't you on the ground yet Beaston?" screamed Start down the cell phone that lay on the desk. He stood in front of it. His face was bright red, and he was leaning on his white clenched knuckles. The crunch, wail and grind of the military vehicle powering along created a great deal of distraction.

"Sir, I did not want to showcase our convoy of thirty-two military vehicles. Which I understand can be viewed from hundreds of vantage points along the valley where our enemy are camped out. So I took a rougher but far more clandestine route over the moors from Blanchland, we are two miles out from the school where we will set up camp."

"OK, OK just get your men on the ground and crush these bastards! I've got the Cornish coming up my arse and the Geordies down my neck, we can't let this escalate. Do you hear me?"

"Loud and clear sir, don't worry we will control this end, do we have drone back up, and what are your orders in terms of contact?"

"Yes drones will be available from later today or tomorrow latest. You meet resistance, you use all necessary force and if you think you are meeting passive resistance, harbouring or human shielding you do whatever is necessary, you hear, whatever you have to do."

"OK sir, thank you, I'll report back at one hundred hours" The phone clicked off. Start looked up from the table at his advisors

"You have to make these calls Lucas" Said Steve Jones, the man who was shadowing his leader closest now and Start was beginning to rely more and more on his kowtowing. It was easier than looking across the table at his old friend Baines, who he remained unsure of.

It was true Baines had pledged his allegiance but Start was all too aware that words were cheap. Baines himself was torn; he currently looked at Start with a face that showed his sadness. He watched everything that he had worked for, his life's work, fall to pieces before him, helpless to turn it around because Start had already gone too far.

It was no longer possible to lead the population into his model of collectivism because Starts thugs had destroyed the trust, they controlled the cities, but the heartland of staple production: the countryside was lost. Now that the food supply and waste disposal services were suffering there was increasing unrest in the cities also.

His vision was slipping away and would certainly vanish under Start. But on the other hand Baines wanted to see the farmer pay for what he had done to his brother and the simplest way to make that happen was to leave Start to crush the uprising. So for now his interest lay in the border war. As he sat watching Start's sweating brow and the rain drops dribble down the window behind his head, he rested back in his chair and let the carnage unfold before him. After the farmer was dead; then he would reclaim his future.

* * * * *

The convoy of heavy military vehicles pulled into the car park and tennis courts of the local school, Beaston gathered his officers to his truck and spelled out his tactics for the day. He took the rolled up map of Hexham that he had studied on the journey, it was a town easily defended with the right organisation. The centre sits high up the valley side from the northern quarter where the out of town shopping, leisure centre, cattle mart and industrial park are located. It was in this location that Beaston wanted his troops to meet the rebels. It was here that the battle would be open and the NSO training, however brief, would prove invaluable for his men.

The small, wiry general was also keen however to stop the rebels entering the higher ground in the town. So he gave particular instructions for a third of his men to blockade the roads leading into the town with the use of the vehicles and it was on these placements that the heavy weapons should be situated.

In a previous life Beaston had toured Iraq, Afghanistan, Egypt and Greece with the Royal Regiment Of Fusiliers. He knew about street warfare and he knew that the rebels could amass and dissolve like a flock of Starlings if they were allowed into the narrow winding streets of their home town with its sympathetic front doors. The NSO force was to move quickly into the streets of the town blockading routes in so that the rebels would have to stand and fight, something he was eager to discover their hunger for.

His men totalled over five hundred at the moment although Start had seen to it that that figure would treble in the next twenty-four hours. He looked up to the night's sky, his sharp nose and chin pointing the way. He was a fidgety man of fast precise movement. He snatched his cell phone from the breast pocket of his woodland greens. He waited impatiently while the phone repeated its monotonous burps. Finally, he heard a voice at the other end.

"Is that Truter?"
"It is, whose this?"

"I'm your replacement, I have orders to shoot anyone or anything which disturbs my operation. So I hope we are going to work well together, now tell me how many men you have at your disposal."

"About one hundred and five" Truter replied with as much disdain as he could muster.

"Are you sure or have some of those been killed by old men in tweed caps?"

There was silence from the other end of the phone; Truter was disabled by his broken arm, he was shocked by the acceleration of events and his confidence was dented by his recent demotion. He was in no mood for witty retorts.

"No don't answer that" came Beastons precise nasal English "I'll be with you in five minutes, where are you, the police station?"

"Yes" Truter responded, immediately after he spoke the line clicked off.

Beaston signalled to his force to move out as he ducked his head slightly and did his trademark half run, half walk to his vehicle. His movement was that of a man whose mind was already a few steps ahead of his current action. His mannerisms were awkward, eccentric and easily laughed at, famed by the troops who had served under him. But he was also a man totally revered by his peers; whatever comedic value his fast-paced mind produced it offered in return absolute attention to detail and unwavering commitment to his cause.

* * * * *

Nat could hear the engines of the military vehicles, a low growl floating across the otherwise still and peaceful night's sky. At that moment, he understood that the NSO knew they were coming, and the vehicles they were moving were not the cars they had been running around in up to this point. He looked across at Amber; she was walking a few yards to his right, eyes firmly fixed ahead of her, concentrating on the hunt. Nat feared for his girl but at the same time he knew she was no stranger to killing. She was a fine stalker, known to be able to get within touching distance of an animal before it was spooked. He looked across again to Stuart on Ambers right again, and the big Scot gave him a solemn grin,

"See you on the other side Nat, you hear the reinforcements too?"

"Aye," said the farmer, his white mane glowing in the night sky.

Looking across the line the rebel force had fanned out sweeping over the whole width of the golf course, a distance west to east of about three-quarters of a mile. Nat was very much at the western end of the formation. As they walked on silently through the night, they saw no movement, no lights and certainly no NSO. They came close to the clubhouse, Amber broke away into the darkness, and Nat and Stuart lowered their shoulders and kept to scrub for cover. The rest of the two hundred or so men and women who were near followed suit ducking into cover or simply low to the ground and there they waited for farmers' next move.

The club house had car parks surrounding it, it was dark, silent and evidently had not been opened for weeks. The putting green in front was overgrown, a rubbish bin lay on its side and as Nat looked closer, he could see that the main double doors had been secured shut with a large security chain. It was of no surprise to him that the regime was not a fan of golf, he wasn't either; there were some positives.

He looked back towards the men who had followed them on an arc around the open space. He gestured to a man behind him who he presumed was in charge because he had seen him talking to Rowell's eldest. His rudimentary signal consisting of a palm held up, a point to his eye and a point to the driveway leading out to the main road running North West out of the town. The other man got the idea and spread the word for the small force to remain where they lay.

Into the darkness, Nat and Stuart moved with pace and silence. Neither were strangers to the world at night, neither were strangers to keeping silent and hunting prey, both felt this was similar but with heightened natural instinct from booming adrenalin. There was no thought for the extremity of the situation because it was reality, this was the here and now and they had to play out whatever was ahead of them and Nat felt good about it. He had all but forgotten about the wound on his shoulder; he felt strong and cocooned by the dark. Most importantly he knew this place like the back of his hand and for the first-time revenge was not his sole motivator; he wanted Claire back safe, and he wanted the regime out of Hexhamshire.

They hugged the eastern flank of the stone wall that led down the driveway. The trees stirred above them in the unnatural silence, the only sounds were the leaves. The occasional stick snapping in the distance and the odd telling whistle as either the rebel force or the regimes troops communicated in the darkness. Nat and Stuart both felt it though, the unnerving energy of unseen human presence, it was in the air like a time bomb ticking and there was no escaping it. As they reached the end of the drive Nat leant back against the wall and turned his head to Stuart

"Not a shot fired, is that good or bad?"

"I have no idea, but they must be somewhere, you heard those engines, that was heavy machinery."

"Aye, but why are they waiting"

Nat took a breath and then poked his head around the corner of the wall. The road ran straight for half a mile in either direction; the fields banked upwards on the far side, and the grass verge was thick with brambles. At first the road looked clear, not a soul in sight. Then as his eyes got used to the distance; in the dark a shape materialised out of the gloom. As he studied it, the form became an armoured personnel vehicle, parked across the road at its narrowest point. Nat thought for a minute then he turned and told Stuart to wait and watch for any movement or change.

* * * * *

Abraham Jones had been at university studying business and international economics five months ago. He had joined the NSO when he had first started his degree course two years previously. The thrill of rebellion and marches had seduced him, and he had bought into Ben Baines politics as his course had taken him through the new world economic order and those flourishing nations. He had seen a real future in the system and was a committed member of the party. Three months before he was due to graduate he had been forcibly conscripted in the regimes military 'elite'. The regime had cancelled all non-essential education, and so all those who found their courses closed were redistributed to work as part of the collective. Seventy-Five percent of men redeployed were enlisted into the military. Abraham was one of them.

As he stood on top of the armoured vehicle staring down his gun sights into the gloom, he had no idea how his life had come to this. He kept repeating to himself that the world had changed and this was for the good of the people. But he couldn't help thinking that back before the revolution, when the rich were getting richer and the poor were suffering a life of reality TV and lager, twenty-two year old economists were not standing on top of military vehicles pointing a very serious weapon down a dark road in anticipation of being attacked by hordes of psychotic farmers.

It was only when a faint light green glow appeared in the centre of his night sights that his heart began to pound, and those moments became paralysing. It was as the dim light green glow became stronger and took the shape of a human being that a tear came to Abraham's eye. It was as Abraham focussed on the weapons that the young man fell off the truck and scrambled over the tarmac to his sleeping colleagues, fifteen in total occupying whatever space they could in the truck,

"They're coming!" he screamed "get you're fucking arses out here now."

The detachment jumped wearily into action scrambling for their weapons and pushing each other out of the way. Few of them had ever fired a weapon at another human being in their life. The man in charge was an ex infantry soldier called Terry Deelam. Out on the tarmac behind the vehicle he grabbed Abraham by the shoulders

"How many are there Abe, what did you see?"

"There's one there's only one out there, but he's walking down the middle of the road and he's covered in weapons"

"What…ONE!" Screeched Terry confounded as he leapt up onto the truck "Shoot him lads, I'll fucking shoot you later Abe!"

As the men climbed aboard the armoured vehicle and set their sights to their eyes. They had a split second to register the green figure about one hundred and fifty yards out, long thin legs, broad shoulders, rifle hanging by a strap off one shoulder. He had a small box shape on the other which as it registered with Terry lit up like a firework in his sights. He was enveloped by calm in that nether world of milliseconds before impact, then the lights went out.

* * * * *

Nat could not believe his eyes when the boy had bolted; he was gambling on the boy's nerves ruining his aim. He had sent the rest of their group through the trees along the side of the road where they were hidden by a stone wall. As he fired the rocket launcher at the armoured truck, the rebels leapt over the wall and charged towards the vehicle. The impact of the rocket had blown the vehicle back about ten yards, the armour on top of the truck had been ripped up and backwards. It was covered in gore from the men who had managed to get on top of the truck and those who hadn't had been crushed by the vehicle.

The rebels quickly counted fifteen bodies; two were still inside the vehicle on impact. Four were still alive, including those in the vehicle and Abraham. All the survivors were going to die from their injuries. Abraham had been hit by the truck as he was still standing behind it when the rocket hit. Nat found his body like a rag doll thirty yards from impact. A scolding shard of metal was embedded in his cranium. He spluttered blood, conscious but oblivious. Nat shook his head as he looked into the young man's fearful eyes. He took out his handgun and shot him dead.

He could hear fighting elsewhere in the town now and he thought it likely that more soldiers would be heading in their direction. He turned to the men with him

"Take weapons and ammo, leave everything else. Get into shadows and gardens. We work our way down this road to the police station, every road we pass leave ten men in wait at the entrance to it. Any NSO coming up or down they should be ambushed once they're in between us and those men in wait."

The message spread down the line and the force split into two moving down each side of the road through the gardens of the houses. As the army passed Eilansgate, they were met by more rebels coming up the hill towards them who had had small skirmishes but no real resistance up to this point. Nat looked down the hill now towards the police station only eight hundred yards in the distance. He paused because the gardens in front of the houses stopped at this point. Therefore, so did their cover. They would have to move en masse and in the open.

The force sat low and quiet as gunfire rang out from a distance, Nat called out to the rebel throng,

"Who's in charge of you?"

A dozen faces stared back, shining and vacant in the darkness. Then out of the shadows appeared two men and a woman, Nat recognised all three but had never spoken to any of them. The first stepped forward, a stoic man wearing work boots, jeans and a camouflage jacket. He wore his semi-automatic weapon across his chest as though he had been born with it. He looked assured and in control and he spoke calm and soft

"I'm Andrew, this is Susan" pointing to a thick-set woman with messy hair and a stud in her nose. "And that's Barty," he said looking at the squat bald man who wore full military fatigues and held his weapon ready. But in a perfect, world he was a good four stone overweight for real combat.

Nat smiled at the three of them in lieu of small talk.

"Where now?" He asked, "We have no cover down the road and we'll lose the surprise if we detour around the streets with this amount of people."

"They're waiting for us aren't they?" Barty commented pointing down the quiet street, the crack of distant shots echoing through the otherwise silent and calm town.

"You've got to imagine yes Barty son they're there."

"Every one of us knew we were going to fight tonight, that we could die here tonight we need to push on, keep the impetuous" Susan interjected. The three of them looked at Andrew. He stood tall unwavering and said, nodding solemnly.

"We came here to fight, let's take the road all at once and fan out as soon as we can and form some sort of platform to attack from."

Nat looked around the gathered faces, he saw the fear but he also saw courage and commitment. They had to keep moving.

"Ok, get your people ready and remember this only works if we are a wave of bodies and bullets." As he finished his sentence Nat looked down the street. Dawn was approaching fast, the deep blue was a shade lighter and in a few hours the stone of the buildings around them would be developing a pinkie hue, was daylight their enemy too? He thought.

* * * * *

Brigadier Quentin Harris observed the rebel army up the hill from his position, he spoke softly over cell phone to Beaston two hundred and fifty yards behind him in the police station. He had sixty men at his disposal against four hundred or so rebel fighters. So he had half his men take up positions in the upper floors of the buildings either side of the road as it widened once more. The other half of his contingent lay in wait behind garden walls. Right now, he spoke quietly to Beaston

"They seem to be having a bloody chat! There is a lot of them so I would advise that you pull back to the school. Wait there for news because if they overwhelm us here they will be on you like lions on a limping goat."

"Ok Quentin, remember reinforcements are on their way, if you can repel them this time we'll smash them the second…"

"I'll see what these boys are made of." He passed the phone to the man by his side and as he looked up the street and saw the mass of bodies charging down the hill. They were roaring like a battle charge from centuries before, he stepped into the middle of the street and shouted to his men.

"It's your ammo against their numbers, remember men I want them to meet a wall of lead." With that, he skipped back across the road and behind his men. There he rested a heavy machine gun across the wall of a pretty garden and squeezed the trigger pumping round after round of twelve point seven millimetre shells into the approaching mass. All his men lit up too and the rebel force was being cut down before they had any opportunity to fire back. The noise was ferocious, sixty weapons firing at about thirteen hundred rounds per minute into the narrow road. The rebels who came within four hundred yards were mown down as they ran; the rest turned and ran back up the street to where they had come. Harris allowed himself a smile but knew that the fluidity of urban conflict might only allow his troops a fleeting glimpse of victory and so commanded them to show no mercy.

* * * * *

As they began running down the road, Nat realised the mistake but it was too late. He couldn't keep up with the younger people, both he and Stuart were left behind and when the shooting began the horror of what lay before them was unimaginable. The violence of lead tearing through flesh and bone with an initial thud and damp fizzing as the rounds ricochet out of bodies. The falling bodies were taking their last agonizing steps. The horrific howls of injured men and women who were helplessly lying in no man's land, screamed above the gunfire. This was the sound of war. Nat watched as Susan was hit by a volley of shots, her body convulsed as it was pummelled. She screamed as though her insides had been set on fire before wilting onto the hard tarmac of the road. Andrew too went down, although he knew nothing of his final moment, on one knee firing aimlessly at the regimes positions, a round hit him in the eye and passed out through his head.

As Nat stood helplessly staring at the mayhem. The taste of blood in his mouth, the air laced with agony, he was unsure what to do until a large hand grabbed his shoulder and pulled him sideways into a gated inlet. Behind which was a garden and house surrounded by high walls. The panicking rebels were crushing into the small turn in between the road and the gate. The gate fell open under the sheer weight of numbers pushing up against it. The stunned rebel force fell over each other into the safety of the garden. The force split into three. Those in the garden. Those running back from where they had come and those lying in the street, the NSO continuing to take pot shots at the living. Nat looked at the faces around him; blood soaked bodies, tears streaming from their eyes, it had been a massacre but they had to counteract the situation, or they would all perish in that street.

Some of the rebels had climbed the trees flanking the high wall and were firing over the wall at the NSO positions. Nat looked around the yard and saw a shed he quickly ran to it and opened the door, there in front of him stood a sledgehammer among more garden equipment. He hurried back to the wall with the hammer, and he swung it hard against the bricks. Within two strikes he had knocked out a brick, another thud, and there was a good hole, ample swing and leverage to fire a gun through. He walked a few paces along the wall and swung the hammer again. The human metronome moved systematically down the wall smashing small holes into it; others began using the butts of their weapons or other implements they were carrying.

Nat looked out over the carnage, the death, the people around him young and old breaking down with the horror. It was the noise that drove them insane, an incessant hammering of gunfire spelling out the danger, the all-consuming screaming foretelling the nightmare of injury and madness. The bodies were everywhere, inert, rushing with activity and rocking with madness; the living sent wild by their proximity to the dead. There was no time for thoughts to reason, to calculate. Nat just kept screaming for people to fire their weapons at the enemy positions. The chaos was all consuming.

Gradually though Nat, Stuart and Barty were able to bring the rebels under some sort of organisation. The men and women who could still face the fight took up better positions and the weight of numbers began to tell as the rebels were able to contain the NSO bullets with suppressing fire of their own.

Once it was possible Nat and Barty ran the gauntlet back up the hill to the rest of the force who were aimlessly waiting out of range and under cover for a sign or an order.

* * * * *

General Harris felt in control, the stalemate suited their plan, and he could sit like this for days. He knew the reinforcements would be here long before that. He moved away from his men, down the side of the police station. He was cocooned between the high wall of the perimeter of the station and the building itself. Behind him was the back of the station and a car park, again there was the perimeter wall enclosing the rear of the building.

The area was littered with rubbish that had blown in on the wind, and there was an overturned salt bin. It was here that he turned and planted his backside. He had a view of his men's positions, and he could see the rebel bullets puffing in dusty clouds off the brickwork. The rebels were keeping his fighters heads low, but they were not killing any of them; so if the rebels were to attempt another charge he would be able to repeat the massacre.

He took out his cellphone and dialled Beaston. The General wiped the dust from his face as he perched on the bin. He crossed his legs by resting his ankle on his knee and he picked at his boot where a scolding hot shell had slightly melted the sole.

"Tell me" Beaston answered

"We have them locked down for now."

"How long can you hold them?"

"I don't know, it depends on what they do next."

"Well, a few hours and we'll have reinforcements."

"That's it I figure we have a bit of a stalemate as we stand…" Harris broke off as he spoke distracted for a second then continued "so if we can…" He stopped again; his words drifted as he sensed something; a presence. Before his brain registered the feelings he felt warm air, breath on his ear, right next to the phone and a small certain voice whispered,

"You'll never win here, this is our country."

As he heard the words, he felt a thud in the side of his neck like a hammer blow, but no pain to speak of, he staggered to his feet the phone still to his ear

"What…what was that? Who said that? What…Harris?" Shouted Beaston down the line.

Harris could only utter a guttural gurgle, the whites of his eyes shining in the darkness and his heart pumping blood harder and harder in an effort to reach his brain. But it wasn't getting anywhere near his brain, his blood was spraying out of the deep wound in his neck which had completely severed his jugular. As he held his free hand to the wound, the blood covered his face and body. As his eyesight began to cloud over and dizziness set in Harris looked down at his assassin. A young woman with auburn hair and vivid blue eyes, her face covered in black mud or war paint. In her hand, an oozing bloody hunting knife a full nine inch blade and fresh from its most recent kill.

As the geyser of red began to wane, Harris the invincible General fell to his knees then flat on that famous face at the feet of Amber. The mobile phone skidded across the floor; she picked it up and hung up on Beaston who turned to Truter

"You take thirty of my men and your ten and defend this position hold it until reinforcements arrive, I'm moving back to the school."

Amber put the phone in her pocket turned ran back into the car park, moving like a cat she pounced up onto the armoured vehicle parked next to the wall and then over the obstacle.

* * * * *

The rebels charged again only this time they had the covering fire of those in the garden suppressing the NSO positions. The NSO seemed in disarray now. The wall of lead was now sporadic, as they ducked the fire from the rebels in the garden and from those charging down the hill.

Stuart was dug-in behind the wall in the garden and had Nat's hunting rifle, he was able to take down a regime soldier with every shot he made. It was slow going, and rebel fighters continued to fall in the charge but the regimes line was soon broken. Rather than bullets the rebels were soon beating those who had massacred them an hour earlier with the butts of their weapons.

The sheer weight of numbers left the NSO no chance and the rebels flooded into the houses either side of the road to clear them of NSO fighters. The incessant mind-bending din and chaos of gunfire now quelled to short bursts as the rebels cleared the surrounding buildings. As the rebels looked back up the hill, it was evident that the victory had been at substantial loss to them and was no cause for celebration. They had routed about sixty NSO troops but lost well over one hundred of their own.

The absolute despair of seeing the piles of mangled bodies heaped in the narrowest part of the road, hit the rebels. With streams of red trickling down the tarmac towards them, the nightmare of war had emblazoned itself on those young men and women in their first sally. As a stunned silence fell over the force, some broke down in tears, others wondered at their lack of emotion, while others seethed with aggression towards this enemy. It was not long before this latter group drove the force on to the police station.

Nat and Stuart caught up with each other now in the simmering crowd energised by the upper hand in the battle,

"Now we get in there get Claire and get the fuck out of this chaos ok Nat?" Stuart exclaimed with a seriousness Nat rarely witnessed from his old friend.

"Aye" Nat responded nodding "let's get this done and back to the country where we can see these bastards coming."

The rebel army surrounded the police station and began by peppering it with gun fire which made no in roads as the NSO troops inside were well organised by Truter. They waited in the body of the building only firing at those rebels who ventured too close. The tactic worked and the battle became a siege.

*   *   *   *   *

As word filtered through that the rest of the rebel force had broken the NSO lines and they were in control of the town running the retreating NSO soldiers down through the streets. Beaston had taken a frantic situation report from a dying commander on the eastern flank of his force. The story was that John Rowell had returned to the battle from the east, he was late but his tardiness meant that the NSO had concentrated their forces on the Northern attack. He had been able to swan into town from an easterly direction totally outflanking the NSO and attacking them from behind, almost annihilating the regimes troops in the chaos.

With word of his forces collapse General Beaston led the remainder of the NSO Troops to a quick retreat up the steep banks of Causey Hill and Eastgate two narrow winding country tracks, edged by high hedgerows. The government forces beat up the steep tarmac with fear powering their tired legs. They occupied the old racecourse as a base and Beaston fanned his thinning force out along the high limestone ridge just north of Causey Hill Road, which cradled the town. This position allowed Beaston and his army an elevated position with a view over the whole town. If they were going to hold off the greater numbers of the rebel force, it was this position that would afford them the best chance.

Nick Christofides

FOURTEEN

The tarmac was lacerated by the battle that had ripped through the street like a hurricane. Two of the Rowell brothers were sitting side by side on the stone wall of someone's' front garden. Whoever's front garden it was would not recognise their house now. Bullets had peppered the sandstone building. It looked as though acid had been thrown at the house. The pock-marked facia seemed to be melting away, the windows gone, expensive curtains hanging in rags and being caught in the breeze every so often.

They were about three hundred metres from the police station. Jesse Rowell stared out at the human carnage that littered the street. His brother Phalin was watching his troops surrounding the police station. He had a necklace in his hand that he had found in the dirt; he was working it through his fingers like it was prayer beads.

As many leaders who had come before him, Phalin was questioning himself. Examining his judgement, observing the loss of life, questioning the war. He knew it was not just his decision that brought all these people to this point. He knew he was the figurehead for a movement that would have taken shape sooner or later, in some form or other. As his trail of thought narrowed on feelings of fate and destiny, his brother nudged him,

"You want some biscuit?" He held out a ration pack biscuit in his grubby and bloody hand. His brother looked at it and his head turned away as though he had been offered arsenic,

"No I don't want any of your biscuits, how can you eat Jesse?" he didn't wait for an answer though, turning back his eyes on the bloody hand,

"You hurt?"

"No, no I'm Ok, just a bit of stone or something caught me on the arm"

Phalin nodded towards the siege

"We gotta get this done fast and sure up our positions in the town, they'll attack again in the morning."

"I saw Mark die tonight and Jennifer and that guy from the builder's merchants…" Phalin put his hand onto his younger brother's shoulder

"I know, a lot of people died, it's down to us to make sure that doesn't happen again. We need to hide ourselves in the buildings and do to them what they did to us in this street tonight" He was as sure as he could have been about his plan.

"Did you call Dad?"

"Yes he's coming with a truck and help to pick up the bodies." As he spoke four men approached them, striding confidently, a slight spring in the step; totally out of place in this hell. Three of the men dropped back leaving John, the other Rowell brother to approach Phalin and Jesse alone. He wore black fatigues but he looked as though he had been in an explosion. His clothes were ripped, his hair was a mess and singed, his eyes bloodshot and face bloody. But he was smiling and walking without injury, he spoke as he approached, his eyes intense and determined. Unlike his brothers.

"What's happening Phalin? There's no time to sit, we need to push on and take Causey Hill."

"No John, there's been enough blood shed for one night, we have the town, we have to swallow them in the streets. Fight in small forces appearing and disappearing, we'll grind them down like that."

John's face fell, Phalin could see he was exhausted, running on adrenalin.

"That's ridiculous Phalin! Why would we let them regroup, re-arm and re-organise!" John shouted

"Because we need to regroup and stuff, we are out on our feet. I don't even know whether this lot will carry on tonight...also we have more men arriving in the night...hundreds I'm told coming in from Haltwhistle way."

"My men will fight Phalin, it's a mistake; the NSO are broken now...they might not be in the morning."

Phalin looked at his feet, these were the decisions which cost lives and he was a cautious man. He understood that the momentum was with the rebels but as he looked around his force seemed decimated itself. He watched as they laid siege to the Police Station. And asked himself the question if they were unable to take that building, how could he organise or push them to take Causey Hill, another fully fledged battle.

"No John, I've made my decision, we rest, we eat, we regroup and attack at dawn, hopefully with reinforcements...what do you say Jesse?"

Jesse looked up at John with sad and tired eyes, "John they need some time" pointing to there forlorn fighters, "A few hours won't ruin our upper hand...".

* * * * *

As the three brothers spoke in the town that lay in the darkness below his position, Beaston spoke to Ben Baines and Lucas Start over the satellite phone. Beaston sat alone in the back of a personnel transporter which was dimly lit by a field light. Beaston was hunched over with the phone between shoulder and ear, he rubbed at some dirt on his hand as he spoke, his mind racing for a way out of this fix. He rarely spoke so slowly

"...Look, don't ask for positives, at this stage there aren't any, we have taken heavy losses, Harris has been killed and we have been pushed back out of the town"

"What about the farmer, is he dead?" asked Baines

"Forget the fucking farmer" Interjected Start "What are you going to do about it Beaston? I brought you in on this because you said you could deal with it, what went wrong?"

"Numbers Lucas, we were swamped, they attacked from three sides and at different times, the men on our Eastern flank got sucked into the Northern attack and then more rebels came in behind us..."

"To be honest Beaston I am not looking for a review of the battle, I need to know you have an imminent plan, a route back to taking this town."

"I have more men in transit. If I get them we might be saved but let me tell you Start if we are attacked again now, we are finished, I'll die here along with all these men. They are ragged, inexperienced and traumatised. We are two hours off getting the artillery set. We are exposed."

* * * * *

John looked around him at the forlorn figures looking for loved ones in the dead, eating morsels of food and cleaning weapons. He could see they were out on their feet. Then he looked up the hill, he could see a glow from lights in the far distance, a mile or so away. A chill ran down his spine as he thought of the NSO being given time to regroup; set up a new offensive. He looked back to his brothers and Phalin said

"Give them a few hours and then we'll attack..."

John shook his head with resignation, "Ok Phalin, two hours. I hope you are right on this one..."

Nick Christofides

FIFTEEN

Stuart was becoming more and more impatient as the rebels were unable to enter the police station; he sat with Nat, waiting and thinking. Nat got to his feet and looked towards the back of the police station. Without so much as a nod he set out up the road, it was only when he was twenty odd yards away that he ushered Stuart to follow.

They turned left into Hellpool Lane, the aptly named road at the end of which the rebels had suffered such losses. They ran up the road and then turned left into a small street lined by Victorian terraced houses with pretty gardens enclosed by stone walls. Fifty yards along this street the road brought them out to the rear of the Police Station. They knelt behind the bushes where other rebels had taken up positions,

"The answer has been staring us in the face, you see there" He pointed to a single storey extension attached to the back of the building. It had a flat roof and small windows.

"I know what you're gonna tell me," Said Stuart

Nat nodded

"They're the cells" They both said in unison

"Aye I should know I've spent a few nights in there myself." Nat said with a wry and rare smile "Long time ago though, when I used to hang around with the likes of you" He added slapping his old friend on the shoulder.

"I bet you that isn't a concrete roof, these weren't designed for any breakouts I'm sure," Stuart said

"Aye that's what I'm thinking"
"Tonight in the dark?"
"We'll have a go." As he spoke he looked up to the sky "It'll be light soon, let's get a move on".

* * * * *

A couple of hours before the morning light broke the darkness, the rebels cleared the dead from the streets. They held the regime troops with suppressing fire at the police station and they prepared for another day of fighting. The Rowell brothers began to organise their forces, reinforcements were trickling into Hexham from the West.

At the racecourse Beaston was sipping hot coffee, his fatigues were open at the collar. He was looking at an ordnance survey map of the town he was planning to decimate as he tapped a sharpened pencil off the table top. He snatched up his mobile phone and hit the green button, he listened to the dial tone for three rings before the call was answered.

"Boyce, where the hell are you?" Beaston spoke urgently.

"Sir we are now in a village called Tow Law, thirty odd miles out from your position"

"Good, good see you on your arrival" There was some degree of surprise in Beastons voice as he was preparing himself to try and hold his position with the men he currently had at his disposal.

It was nearly an hour before the rumble of heavy machinery travelling slowly and precisely could be heard. Beastons mood transformed from dark to bouncing arrogance, he leapt out of his chair, grabbing his sergeant by the shoulders

"Those stupid bastards had us, I want the artillery ready to fire in fifteen and troops mobilised and in position immediately."

As the military convoy rolled into the racecourse, Beaston could see that Start had not let him down. The top table were serious about quashing this rebellion and for once they had given him the right tools to complete the job.

He now had at his disposal two units of heavy artillery, twenty-three mortar squads, three drone teams and nine companies of infantry. The tables had turned dramatically in terms of weight of numbers and also firepower.

Beaston deployed his men in an arc curling round the high ridge south of the town from Gallowsbank wood in the east to the Allendale Road in the west. Tactically it was a superb position at least one hundred and fifty metres above the town with a clear view of the whole theatre. He sent the drone teams out in the darkness and they flew high over Hexham with heat imaging equipment recording concentrated areas of heat then the artillery and mortar squads were positioned on these areas for initial attack.

Beaston pranced around his makeshift command centre high on the titillation of control and the excitement of anticipation. He had been in this position many times before, he knew the rebels didn't stand a chance and he needed to show his troops that winning was easy. He couldn't understand why the rebels hadn't carried on the rout when they had the opportunity.

"We'll be having a brandy with lunch today." He said to his team as the data from the drones filtered in showing a line of heat images running across the foot of the ridge and another concentrated around the police station.

"Make sure your gun bunny's over compensate on their AOR's" Beaston commented quietly but firmly to his artillery commander "I want them legless and mentally ruined."

* * * * *

As they sat under the stars the grunt and groan of heavy vehicles and massive activity rumbled down the hill to the rebels in Hexham. John felt his heart sink, betrayed by his brother's caution. Phalin looked at Jesse "I don't think we can attack, we need to dig in and hold the town. We can't send these people up that hill, all that is waiting for us at the top" he nodded up the hill towards the mechanical din of an army preparing for war.

"Aye, agreed, we won't match them now and they have the higher ground, we'll hide ourselves in the town and fight in the streets."

"I think we make small sniping attacks on their lines, suck them back into town and take on smaller groups street to street."

"That's the way I see it." Accepted Jesse, both men realised the opportunity they missed in pushing on up the hill when the chance was there. But this was no time for reflection or accountability. Now with the new sun came the dawning realisation that war was a constant. The enemy didn't just run away, they would always return, a little more knowledgeable, a little harder and a little more desperate. There was no control over events now, Jesse and Phalin had started something they could not have imagined before. They had led their peers into war, its very nature one of suffering and tragedy. When they looked briefly into each other's eyes, they could see that flickering melancholy and doubt. Whether they won or lost this day, there would be no excitement or glamour in the tales of battle. Only sadness and a hollow in the soul of those who experienced it for all those whose lives were obliterated by the madness.

* * * * *

Nat and Stuart could hear the reinforcements, both men knew that the next battle was going to be worse than the first. As the clangs, the engines and the yelling of orders echoed through the trees and houses the chill of impending doom ran up Nat's spine like icy water.

"We need to do this now," He said to Stuart, who nodded and pointed to their right.

The two men bent low crept towards the red brick community hall which stood alongside the police station, it had a drive running along its flank wall leading to a car park at the rear. The drive was bordered by a low wall which the two men used as cover. The wall stood approximately one metre on Nat and Stuart's side but two and a half on the police station side dropping into the car park which remained full of cars. If they could get over the wall without being seen, the rest was relatively straight forward.

They were on all fours behind the wall, Nat looked at Stuart as if to say 'what now' Stuart gave a slight laugh

"We gotta do something because my back and legs are gonna cramp up."

Nat raised his head slightly above the wall and a single shot rang out from the police station. Before he had registered the noise Nat fell back as dust and concrete chippings stung his skin, lying on his back he looked at Stuart, eyebrows raised; stunned.

Then Stuarts face clouded, he took his weapon off his back and checked the magazine. He looked solemnly at Nat and without a word shrugged his shoulders and leant on the wall unleashing the contents of his magazine on the building. Shots were returned, hitting the wall and fizzing over their heads but no sooner had Stuart began shooting then the whole rebel contingent seemed to follow suit. The building was shrouded in dust as the bullets rained down upon it.

Stuart took his chance and leapt over the wall, Nat followed suit and they found themselves sheltering behind a red car as the shots flew above their heads. They ran crouching under the deadly storm, moving across the car park and up hard against the window-less single storey wall.

Here they waited for the rebels firing to wane then Stuart leapt onto the roof of the car next to him and then up onto the roof of the single storey extension. Lying on his belly on the flat roof, he hung his hand down and pulled Nat up behind him.

In the middle of the extension was a square light well or yard where prisoners could be brought in or taken out of the cell block. An important aspect of this yard was that the walls had been built up higher than the roof, like a turret which now obscured Nat and Stuart from the view of the regime troops within the building.

The roof had been chewed up by rebel rounds and they could see through the gnarled fibreglass to rafters and ceiling board below. They were in business, but the plan would only work if Claire was this side of the yard. They looked at one another, nodded and each shifted to the nearest hole where they began chipping through the exposed plasterboard of the ceiling below. They worked systematically across the roof creating small holes, calling out quietly, hearing nothing and moving on.

It was the fourth opening that Nat broke through, making short work of the fibreglass, he looked through the small hole as tracer rounds flew over his head momentarily lighting up the sky. He saw a whisper of ivory skin in the darkness below. It was just a flash, but it was enough; as his size elevens smashed chunks of fibreglass and plasterboard away, he caught Stuart's attention. Without a word, he dropped through the hole he had made and Stuart dived onto the gap and peered blindly into the blackness below.

Nat landed hard on the concrete floor. Although the ceiling was fairly low, the darkness had extended the drop and he couldn't prepare his landing. He rolled on the floor in a heap, a deep throbbing pain rising through his feet and shins. As his palms touched the cool, smooth floor his fingertips brushed another object alien to the flat surface. He reached for it and felt a thick woollen sock covering a bony little foot, attached to the foot was a jean covered leg and a soft woollen covered body which smelled of Patchouli.

Nat knew Claire was hurt, she was limp and dazed in her seat, hardly reacting to his sudden presence in the darkness. He felt the pulse in her neck which was strong enough, so he began to tap her cheek, but stopped immediately when he touched her swollen face, not least because she recoiled in agony. He moved quickly around to the back of the chair which she sat on. He cut the plastic ties which bound her hands and he whispered in her ear, as softly as his vocal chords, gnarled by the changing seasons of passing years, would allow

"Hold on now lass, I'm gonna pass you up to Stu, ok?"

Her arms wrapped themselves tightly around his neck and he crossed his forearms under her buttocks and lifted her smoothly and easily up out of the chair. He then used his foot to guide the seat under the flashing hole in the roof. Once in position he stepped carefully onto the metal and plastic chair, it gave a little but took their combined weight. He moved his hands as gently as he could under her bum and pressed her, dead weight over his head. Claire guided herself through the jagged hole in the roof and then two meaty hands took her wrists and the woman levitated up through the roof, into Stuart's arms.

Stuart's head came back through the hole,

"She says there's someone else down there, a Rory?"

"Ok," Nat whispered and he called out quietly in the darkness "Rory, where are you man?"

A murmur came from his right and he found the curled up frame of a man against the cold concrete wall. Nat pulled him to his feet,

"You injured?" He asked "You gotta pull yourself together, dig deep because I can't lift you out of here."

The broken man stumbled to the chair and with Nat's help and Stuart's brawn he too rose up off the chair and through the hole in the roof.

Moments later a hand came back through the roof and Nat could see Stuart's head silhouetted against the flashing dawn sky.

"Come on Nat let's move" He called down. Nat clapped Stuarts palm with his own and called back "I'll see you back at the farm."

"Don't be fucking stupid Nat, I'm not leaving you in there!" Snarled Stuart exasperated.

"You will Stu" He replied calmly "You'll go now, get them and Amber safe on the farm. I have business here with the South African and the other one. Then it's over, I'll be back before the sun's out." Stuart looked around at the rising sun and flashed a look back at Nat in ridicule of his promise.

"There's plenty of time...not now..."

"Go Stu get Amber, go!"

Stuart growled in frustration as he looked at Claire shivering with fear her back against the wall that separated them from the NSO guns. Then his silhouette disappeared from the hole in the roof and Nat was left in the relative silence of the cold cell.

He stood for a short while in the darkness, he could taste the concrete. His heart pumped blood through his body like the fire in an engine, his muscles twitched and his mind was as clear as crystal, lucid and focussed on his imminent future; the hunt. Right now, he didn't notice the ringing in his ears, his burning shoulder from the bullet wound or the open wound in his neck. An oozing mess created by a golf ball sized piece of brick which struck him during the fighting. The horrors of recent days weren't haunting him now, he was entirely absorbed in this moment and nothing else entered his mind.

He walked across the empty room until he hit the wall. From there he moved left, hands flat on the smooth painted concrete, slightly tacky to the touch from condensation from the high gloss paint which covered it. It was only a few feet before his hands fell away into a gap and hit the frigid iron cell door. He felt around the frame of the door and found hinges on the near side; the door would open out ways from the side he was on leaving whoever was coming in further away from him. So he moved to the other side of the door, back to the wall he set himself.

He strapped his assault rifle tight across his back, he took out his handgun and changed the magazine to a full one. Then he slipped his twelve inch hunting knife from its sheath, the blade managed to attract whatever light was rebounding around the darkened room glinting slightly.

He took deep breaths as he thought about the best way of getting someone to open the cell door. He had time and so he went for a lure rather than an alarm. He turned his gun around, holding the barrel he began to hit it against the concrete of the door frame. No more than firm taps, the sound was not loud, but it resonated through the steel door. He hoped that somebody would be passing and at best think Claire was trying to escape, at worst become inquisitive as to what the sound was.

The minute's past and Nat was becoming impatient when suddenly the viewing slot in the metal door slid open aggressively. Torchlight beamed into the darkness and waved around the empty space, settling for a moment on the empty chair in the middle of the room and then slowly ascending to the hole in the roof. Nat held tight against the wall to the side of the door, his scalp rested on the cold wall and his breathing was slow and steady. He heard a voice "She's only fucking gone through the roof."

"Open the door, let me see..." Said another voice.

Nat stood calm as he heard the clink of keys, the metallic grind of the correct key in the lock, the clunk of the solid lock unlocking and the wash of light as the door cracked open. His grip tightened on his hunting knife as the two men entered the cell, their attention fixed on the chair and the roof.

"She must have been helped, Truter almost killed her earlier," Said one as the two men stood a few yards in front of the shadowy hunter set to pounce behind them. They looked vacantly up the shaft of torchlight pointing at the hole in the roof when Nat made his move. He took one step forward and swung his right foot with all his power. His boot came into contact with the man on the left-hand side. A full unadulterated boot in the groin from behind. It hit with such force that he was lifted off his feet and thrown forward landing painfully on the chair sending it flying and the torch skidding across the floor, plunging the room once more into darkness.

Before the light or the man had come to rest Nat had spun the distance between the two regime troops. He plunged his knife into the second man's side. Shock took the man before death was close, he staggered in the darkness and slumped against the side wall of the cell, his life draining away in the blood which flooded the floor.

Nat moved back to the first man who was wailing from his belly in uncontrollable bass groans, fighting for breath over the seismic waves of gut rot pain. Nat knelt beside the sorry heap and sunk his blade deep between his ribs. Silencing his din. As two lives in the cell extinguished the third stood tall, breathed the fresh air laden with the smells of war; hot copper, wood smoke and dust. He was at the height of alive now, his every sense burning for the next confrontation and his focus firmly on hunting down the South African.

At the open cell door he darted his head into the corridor back and forth in either direction, there was no one there. He thought about where he was in the building and imagined that left would lead him to the central courtyard and on into the depths of the building. He turned left and moved quickly, his back to the wall.

He reached a closed door and opened it slowly. As it cracked a voice came from the other side "Has she tunnelled under the wall?"

Nat turned his slow motion into fast forward he threw the door open and the flashing sky above illuminated three figures sheltering against the walls in the small open courtyard. Nat's handgun flashed with a metallic thump three times in quick succession and the three men remained where they lay. He searched the bodies taking three grenades and a set of keys.

As he turned, he heard the sound of a heavy metal ball rolling on concrete. His brain immediately registered the dark rat-sized lump coming through the open door on the far side of the courtyard as a grenade. Reacting, he scragged the man who lay at his feet by the scruff of the neck. He heaved him up off the ground like he had done to a thousand bales of hay in the past, he turned and threw the dead weight across the yard with all his might. The limp body landed belly first on top of the shell. The farmer had seconds but managed to throw himself against the wall while pulling another body over his, he lay as flat as he could when the courtyard turned into an instant pressure cooker.

First Nat was blinded by light, then thin air crushed his body in a wave of pressure and finally he felt his skin burn in an instant. His ears felt as though they were plugged and a high pitch ringing was the only thing that came through. His eyes registered a white light speckled black. But there was no time to waste on acclimatising; if someone threw a grenade through the door, they would follow the explosion.

Without moving the mangled corpse that had taken the brunt of the explosion Nat loosened the strap of his assault rifle and pulled it around to face forward across the courtyard to where the door was. Although his eyes were settling once again, the room was cloaked in a thick soup. As he saw dark blotches appear in the smoke, he opened fire, some of his bullets hitting their targets as the shadows fell to the floor. But the thumping bloody corpse which lay on him took rounds on his behalf also.

He needed to move so as the shadows fell he threw the body to one side and jumped to his feet, skirting the side of the courtyard and around to the side of the open door. He saw three new bodies lying in the doorway as the smoke began to clear. There were more grenades, wasting no time he took two, pulled their rings and threw them in either direction down the hall outside the door. He waited counting the seconds, reaching seven he heard the two ear-splitting bangs in quick succession.

He followed the explosions directly looking blindly left and right, choosing right this time he hugged the wall in the smoky darkness. He tripped over a body as he approached another door. 'Another door!' he thought all unknowns and dangerous for him, he knew he could only ride his luck for so long.

He pulled another grenade from his pocket as he looked through the small square window in the door. It was reinforced with wire, little squares which disappeared as he focussed on the corridor behind. The lights were on and it was empty, it turned to the left after ten or fifteen yards, Nat wasn't going to chance it. He repeated the action of clearing the passage with a grenade. As he rounded the corridor the walls were covered in gore there were three people. Two dead the furthest dying, Nat put him out of his misery and moved to the next door which gave access to the main central hall in the station.

The farmer slipped through the double doors and into the dark space. At first the dimly lit area seemed empty, the tough lino floor squeaked slightly under his feet. Notices spanned the walls and a large varnished wooden desk ran to his right, behind which there were various metal filing cabinets. The large room still smelled clean and clinical. Nat immediately calculated the risks, the door behind was not going to produce any surprises, the door at the far end of the hall led to the foyer then the street. There were two doors behind the desk, Nat edged towards the counter in silence, a large clock ticked on the wall above the doors. The noise outside the station seemed to have stopped, he couldn't make out whether it was because he was deep in the guts of the building or whether the fighting had slowed outside.

As he stepped slowly through the quiet, his weapon shouldered, eyes straight through the sights, index finger resting gently on the trigger. His breath was calm, in-out, in-out. Deep, controlled breaths, his mind calculating, concentrating and beginning to react to an instinctive feeling that something was about to occur. His mind concluded that whatever was about to happen in this situation was most likely to be at his expense. So he side stepped twice quickly turned and slumped down against the desk so that it stood solid between himself and the doors.

His breath was faster but under control, he sat and looked at the blank white painted wall opposite. It was not white now as the room was dark, but he could see it reflecting the scraps of glow that entered the space. There was silence now, no movement to discern, he heard the occasional crack of sporadic firing from outside and within the building. But it was all outside his microcosm. His backside ached on the concrete floor as his tail bone rested hard on it. He shifted onto one cheek as he contemplated his total lack of a plan. The red mist had undone him, how could he really think that he could enter the building on his own and survive? He looked to the front door and immediately went off the idea of running the gauntlet of 'friendly fire' as he exited the building and NSO shots at his rear.

Thinking of Esme's smile he was at peace with death as he sat in the silence, his weapon resting vertical between his legs, his forehead leaning against the hot metal of the barrel. The pain of her loss was unbearable in the moments of calm and solitude, it would be a mercy to be released from his grief. Then he thought of Amber and his stomach turned, she was only eighteen.

The doors behind the desk opened with a slight metallic creak of the hinges and the squeal of wood against wood on the floor. Then he heard the soft steps of a number of men stepping into the room with their weapons leading the way and their eyes firmly down the sights.

He sat with his head lowered as eight men rounded the desk with their weapons trained on his head and body. They had torches mounted on their guns and so his sight was compromised by the lights shining directly in his face. He kept his head down figuring that either someone would kill him. Or they wouldn't, yet.

* * * * *

"Looks like he's had enough," said one of Truter's soldiers as the South African joined them in the hall with Bell slumped on the floor in front of the desk. Truter was not as quick to write the old farmer off so he kept behind his troops and their blinding torches, safer for him to be unseen, but not unheard,

"If I had known then what a pain in the arse you would become Bell, I would have tortured your wife. As well as let those dogs rape her, they were horrible boys those; poor woman. You should have been there Bell."

As he heard Truter's accent, the farmer's head rose, his white hair and teeth glowing in the bright lights. His sweating brow wrinkling around those cobalt eyes. Every man with a weapon trained on him tensed as his eyes blinked in the blinding beams of the torches. The farmer didn't speak, he simply grimaced into the light, and searched it for his prey.

Truter opened his mouth to give the order to shoot the cornered man when a deafening clap resonated through the building, the sound was enough to drop the men to their knees. Then an instant passed before flame leapt from the doors behind the desk and a wave of energy carried debris, bricks, rafters steel beams through the air towards the men. The ceiling collapsed and no sooner had dust filled their lungs than the weight of the building was upon them.

* * * * *

Nat stuck fast to the desk as hell broke free above him. The explosion tore at the solid wooden structure, but it held and for the most part protected him. As the ceiling came down he got on his hands and knees, covered his head and pulled in tight along the bottom of the desk. The joists of the ceiling came down in one and lay across the desk sloping down to the floor, saving Nat's life as he nestled in the suffocating dust of his lucky capsule. His face and mouth and nostrils were caked in masonry obliterated by the blast. He tried to wipe it away and take a lung full of air, but it felt as though he was inhaling cement. He choked violently as he pulled a rag from the t-shirt he was wearing under his coat and tied it over his mouth and nose.

He crawled through the rubble and squeezed between the fallen ceiling joists and desk, as he stood in the glowing dust ridden space he saw nothing but carnage in front of him. His mind registered the destruction the earth shook again and another deafening boom dropped him to his knees. As he began to get up again another explosion shook the world; Hexham was being flattened by artillery. The gauntlet thrown down by the rebels had been taken up by the NSO in no half measure. War was upon them and the farmer realised he was in the eye of the storm. That however was not enough to make him run just yet. He checked his weapon and move through the rubble, he saw some of the NSO troops mangled bodies, arms and legs sticking out of the rubble. There was only one, in which he was interested; the South African.

The heavy dust born of the demolished building and pulverised masonry was thick in the air and the flames that roared from the impact zone created ample currents within the air to keep the particles airborne. The same flames gave off a flickering orange glow which provided Nat some sort of vision in the confusion. The stench of burning materials and flesh hung heavy in the air. Nat was thankful that he could see the dawn sky when he looked up as he feared he would have asphyxiated by now had the explosion not taken the roof off the building.

He climbed through the rubble as it tore at his limbs; the splintered timbers were the claws of mythical beasts and the rubble the knuckles of giants beating at some part of his body with every step. He could see the white painted wall he had stared at earlier. Now it was mostly a Jackson Pollock of charcoal black, dusty brown and bloody red. But it was the same wall that the South African had been standing in front of so if he was alive that is where he would be.

Nat found him unconscious but alive. His skin was caked in the thick dust, he had a gash on his skull and his leg had been badly crushed. Nat grabbed the back of his black jacket and pulled hard, tearing his leg away from the rubble that pinned him down. Truter came to immediately screaming out in pain as the bloody mass of his leg came free, his arms flailing at Nat's grip in a futile attempt to fight. As they reached some relatively bare ground, Nat threw the man against the same white painted wall; Truter slumped against it, his eyes shone in the orange light. He looked up at Nat; the fear reduced his years, Nat could see him as a little boy now, innocent and vulnerable.

"Those weren't the eyes that looked at my wife when you had your fucking hands on her. When you took everything she had and replaced it with filth and misery; and then you left her to bleed."

"I...I..." He attempted but stopped as Nat, a face as harsh as the north wind, lowered himself down onto his haunches and drew his hunting knife.

Those sapphire eyes connected by an invisible force to Truter's. Puncturing deep into those fear-filled orbs, he swamped the injured man's mind. Without a word and without wavering eye contact Nat raised his hunting knife high above his head, Truter screamed and covered his eyes with his forearms. Nat shouted over the din of pulverising mortars.

"Look at me! Look at the fucking man whose wife you killed."

Truter's arms came away from his head, palms up pleading for mercy. As their eyes connected once again, Nat brought the blade down hard on the South Africans leg as though he were stabbing the knife into a block of wood. The steel split the knee cap and tore through ligament and skin before hitting the concrete floor. Truter screamed again in agony and clenched his knee with his hands one already in a plaster cast from his broken arm. He sat up as he grabbed his knee and Nat grabbed his head as it came close to his. He held it between hand and forearm and brought it in tight so Truter's ear was next to his mouth,

"You won't be walking anywhere now."

As he spoke he held the man close and pulled the knife from his knee, Truter screamed once more. Then Nat whispered in his ear again.

"You know my wife was still alive when I got back." He drove the blade deep into Truter's stomach.

"She was drowning on the blood which was entering her lungs caused by the bullet which hit her back."

He now rested Truter back against the wall and those sapphires found the South Africans soul again.

"You even shot her in the back, was that before or after you raped her?"

He spat the words in the dying man's face as he watched the blood rise up into his mouth. He watched the uncontrollable fear in his eyes dull, to a fading grey.

Truters vision diminished, tunnelled, soon to be left with just a white light that Nat would wait and make sure he went towards and through.

Truter writhed in agony as his bile mixed with blood and burned his insides. Even with access to the best medical teams there was no saving him from such a severe knife wound to the stomach. But that did not mean that he would bleed out quickly; Nat crouched next to the South African for eternal minutes.

At first he begged Nat to finish him off, but Nat told him to look into his eyes and see the man that would make him suffer to the end. Then he tried to move but Nat pinned him to the wall. Then he screamed and spat and cried. Then he fainted. Nat slapped his face until he came around but now much more subdued and as the breaths became shallower, faster, Nat knew he was on the way out, he couldn't feel the pain anymore. Reality would be a blur of consciousness with little lucidity. So the farmer stood, he wiped his bloody knife on Truter's blood-soaked clothes and he turned towards the entrance of the building.

Leaving the last of the men who murdered his wife; to die and burn in the belly of the police station.

* * * * *

General Beeston stood on the ridge south of town admiring the carnage he had caused. Although he understood all too well that had the rebels carried on attacking up the hill through the night he may well have been routed. Victories are won on small margins and as he watched with marvel the carnage that lay before him he knew how close he had come to ruin.

It was a crisp morning, flames leapt from piles of rubble along the centre and southern reaches of Hexham where the rebel army had paused its advance. The buildings were flattened, it was unrecognisable and Beaston was certain that the rebel army was decimated. His phone rang:

"General Beaston its Ben Baines, how are you getting on up there?"

"I think we've finished this little uprising already but the troops will be entering the town shortly so consider the mission a success".

"And the farmer?"

"Which farmer, they're all farmers."

"Bell, the one that's been in the news..."

"I have no idea, we've just pulverised the town with artillery, he could be lying in there waiting for us or he could be an unrecognisable jam, who knows!"

"Well, you better put it on your list, I want a body; you get me proof that that bastard is dead or you hunt him down and bring him in. You hear me?" Baines lost his usual calm, his charisma dissipated and Beaston was left listening to the bare bones of desperation and anguish.

"I'll get him for you sir."

"I'll be waiting..." replied Baines as he hung up.

As Beaston looked out over the devastation, he had caused he mumbled to himself ironically.

"Thank you, General Beaston for solving our problems up north" As he spoke he turned and walked casually back to his vehicle. Climbing into the RV, he picked up the radio and ordered the troops to enter the town. He explained that their mission was clearance of all rebels by whatever means and their primary target was the recovery of the body of Nat Bell; dead or alive. He climbed back down from the vehicle and counted the minutes. Eight had passed in eerie silence before the crack of high-velocity rifles signalled the snipers opening fire on rebel positions. It was fifteen minutes before the heavy diesel engines could be heard thundering into the ruins of Hexham. The sporadic rapid fire of his troops clearing buildings drifted up the valley sides like the thick black smoke from the bombing.

Beaston knew that the slaughter of innocents was occurring, but he also understood that the theatre of war was hell and a 'humanitarian' conflict was impossible. He had experienced the enemy taking advantage of the passive population in so many conflicts that even when ordered otherwise his armies treated everyone in the conflict zone as the enemy. Something successive governments had turned a blind eye towards in preference of getting the job done. The NSO were no different; in fact they encouraged his hard line.

* * * * *

Nat squeezed his way through the rubble and out into the bright morning. He found himself standing on the steps of the police station, he stood up to his full height and took in the scene. In that single moment, it dawned on him. The futility of war. Conflict was ever escalating destruction which inherently sort to enslave the defeated. It had no place in the natural order of the world.

As his eyes ripped right to left across the devastation, the deep wrinkles in his skin hardened and his gritted jaw fell slightly ajar. The town he had known all his life was gone, to his right the terrace of houses had been levelled, burning debris piled high in their place. In front of him, a lone facia remained standing but everything behind it had gone and the same hell stretched off to his left. Where his view had previously been four-storey terraced houses from the station steps, he could now see over the piles of rubble and onto Hexham Abbey half a mile to the North East. As his brain acclimatised to this new topographical reality, the details began to pounce like demons from the wreckage. The gruesome hand lying on the tarmac at the foot of the steps. The old lady staggering aimlessly through the carnage, covered head to foot in a coagulating mass of blood and masonry dust. The countless bodies were strewn in the street.

His feet were stuck to the hard concrete and his lungs felt like they were filling with a fine porridge as he inhaled the dust and smoke that hung thick in the air. Unconsciously he moved to run his fingers through his hair but he could not push them through the matted mass. He was covered in the thick white dust from head to toe as much a ghoul as the old lady who still wondered from nowhere to nowhere.

After long minutes of horrified awe, Nat recovered his composure and forced his legs to move. He knew all too well that after the area was flattened the troops would flood in to secure the NSO victory. He had to move north, quickly.

Nick Christofides

SIXTEEN

He measured and staggered through the rubble and death that blocked his path. He was heading the same way out of town as that which he had entered. The going was just as difficult now but in place of the wall of gunfire he now had bodies and mangled cars and crumbled buildings lying in his path.

It was not the death which disturbed him most but the fact that every other face intact enough to recognise was someone that he knew. And his horror was that the next one would be Ambers. He hoped to God that they had escaped before the bombing and that he would meet them back at the farm.

Thick smoke wafted across the scene every so often blanketing his view with a hellish acerbic blackness. As one such cloud cleared his boot caught on some jagged brickwork lying in the middle of the road. He struggled to maintain his footing, his hands went down towards the ground where he saw a shock of auburn curls matted and spilling from a pile of rubble that banked steeply up to his right. He caught his breath as shock paralysed his muscles. Then he fell to his knees and began to rip the debris away to find the head that belonged to the locks of hair and the confirmation that his daughter had been killed as well.

As his hand touched the back of a bloody scalp, a bullet whistled passed his nose and thudded into the masonry to his left. The velocity and size of the snipers round told him that the well-armed NSO troops were closing in, and fast. He rested his hand on his daughter's head for a short moment then he was gone.

With agility and speed he traversed the rubble, putting the pile between himself and the approaching force. He found himself at the top of Westbourne Grove, a small steep road which would take him down the valley side onto the flood plain of the river Tyne. And into the industrial sector of the town where he would be able to find a vehicle in one of the many garages there.

He jogged down the middle of the street, he was not alone; there were other rebel survivors beating the same retreat, many wounded, others shell-shocked and crazy with the chaos. Nat was once more focussed as a thrown stone, his heart was now destroyed and his trajectory was already being calculated as his heavy feet stamped down the hard concrete.

He heard the crack of small arms fire behind him, he realised the army was already coming down the hill, killing whoever stood before them. His heart pounded and his lungs burned as his legs kept pace with the incline of the hill. He had not run so fast in years, but the swarm of troops was too close for comfort. Just out of sight up the hill but he could hear rounds whistling through the morning air and he could feel the Reaper walking by his side.

As he ran his eyes darted left and right for an escape or at least a place to hide. As the road began to level he was hit from behind the impact knocked him off his feet, and he could not catch his breath as his shoulder and chest began to burn. As He pushed himself to his hands and knees, he spat blood on the tarmac and coughed to find air. Then he was hit again, this time through his calf. His leg felt utterly useless and he had to fight the shock as his brain told his body to give up. He felt the warm sticky ooze flowing freely from his chest, about four inches above and to the left of his heart. He wondered whether the round had passed through his lung. He wondered whether he would live for more than a minute.

He heard shouts, whoops, and barbaric cheers as he balanced on his hands and knees. He looked up the street and saw the soldiers running towards him.

The farmer heaved himself up and ducking across the street, he fell over the wall which dropped him back into the stream from which he had pulled himself a few days earlier. The Cockshaw Burn went underground again after about twenty yards. As Nat disappeared into the shadows, the NSO guards hit the wall above him and sent a couple of shots after him but none were keen enough to jump into the icy water also. He dragged himself through the dark tunnel, fighting his desire to rest with every movement.

After what felt an eternity, he was behind the wheel of a thirty-year-old Toyota. He had roughly tied off his calf with a strip of material ripped from the shirt he was wearing. He had tried the same for his chest, but he was unable to do it so he left it to bleed, preferring to escape first and worry about his injuries later.

He took out his knife and prized off the access cover underneath the steering column. Bent double with knees around his ears he grabbed the wiring harness connector and pulled it out giving access to the wires behind the ignition. Taking the two red wires and some insulating tape from his pocket he stripped the ends and wound them together; securing them with the insulating tape. Finally, he took the brown wire and touched it to the end of the reds and the engine fired. He revved it a few times in the deserted garage and let it turn over as he pulled the dead agents telephone from his pocket.

He brought up the dialled numbers, there was only one so he pressed the green button and put the phone to his ear. He listened to the dial tone, three, four, five rings and then it was answered.

"Yes" came the voice of Baines, Nat could hear query, hatred and anger in the tone, he could imagine Baines hoping that he had been killed in the bombing. He could imagine him praying that this might be an NSO operative calling the number he found in the phone on the outlaws body. But it wasn't...

"I have nothing left to live for...," said Nat his voice a whisper, even though he tried to disguise his laboured shallow breaths with a guttural growl.

"Why don't you just fucking die then?" retorted Baines with a sudden lack of control.

"I have nothing left to live for" repeated Nat ignoring the outburst "except for the day that I have your blood on my hands; I'm coming for you Baines."

He did not wait for any response, he pressed red and threw the mobile onto the passenger seat. He gunned the old Toyota out of the car lot.

On the approach to the bridge out of Hexham, Nat saw two large trucks parked across the road and a heavily armed contingent watched the out of town approach. Nat didn't notice whether any troops saw him as he veered left off the main road about half a mile short of the road block. He was racing along Tyne Green parallel to the river. He gunned the old Toyota aiming to cross back over the river at the point the rebel army had the night before.

The road ran out, but he gave little on the throttle as the car bounced up and lurched over the uneven surface of the golf course. The road tires struggled for traction on the wet grass, but he pushed on bleeding and in pain. He was a good eight hundred yards short of his destination when he lost control of the vehicle. The jalopy aquaplaned over the grass and fell sideways into a bunker in front of one of the greens. The car rolled onto its roof and wet sand oozed through the smashed windows. Nat fell from his seat, landing on his injured shoulder wincing with pain and then curling up as the delayed effect of having the wind knocked out of him took hold of his abdomen.

He pushed himself out of the car and made sure nothing was broken as he sucked air into his lungs. His calf was agony, but he had to walk on it now so he put the pain to a corner of his mind and he began the walk back to the rebel vehicles at waters meet. It took agonizing minutes to cross the ruins of the railway bridge. His injuries heightened his sense of vulnerability. He was concerned by his exposure to attack as he crossed the metal girders of the bridge. And he was also struggling to balance on the relatively narrow metal with his gunshot wounds making him lame and his left arm almost useless.

Noise of the rebel slaughter echoed out of the town like the howls of ghoulish beasts only to be overwhelmed by explosions and the rumble of falling buildings. As Nat passed the shrine of personal belongings left by the rebel soldiers, he saw the necklace that Esme had given to Amber. He snatched it up with a massive hand and buried it deep in his pocket. His face showed no emotion except for that ever present grimace, but that small contemplation of the dirt at his feet and the slight shake of his head betrayed the disappointment and regret that ate away inside him.

There was no one else at waters meet, he could not see a soul, just evidence of the army, rubbish, clothes, vehicles everywhere but no people. It didn't take him long to find a vehicle with the keys in the ignition and his battered carcass slumped into the driver's seat. He pulled away from the ghostly Waters Meet, heading for home once again.

SEVENTEEN

The earth moved just as Amber's foot had touched the ground stepping out of the transit van that they had used to escape Hexham. She turned and stood stiff as the bank of fire erupted high above the town like the walls of hell ripping through the air in a churning billowing mass of fire and smoke. The ground trembled under the waves of explosives which thundered down. The shock-wave reached them a few seconds before the crack which rolled and rumbled on after its initial percussion. Amber fell to her knees as she saw the carnage. There wasn't a square inch of the southern side of Hexham which was not engulfed in flame and she could not imagine any shelter in the pulverised streets.

She felt Stuarts hand on her shoulder and the deep voice she knew so well spoke softly

"I'm sure he'll be long gone child, don't you fear."

"Can you swear to that Stuart?" She tested looking up into his ruddy face, dark eyes looking down at her

"No, Amber love, no I can't" His eyes searched the middle distance for more words but there were none. He placed his hand gently on her head, much as Nat had done in the rubble to the body he thought was Amber.

Twelve of the rebels had escaped the fighting in the transit van that now stood on the gravel at Carlins Law. Claire lay battered in the back of the van, a woman, another nurse, was tending to her injuries with a rag and some water. Stuart turned to the people who had spilled from the van to watch the maelstrom unfold in the valley below.

"We need to get back on the road north. That does not look like they're taking prisoners, we need to beat them to the border!"

He turned and clapped his hands, bustling the forlorn gang into the back of the van. Then he turned and his hand ran across his whiskers as he looked pensively at Amber, still kneeling and facing towards Hexham, away from him. He moved over to her and lowered himself to her level,

"C'mon girl, we gotta go, we can't stay here."

"I'm staying here Stuart, this is my home, my mum, my dad, where will I go?"

"With me lass, till we find your father, c'mon please don't do this, I can't leave you."

"I'll be ok, I'll stay in the woods, like Dad, he'll come back, he'll find me."

"No lass, it's not happening that way, you come with me now, then in a few days when the dust settles we come back and catch up with your dad."

Her face turned to look at him. The morning light made her glow with a vivid, striking beauty, pale skin, glowing freckles and stunning eyes blinking in the cold breeze or fighting tears, Stuart could not tell. The same breeze caught her locks and made them ebb like an autumnal tide.

"I know what you mean Stuart and I understand but if I leave I won't know, I won't be able to help and he might need me, he might be injured..."

"I know all this but look at these people they can't survive in your woods. If you stay, I have to stay and we all will probably get hunted down. If we go, we get them safe, we escape this army." He pointed towards the burning town. "And we can come back, you know your father, he'll either find us or he'll be here when we get back."

"Sounds like what he said when we left the last time and my mother died"

"Don't do this to them Amber! Don't make the same mistakes your father has made!" he said the grit showing through in his voice as time began to fray his patience. The young woman's head dropped, she knew he was right. She got slowly to her feet and closed the back doors of the van with a hollow metallic slam, then as Stuart rose and turned she climbed into the front passenger side. He ran to the driver's side and wasted no time in gunning the white van away from the farm.

* * * * *

Nat's foot was flat to the floor as he sped along the military road. He hit the roundabout at the Errington Arms at seventy-eight, his tyres screamed on the tarmac and out of the corner of his eye he saw a white van heading north and fast on the A68. It was the only other vehicle he had seen on the road and it worried him a little to think that there may already be NSO troops in the countryside. The car didn't slow; he took the next turn off the roundabout and carried on hammering the engine.

He was completely oblivious to the hand that fate had dealt. The white van had gone from his mind and there was never a thought that the occupants could have been his daughter and his old friend. Their lives' diverged at the mercy of straining diesel engines and Nat's reality that his daughter was dead remained intact; as did the same belief of his fate by his daughter.

He was back at his ruined home within ten minutes of leaving the roundabout. He smelled diesel in the air and his instincts kicked in. He scanned the surrounding rubble, buildings and landscape for signs of life, signs of an ambush; had someone been dropped off to await his return? He tasted the air and studied the places that a hunter would choose and he knew there was no one waiting, no one watching him; for now he was alone.

He went to the barn and grabbed some more clean items of clothing and some towels. He kept whisky in there and it was the only thing he could lay his hand on to clean his wounds before dressing them. He took a bottle and the first aid kit.

His head pounded, so he drank from the tap to slake his thirst; relatively unsuccessfully. He slumped stiffly down in the dusty light of the barn, his back against the cupboard under the sink and took stock of his injuries. He was no doctor, but he was pleased to see that both bullets had passed through him. The pain beat through his body like a drum. The wounds burned as though he was being stabbed with a red hot poker. His internal organs ached and shot with pains. His muscles were limp and his mind was dizzy. He had to fight the shock and he had to fight his natural desire to bleed out.

He ripped off the beaten wax jacket and his sodden clothes. Taking the hose from its circular rack he turned the stiff tap until a jet of icy water tightened his clammy skin. He washed himself down quickly then towelled himself off. The towel was damp but did the job. The remnants of a past life.

From the first aid kit, he took strong pain killers and crudely sewed his wounds shut. Then he tied them off tight with bandages. The painkillers gave him some relief from his wounds, but he was disorientated. He stuffed the first aid kit into his pack. Then he grabbed some fresh clothes which had been sitting in the dryer since the day his life had been turned upside down. He thanked Esme for insisting the washing stuff was in the barn. He took another wax jacket and he took no small comfort from the feel of clean, dry clothes on his skin.

Warm, clean, dry and drugged against the pain, he moved back to his supplies. He strapped his hunting rifle across his back once more, his hunting knife into his belt, stuffed his poncho, a few items of clothing and some tins of food into his pack. He walked quickly towards the door and spilled once more into the open.

He stomped up the hill towards woods where he would decide his future. His mind was cold, he had locked the sadness away, connecting only with the pain; he thought only about survival.

He dug in close to the edge of the tree line overlooking the approach to the farm. It was a mild morning, thick acrid smoke billowed high up above Hexham and he could hear the murmur of sporadic arms fire drifting up the valley. In the fields below him, his sheep grazed across the pasture and he knew the weather was going to remain good. He noticed a ewe in the bottom field, it was lame, he could not do anything to help it, but it would feed him tonight. He lined it up in his sights and watched it for a few minutes. Its front leg was broken or infected and it was tired, struggling just to feed, he imagined the fox would have it that night if he failed to get there first.

A twig snapped behind him, drawing his attention away from the lame ewe. He had covered himself with the poncho and foliage, the broken stick was behind him. He was trapped at the mercy of his hearing, his smell; as any movement would definitely betray his position.

He lay close to the dirt in a thicket of brambles, the rich soil filled his nose with earthy tones and he could smell the sap of the foliage around him. He could hear something approaching him. The noises were small, quiet but relatively constant, whatever was behind him was on the move.

Silently he rolled slowly onto his back and concentrated on the camouflage material of his poncho and the direction of the intermittent rustling. A translucent spider danced across the material, it captured his attention until the brambles to his right scragged and shook. His eyes darted and head turned, both beasts were less than two metres from each other.

The Roe deer was an adult buck standing at about two and a half feet tall. He was a fabulous specimen with good twelve inch four pointed antlers. The deer's coat was almost black from the long winter and Nat watched him as he stared straight back at the hunters hide. The deer did not flinch, he did not run but he could sense a presence, he just couldn't see Nat or smell him. Nat was happy with his hide, if this wily old prey couldn't see him it was unlikely humans would.

The old farmer relaxed his grip on his knife and slid it back into its sheath as the deer skittered away with long bounds through the undergrowth. Nat rolled back onto his front and his eyes settled once again onto the ruin that was his farm.

As he looked on his mind drifted back to life before the NSO, they would often lay down in the thick grass and look down on the farm; Esme, Amber and him. They would talk about the business, about the neighbours and people around; as families do. They would talk about Amber's future and Esme would be the reason to his anxiety. He had always been hard and capable physically, but Esme had been his latitude, his liberalism and adventure. The world outside the farm scared him, it was full of threat and deceit. It wasn't so much the physical threat to himself that he feared, it was for his daughter and his wife. He felt that society had created a greed that would always leave those without the power short. It was his wife that quashed this paranoia, she would joke with him and reason. He missed her so much and he shook himself as he thought about his current predicament; everything he had ever feared was now real.

As he daydreamed it dawned on him that he had to move, he had to leave the farm and Esme or sooner or later they would find him there and burn every square inch until he was dead. In that instant he decided to make a break for the border, he got to his feet and left the safety of the tree line. His long white mane waved in the breeze, piercing blue eyes framed by that harsh wrinkled squint and those white gritted teeth shone through tight lips and ever thickening stubble. The hard man turned hobbled down the hill, labouring on his lame leg and his chest pain defeating the painkillers. The open air of the middle of the field gave him a feeling of freedom he hadn't felt for a while. He looked up to the vast sky and sucked the fresh air, deep into his ailing lungs.

Nick Christofides

EIGHTEEN

"He does have the ability to survive..." Beaston spoke urgently but calmly delivering the bad news. He kept his sentences short. He didn't elaborate; elaboration invited questions, prolonged the agony. He couldn't stomach failure, "...but we are turning his land over now. We'll find him, that's all I can say right now."

"Can you be sure he survived?" Asked Baines obsessively

"Well, his body has not been found in the rubble in town."

"Look, this is your only objective...find him."

Baines put the receiver down; he understood all too well that the man at the other end of the phone didn't have anything to go on. But he also understood that that was Beaston's problem. The death of his brother had made him see things in a new light. He had entrusted too much power in Start and his deputies. His failings would lead some men to destruction or to fade into obscurity. Not Ben Baines, he was in the process of subconscious transformation, re-invention. He was not going to let his importance slip through his grasp, especially now that the one person who anchored him was gone. For his whole life nothing had been more important to Baines than his brother's admiration. He had no family now, no wife and no children. But he did have Lucas Start; he had The Party, and he had power. He was not in the wilderness yet, and he could enjoy a good life now; if he took advantage of his position.

It was in this thought process that the farmer was losing his importance to Baines already. Baines would make sure that Beaston spent the rest of his days hunting Bell down. That was a certainty. But Baines also had a revolution and the country to stabilise; he had to take control of Starts government and set it straight once again. He knew he could do it, and he felt alive with the challenge.

As he looked at the dark colouration of the desk beneath him, he swept the hair off his forehead; his tanned skin shone under the low lights in the office. His brow was furrowed and he rubbed his chin like the chess player agonizing over the move that would lead to checkmate. Then his forefinger came down on the mahogany twice, and he pushed himself up from the desk and marched decisively out of the grand room.

He tapped on Start's office door before entering. As he pushed the heavy door open and stepped onto the dark varnished floorboards; he saw his friend, his colleague and his adversary hunched over his desk. He sat lonely like a bull squashed into a stall. The only light in the room which shone was his desk lamp. The light was dim and the shadows were long. For a newcomer to Start's domain, it would be a sinister glow and a foreboding space. Baines was no newcomer though; he waltzed into the room and slumped casually down in the seat opposite his old ally.

"Tough at the top eh, Lucas?" He said jovially. Starts bullish head rose from the papers he was pouring over, already there was a twinkle in his eye. They say that ninety-five percent of communication is unspoken and Start seemed to understand.

"What can I do for you Ben, I've got a lot to get through?" He lifted the articles slightly from his desk.

"What's that then?" Asked Baines

"Where are you Ben, are you on my side?" Starts eyes narrowed and his gaze didn't waver from the eyes that sat slouched in the chair across his desk. Baines locked his eyes to Starts and sat up in the chair. He was a master at making grabbing attention and Start lapped it up.

"I had my doubts when you usurped me, if I'm honest. But I'm no baby Lucas, what am I going to do, creep around in the shadows while you struggle on. You need me and I need you; just like it always has been"

Start said nothing but pushed himself up and walked the couple of paces to a small occasional table on which stood a cut glass decanter and two glasses. He lifted it and turned from the waist raising the decanter in Ben's direction. Ben nodded maintaining the silence as he allowed Lucas to pour two hefty drams of single malt. The big man took his time, enjoying the tinkling of cut glass and the warming sound of flowing spirit. He turned with the two glasses in hand and returned to his seat, placing the glasses one on either side of the desk, all the while looking searchingly at his old compadre. He allowed himself to fall back heavily into his commodious leather desk chair. His fat hand came up to his mouth, and he pinched his bottom lip between thumb and forefinger.

"Let's not ham this up too much Lucas. I'm here and God only knows you need my help" Ben leaned forward and raised his glass to the other man then took a healthy swig of the brown doctor. Calmly Start responded

"How about your relationship with Eastman and the toffs?"

"I spoke to him once Lucas...look you screwed me, what do you think I was going to do?"

Start contemplated for a moment then abandoned his hand.

"Of course I bloody well did you idiot. I knew something like that would happen. I'd just stabbed you in the back. For fuck sake Ben, if I had been in your shoes I would have jumped across the table and strangled me there and then."

"Well, if you know about that then you'll know I've had no further contact...nothing was compromised."

"I'll take your word for that, the way I see it, it is not your style to be a double agent creeping around the darkness. Your beliefs are too strong and your ego is too big. And God you are right I could do with your help. I've got the heavy hand bit down to a tee, but I have no control when it comes to policy and balance. I need your brains and your diplomacy Ben...I'm big enough to admit it!"

"And I need your thuggishness, backstabbing, your paranoia and your scheming," Baines said slowly

"Well, thank you very much! The dictator and the politician"

"Jesus Lucas you have a phenomenal sense of self."

The two men raised their glasses and saw off the whisky they had left. As they savoured the smooth heat of the peaty alcohol and felt it warm their insides, Lucas tilted his glass at Ben again to silently ask if he wanted another. Ben slid his empty glass across the desk,

"God yes, keep them coming, I could do with a soaking."

As the big man once again rose from his desk, he pointed Ben over to the other side of the room. There were two high back armchairs positioned in front of a huge fireplace. Ben nestled into his armchair, he smiled and raised his glass. Lucas reciprocated and after a moment, sparked,

"Hey, did Beaston get that bloody farmer?"

"I don't know, I think he annihilated everything else in the vicinity and by all accounts he certainly quashed the uprising but I think the slippery little bastard got away."

"You can't obsess about him Ben. There are thousands like him causing trouble now. It is a cancer which is really threatening my...or should I say...our" Lucas checked himself and his eyes darted to Ben in apology "regime".

Ben chuckled at the slip. He didn't care as he knew that this merry dance would be enjoyed by both of them until that time came when one could destroy the other.

"Your judgement has been clouded by the pressure Lucas; you were the one who said to me that Civil War was our friend. Think about it; instability and fear focuses the mind, gives a siege mentality. People won't be worrying about the finer points of education and health care if they think that somebody is about to kill them and steal their home."

"I know all this but how do we stop the tide turning against us?"

"Politics my friend, politics, the flock will follow if the words are right"

The room fell silent and both men sipped at their drinks, the shadows loomed like the masquerade of their friendship. Lucas slouched down in his seat and pointed with his glass toward Ben.

"I am sorry about your brother Ben, a ruddy mess and a great man lost."

"You know, I really don't think he would have minded going like that. To live the way he did for so many years, he was tortured; never been normal since we lost our parents."

Ben stared into the distance living the memories of the most momentous and horrific time of his life. He was only young when his mother had been chosen for a two-month stint working in New York. It was the first week of her stay when the twin towers came down. She had been in a meeting on the ninety-first floor. Two days later Bens' father had turned to drinking the grief away in a London pub. At three in the morning he was mugged forty yards from his front door, in his stupor he fought back and was stabbed. He bled to death in the quiet street whilst his attacker escaped with eighteen pounds. He was not even carrying his mobile or wallet because, in his drunkenness, he had left them in the bar.

It had been a couple of days after the funeral that Tom had joined the army. Ben had never spent more than a few hours at a time with him after that day and in recent years it had been limited to a few words every few years. So their recent contact had been a real pleasure for Ben.

"Yeah well, it must be hard on you, we will find that farmer you know."

"Someone was going to kill him sooner or later. Luck was with him for forty odd years. I know we'll string that bastard up but you know the reality of death is that life doesn't even skip a beat. My parents, now my brother; if I stop to grieve we lose ground and we can't lose ground now Lucas"

And so it was that the new bond had been forged. It was at that point that Start regained his composure, the confidence returned. The heavy hand of power began to rise above the country again because he was absolutely sure that Ben Baines could return justification, reason and empathy from the general population for the war against its own people.

It didn't matter that both men knew that the other would finish him when the opportunity and the timing were right.

Nick Christofides

NINETEEN

The walk back down the hill was hard going on Nat, his calf muscle was next to useless. Every time he put weight on the leg the pain was fierce. His face felt contorted from wincing.

His leg was painful, but he had no idea of the damage the wound in his chest had done or was doing, he needed medical attention and he needed it fast.

He staggered towards the car; he touched the cold handle of the door and no sooner had his hand made contact than he heard the engines. His heart sank as his head spun to see seven or eight military vehicles snaking along the narrow country road below his farm. He watched for a second or two then turned to his wood. The land that he knew so well was his only chance of escape; it was not an upper hand against these numbers but if he could get into the trees, he could disappear.

Jumping into the car, he fired the ignition and the engine sparked first time. He slammed his foot on the accelerator and pulled off the clutch; the vehicle leapt into action, tearing for bite in the loose gravel. As the tyres gnarled at solid earth, it lurched forward. He spun the wheel to point the car at the gate leading into the field and onto the woods. He clattered through the wooden gate which had bridged the gap to the top field for over fifty years. He kept his foot flat as the car revved in second gear up the steep incline. The land was not too boggy and the car's tyres managed to grip enough to push the lump of metal up the hill. The engine whined as he approached the gate to the wood. Again he drove straight through it and then veered the car into the ditch with a violent rocking thump. He shook off the impact and rolled out of the car.

Scrambling through the undergrowth, bracken tearing at his skin he fell on the top of a knoll just behind the stone wall which separated the wood from the field below. He had a clear sight of the farm below; the vehicles were stopping, lined up on the gravel and the drive. He watched as troops jumped from the trucks and were directed to fan out across the field and approach his position.

He rested his head in the soft wet grass as he thought. He was desperate now, he felt cold and tired. He had three full magazines for his rifle and he could drop some of the men who wanted him dead now. Or he could run and leave them guessing where he was. But they saw the car. They must have seen him driving up the hill.

He raised his head to the telescopic sights and he lined up the first, unlucky, anonymous shadowy figure. He settled his breath, in, out, calm, steady and then he squeezed the trigger and he felt the kick and he heard the pfft of the silenced shot and the dark figure fell.

After the first shot, Nat stopped. He rested his head again in the wet earth he had no stomach for killing faceless men anymore.

He looked again at the approaching soldiers and beyond. Then he noticed the NSO commander by the trucks. Without hesitation he put his eye to his weapon and fired twice, he hit the man in the shoulder and he watched as he scrambled out of sight behind the vehicles. It was less than a minute later that he saw the black dot parting the smoke over Hexham in its violent down draught. He paused for a second as if for confirmation of what he already knew. There it was, soft, almost inaudible the pulsating throb of rota blades beating a course for his position.

He wanted to lie there forever, but he had to move. Digging into the depths of his determination he pushed himself through the pain and to his feet and he ran as fast as he could into the thickest part of the wood. He didn't stop; he knew he had many acres to lose himself in.

* * * * *

"I want him pinned down, but I don't want a kill from the air; you understand me?" Beaston spat over the radio to the pilots in the helicopter. "I want to see the whites of this bastard's eyes" He muttered to himself after putting the receiver down. He sat on the tailgate of one of the trucks; his shirt was pulled down over his broken shoulder. Nat's bullet had passed in through the meat of his upper arm. A medic worked quickly to stem the blood and make the injury stable. The General would live, but it was another infuriating dent in his pride.

As the chopper roared overhead, Beaston was brushing the medic away and barking at his troops to form up. There was no time to lose, now was the time to rid the dog of this tick.

* * * * *

Nat scrambled through the thick coniferous wood. The bare branches at ground level were hard as bone and ripped his skin as he ran. The strong sticky sap filled his nostrils with its reassuring smell. He ignored his injuries as best he could, but he knew that his movement was laboured and that he was still losing blood; he felt light headed. He focussed on surviving the next hour. His goal was to reach an outcrop of rock which would give him a rocky shelter from the searching helicopter and also give him some elevation from the approaching NSO men.

He was about two hundred yards from where he wanted to hide. To his left were the deepest darkest coniferous trees in the woodland. To his right was the edge of the steep ravine which gave passage to where Esme lay buried. He hugged the edge of the drop because the going was much easier than in the thick of the trees. As he ran he tried to duck a fallen tree trunk but he caught his back on the bow, he was knocked off balance and he veered over the edge of the ravine. With no conscious decision, he threw out a hand and grabbed a thick branch which hung from the leaning tree. He hung, his legs scrabbling on the steep unstable slope. His hunting rifle fell from his shoulder. It hung on his wrist on his injured side, he had no strength to swing it back up onto the flat ground so he wriggled it free and let the weapon slip away down slope.

The thud, thud of rota blades was loud in the air now. He was a sitting duck hanging helplessly over the edge of the ravine. His good hand held his weight, but he had to move. He swung himself up and grabbed with his left hand, the excruciating pain shot through his chest as he grabbed another branch on the trunk. He screamed out in pain as his weakened body took the strain. He was then able to walk his legs up to the top of the incline. His calf was also hurting but nowhere near the pain in his chest. He blinked and breathed heavily as he contemplated moving his sound arm. Finally, he took the full weight of his body on his left arm and grabbed the next branch with his right. The bark now tearing at his hands, but he was there, able to use his stronger right arm to lift himself up and onto safe ground. He lay quietly for a short while catching his breath and collecting himself. All composure had gone; the farmer began to understand that his injuries were making it impossible to keep running. But one thing was certain; he had to get up and get into the rocks or he didn't have a chance.

Nick Christofides

TWENTY

The white van trundled over the undulations of the North Northumberland highway. Few places on earth offer a sky vaster and a landscape wilder. Amber sat staring out across the browns of the moorland as it stretched off for miles before hitting the blue sky with its huge billowing clouds. Stuart did not look up from the road; they hadn't spoken since leaving the farm.

Stuart swung the van off the road at Catcleugh Reservoir and followed the rough woodland track through Castle Crag Forest to hit the border a few miles north at a crossing the Scots had opened for the retreating rebels. They had travelled a short distance when Stuart skidded to a stop. Coming the other way were a number of vehicles which pulled to a stop in front of Stuarts van.

The door to the first vehicle opened and Jesse Rowell jumped down from the four by fours driver's side. He ran to Stuart's window

"You made it, good to see you Stuart, Amber" He looked through to Amber and smiled warmly

"Likewise Jesse, is the border shut up ahead?"

"No its open but we have had word from friendlies in the NSO that, Amber, your father is alive."

Amber moved immediately to leave the van

"I'm coming with you then," She said

"Woah lassie" Said Stuart "We'll both go, but we gotta get these guys safe first" he indicated to the back of the van.

"We haven't got time for that Stuart" Jesse butted in "Word is that they have him on the run at Carlins Law. And they have men in numbers combing the land to flush him out...we need to get down there and meet them head on from the north, see if we can get him out of there."

Stuart looked across at Amber, thinking.

"Ok, we'll come with you if there's room, someone in the back can take this one on to the border."

"Not a problem lets go."

Stuart and Amber jumped into the flatbed of the truck, it was cold but they were joining ten other bodies huddled in there. The convoy moved out to save the farmer who had become much more than a mere fighter in their struggle against the regime.

* * * * *

The helicopter flew low and virtually over his head. The trees rocked wildly under the down force of the rotas, and the noise was immense. Nat couldn't think, undergrowth slapped him across the face and filled his eyes with vicious specks of dirt. He clenched his fists and beat the earth pushing himself to his feet. He staggered towards the rocky knoll and slid between the crags. He covered himself with his poncho, and he searched the raging sky for the helicopter. To his dismay the helicopter hovered low above his position, and he knew that it was guiding the men to where he was.

He watched as the chopper spun slowly, about fifty feet above his position. He wondered whether a bullet would pierce the windshield. Then he looked at the tail rotas and he watched as it came around. He had a clear shot straight up below the tail and it was moving slowly enough, he thought. He had no idea whether the rounds from his handgun would penetrate the metal or affect the mechanics, but it was worth trying.

The pain of aiming the weapon was excruciating, but the need was greater. He took the strain and watched as the tail of the helicopter slowly spun around to show itself above him once again. His eyes were locked on the tail and he knew he'd make the shot.

As the tail came to its closest point, he released a burst of five shots, smooth as a whisper and his shot was straight and true. It penetrated the underside of the tail where the rotas components were positioned and seemingly shattered the blades of the small rear rota. Then there was nothing, the helicopter carried on circling as it was.

Nat's head dropped; there was nothing more he could do. Then he heard a slight change in the sound above him. He looked up again, his eye caught the wisp of black smoke coming from the rota. He must have hit the mechanics, he could see the helicopter was making more erratic moves. He watched carefully, the smoke became thicker, the tail began to spin more quickly. It was as though the wind had dramatically picked up all of a sudden, and the helicopter banked off to the east, the pilot was losing control, and the rear rota was smoking heavily now. The aircraft went out of view below the trees to Nat's left, and he heard the deafening grind of rotas on wood; like a giant lawn mower running over sticks. Then there was an enormous crash and the noise of the engines stopped.

The wood was silent; peaceful. Nat lay against the rock, his breathing was shallow. Blood was oozing from the wound in his chest. Right then, he felt like he would never move again. The sounds drifted through the trees. He could hear the faint rustles and snapping branches of the approaching soldiers. He lay prone against the cold stone, slumped and lifeless. He was shivering, struggling for breath, concentrating on the necklace that Esme had given to Amber. He waited.

* * * * *

The convoy made a sharp left turn off the A68 and sped along the narrow country lane running along the north border of Nat's land. The vehicles pulled up hard as the road ran parallel with the Fairspring Burn and the rebels leapt down into the lush grass verges.

They were about two miles north of Nat's position. They could see the helicopter hovering low above the trees.

"I know where he is" Screamed Amber "Follow me, follow me" She called to the others as she climbed the stone wall into the next field. They were in no formation just running as fast as they could, attempting to cover the ground between themselves and the cornered farmer as quickly as possible. As they covered the open fields, it looked like an infantry charge of old, there were about fifty of them. They were just sprinting in silence en masse towards the woodland, the wisp of rye grass under their feet.

* * * * *

Nat waited; his beloved trees surrounded him, enveloped him and made him feel safe. He could feel Esme and Amber there with him. He could see mist ahead of him, or was his sight failing him? He had no idea, but he felt heavy, he felt no pain. He watched as dark figures became evident in the trees. They stopped and fanned out in a ring around his position. No one fired, and no one spoke. Nat sank as low as he could, but he was confused, in full view lying, dying in the undergrowth. He understood now that he didn't stand a chance.

The first few drops of rain pattered down through the foliage but were followed quickly by a heavy deluge which made a real noise through the wood. Nat laid in his nest, the water beating off his poncho, watching the men who had come to kill him and listening to the drumming of rainfall. It was a good few minutes before the voice was heard

"Bell, I am General Beaston, can you hear me?" The words echoed through the trees. Nat sat silently watching, he could see a figure who spoke but he was shaded by the trees; he could not make out any features. The voice came again

"Well, I'm going to try again, Mr Bell. I want to parley with you, we need to have a conversation before whatever happens here happens." The Generals voice was strained as he winced with the pain from the wound that Nat had inflicted in his shoulder.

Again the wood went quiet, Nat listened to the drops of rain landing on foliage, a cough from one of the enemy and then he decided

"I can hear you" He shouted at the General.

"You stamped on a nest of hornets Bell, we have to take you in now or this area will never settle, you understand."

Nat looked at his hands, they were black with dirt, cut and bleeding from injuries he had not even registered, he was so tired; finished. He shouted back

"I'm done running, I'll come in, and I've got nothing left to fight for now."

"I can see that Bell, I reckon you've got about fifteen minutes at best. It comes to us all son, war is lost when you have nothing left." Beaston took a few careful paces towards Nat. Nats blue eyes focussed and the two men looked intently at each other. "I was very unfashionable for a while. You know why?...because I knew that you could not win a war with hearts and minds. War is about stopping hearts, enslaving minds and crushing hope. That's what I do very well."

Nat shifted painfully on the wet ground. As he moved, he heard the amassed soldiers shoulder their weapons and train them on his body. He mustered all his strength to sit up slightly to face Beaston.

"They were innocent people who died in Hexham." He said.

"There are no innocents in war Bell." Beastons voice was raised, irate. "I never understand you people. It always baffles me, people in this country, I don't know why you're surprised I mean we've spent the last three centuries fighting wars in other people's countries. I always knew that one day we would have to fight on these shores, I thought it was going to be the bloody Islamists but then along came the anarchists and changed everything. It is not like you have never seen the news, all those conflicts across the globe, what did you think; that only military personnel get injured. I mean it amazes me; you people never got upset when all those people in foreign lands had their lives torn apart by war. That's what war is, it is hell. It is destruction, and it is only good for the protagonist who has the most to gain...and of course me, I'd be out of work if I weren't bringing hell to the masses. So don't blame me anyway, I'm just the hammer, I perform the will of others."

The General made Nat sick with hatred. As he listened to the words he carried on edging up the stone, his arms spread, his poncho flapping in the breeze.

* * * * *

Amber cut through the trees far quicker than the others; she could hear nothing over the padding of her feet on the wet soil and the scrabbling of twigs in her face and across her body. Then the rain began to fall and masked even those sounds. She could see the craggy outcrop, and she was sure her father would be holed up on the other side. She stopped momentarily to see where the others were, and she could see the figures moving through the trees behind as though the forest were coming alive, so she turned again and moved on. She had about three hundred metres to cover. She skimmed through the tightly packed trees like a roe deer on the hoof. She cocked her weapon and pushed herself harder to cover the ground.

* * * * *

"Stop there Bell" Beaston called out from the shady bow of a great oak tree. Nat stopped shuffling, he was almost to his feet. He tried not to show his weakness, but it had become impossible.

The lower leg of his left leg was sodden, a dark burgundy soaked the material and the left side of his poncho betrayed his chest wound with a large blood red stain, shiny wet in the middle. His face was ashen, the lines deep and pronounced by the pain. His beard hung wet as did his shock of hair, his eyes however still shone azure and sharp.

Beaston leaned against the tree relaxed, his hand above his head against the rough bark, his injured left arm strapped roughly across his body. He watched the man in front of him. After a few moments, he pushed himself off the tree and walked slowly towards Nat. Blood showed through the field dressing on his shoulder too, but only a patch. He had a pistol in his other hand which he swung freely. His brown hair was wavy, verging on foppish; his military greens were well worn but clean and ship-shape. He wore desert boots, and he covered the ground with a certain contempt for its nature, its uncultivated beauty was an irritation to a man like Beaston; nothing but a logistical quandary. He came within ten yards of the farmer who lay against the rock to support his dead weight.

"That's better, I can look you in the eye now Bell." Beaston's eyes were wide set, he was a handsome man but, like Nat Bell, his face had seen many hard years and the life he had lived was written in his skin. His eyes were dark and intense, the left misshapen by a scar.

"You remind me of the Taliban Bell, you've got your own set of ideas and to hell with the rest of us eh?"

Nat said nothing but his heart beat enough blood for his brain to calculate. Beaston continued

"When I was young I was like you, not young teenage, I mean really young. One day we had a big family lunch and my father wanted us all to play some damn game. Well, I didn't want to play inside; some fucking charades or some such, I wanted to play outside with my cousin. But he was too scared of my father, so I went out alone. I was playing with a ball in the garden when my father came out. He took me to the greenhouse. I was a little scared at this point; I knew I was in trouble. The old bastard took me by the neck, and he pushed my head down into the water butt. I thrashed about and pushed and pulled but my god man I was only eight or nine; I was no match for his power. He held me under water until I passed out" Beaston paused for breath; he nodded at Nat as if to re-affirm the story. Nat stared back at the man who had come to kill him.

"When I came to, my father told me that the first lesson in life is that other people are in control of your life. You might not want to do what you have to do, but if you don't do it the whole system fails." again Beaston paused nodding letting the point sink in. "I think you could have done with a lesson like that Bell. I'm the hand holding you under son, but I'm afraid there's no let up here, you went too far when you started killing people."

Beastons face hardened, Nat's eyes narrowed and his clenched teeth shone below his matted whiskers. The troops behind Beaston pricked at the flashpoint of unspoken energy.

* * * * *

Amber came upon the craggy knoll and she was sprinting as she rounded the outcrop. That was when her father came into view, her heart rolled over as she saw him leaning against the rock visibly wounded and about ten feet from another man. They were like gunslingers at noon. She dropped to her belly and aimed her weapon, momentarily she registered the NSO troops in the trees behind so she waited for the others to arrive.

As she paused for no more than a second, her brain unravelled the situation. Her mouth opened to scream and her finger squeezed the trigger as Nat Bell moved like lightning drawing a handgun from his belt he fired once hitting Beaston in the head. The General screamed an involuntary wail and fell to the floor. Nat stood his gun outstretched as all hell broke loose from the trees, the rounds pumped into his body for what seemed like an eternity. Amber watched as his body convulsed absorbing round after round. The stone behind him splintered as the bullets ricocheted off it. His blood misted the air in front of him and he fell sideways into the bracken that covered the woodland floor, his blood flowing free into the land.

Amber watched the horror of her father's death, the reality felt like a dream in that desperate, visceral moment. She screamed a banshee's wail as she fired indiscriminately into the trees. She got to her feet and began to charge down to where her father lay, but a huge arm wrapped around her waist and pulled her back to safety leaving the other rebels to fight the regime troops.

As the young women kicked and thrashed and smashed the butt of her weapon into Stuarts face something numb was spreading through her veins. As she screamed and wailed, cried and spat a dark mist was descending in her soul. As her brain registered the horror she had witnessed, she became numb, her mind became lucid, she stopped thrashing, breathing heavy, hatred blackened her heart and life became death in the name of vengeance.

As the rebels overwhelmed the regime soldiers, the pair stood in the leafy clearing. The rain beat down upon them, upon Nat's forlorn body lying in the scrub. Amber stood calm contemplating the misery. Stuart watched her face harden, her eyes steel and her soul retreat from the comfort of his support to stand alone in the face of her enemy. The big man's heart sank and tears came to his eyes as the cycle of tragedy began its second revolution.

The End

Nick Christofides

Lightning Source UK Ltd.
Milton Keynes UK
UKOW06f2144200315

248254UK00001B/1/P